A Mother's Love

By Danielle Steel

A MOTHER'S LOVE · A MIND OF HER OWN · FAR FROM HOME · NEVER SAY NEVER
TRIAL BY FIRE · TRIANGLE · JOY · RESURRECTION · ONLY THE BRAVE
NEVER TOO LATE · UPSIDE DOWN · THE BALL AT VERSAILLES · SECOND ACT
HAPPINESS · PALAZZO · THE WEDDING PLANNER · WORTHY OPPONENTS
WITHOUT A TRACE · THE WHITTIERS · THE HIGH NOTES · THE CHALLENGE
SUSPECTS · BEAUTIFUL · HIGH STAKES · INVISIBLE · FLYING ANGELS · THE BUTLER
COMPLICATIONS · NINE LIVES · FINDING ASHLEY · THE AFFAIR · NEIGHBORS
ALL THAT GLITTERS · ROYAL · DADDY'S GIRLS · THE WEDDING DRESS
THE NUMBERS GAME · MORAL COMPASS · SPY · CHILD'S PLAY · THE DARK SIDE
LOST AND FOUND · BLESSING IN DISGUISE · SILENT NIGHT · TURNING POINT
BEAUCHAMP HALL · IN HIS FATHER'S FOOTSTEPS · THE GOOD FIGHT · THE CAST
ACCIDENTAL HEROES · FALL FROM GRACE · PAST PERFECT · FAIRYTALE
THE RIGHT TIME · THE DUCHESS · AGAINST ALL ODDS · DANGEROUS GAMES
THE MISTRESS · THE AWARD · RUSHING WATERS · MAGIC · THE APARTMENT
PROPERTY OF A NOBLEWOMAN · BLUE · PRECIOUS GIFTS · UNDERCOVER · COUNTRY
PRODIGAL SON · PEGASUS · A PERFECT LIFE · POWER PLAY · WINNERS · FIRST SIGHT
UNTIL THE END OF TIME · THE SINS OF THE MOTHER · FRIENDS FOREVER
BETRAYAL · HOTEL VENDÔME · HAPPY BIRTHDAY · 44 CHARLES STREET · LEGACY
FAMILY TIES · BIG GIRL · SOUTHERN LIGHTS · MATTERS OF THE HEART
ONE DAY AT A TIME · A GOOD WOMAN · ROGUE · HONOR THYSELF · AMAZING GRACE
BUNGALOW 2 · SISTERS · H.R.H. · COMING OUT · THE HOUSE · TOXIC BACHELORS
MIRACLE · IMPOSSIBLE · ECHOES · SECOND CHANCE · RANSOM · SAFE HARBOUR
JOHNNY ANGEL · DATING GAME · ANSWERED PRAYERS · SUNSET IN ST. TROPEZ
THE COTTAGE · THE KISS · LEAP OF FAITH · LONE EAGLE · JOURNEY
THE HOUSE ON HOPE STREET · THE WEDDING · IRRESISTIBLE FORCES · GRANNY DAN
BITTERSWEET · MIRROR IMAGE · THE KLONE AND I · THE LONG ROAD HOME
THE GHOST · SPECIAL DELIVERY · THE RANCH · SILENT HONOR · MALICE
FIVE DAYS IN PARIS · LIGHTNING · WINGS · THE GIFT · ACCIDENT · VANISHED
MIXED BLESSINGS · JEWELS · NO GREATER LOVE · HEARTBEAT · MESSAGE FROM NAM
DADDY · STAR · ZOYA · KALEIDOSCOPE · FINE THINGS · WANDERLUST
SECRETS · FAMILY ALBUM · FULL CIRCLE · CHANGES · THURSTON HOUSE
CROSSINGS · ONCE IN A LIFETIME · A PERFECT STRANGER · REMEMBRANCE
PALOMINO · LOVE: *POEMS* · THE RING · LOVING · TO LOVE AGAIN
SUMMER'S END · SEASON OF PASSION · THE PROMISE
NOW AND FOREVER · PASSION'S PROMISE · GOING HOME

Nonfiction

EXPECT A MIRACLE: *Quotations to Live and Love By*
PURE JOY: *The Dogs We Love*
A GIFT OF HOPE: *Helping the Homeless*
HIS BRIGHT LIGHT: *The Story of Nick Traina*

For Children

PRETTY MINNIE IN PARIS · PRETTY MINNIE IN HOLLYWOOD

DANIELLE STEEL

A Mother's Love

A Novel

Delacorte Press | New York

Copyright © 2025 by Danielle Steel

Published in the United States by Delacorte Press, an imprint of Random House, a division of Penguin Random House LLC, 1745 Broadway, New York, NY 10019.

Delacorte Press is a registered trademark and the DP colophon is a trademark of Penguin Random House LLC.

Library of Congress Cataloging-in-Publication Data
Names: Steel, Danielle, author.
Title: A mother's love : a novel / Danielle Steel.
Description: First edition. | New York : Delacorte Press, 2025.
Identifiers: LCCN 2025009022 (print) | LCCN 2025009023 (ebook) |
ISBN 9780593498736 (hardcover ; acid-free paper) |
ISBN 9780593498743 (ebook)
Subjects: LCGFT: Romance fiction. | Novels.
Classification: LCC PS3569.T33828 M68 2025 (print) |
LCC PS3569.T33828 (ebook) | DDC 813/.54—dc23/eng/20250227
LC record available at https://lccn.loc.gov/2025009022
LC ebook record available at https://lccn.loc.gov/2025009023

Printed in the United States of America on acid-free paper

randomhousebooks.com
penguinrandomhouse.com

2 4 6 8 9 7 5 3 1

First Edition

The authorized representative in the EU for product safety and compliance is Penguin Random House Ireland, Morrison Chambers, 32 Nassau Street, Dublin D02 YH68, Ireland, https://eu-contact.penguin.ie .

To my darling children, Beatrix, Trevor, Todd,
Nick, Samantha, Victoria, Vanessa, Maxx, and Zara,

May you be ever blessed, ever safe, always protected,
may the forces of evil never touch you,
and may your only memories of the past
be filled with the knowledge of how greatly you are loved.

With all my heart and love,
Mom/d.s.

A Mother's Love

Chapter 1

It was a beautiful early October day, the weather was warm, the leaves were starting to turn in a riot of color, and the wedding had gone perfectly. Halley Holbrook sat in a quiet corner of the peaceful terrace overlooking the exquisite garden of the Connecticut estate she had rented for her daughter Valerie's wedding. The bridal couple had wanted a daytime wedding, with a morning ceremony, a celebratory lunch, and an afternoon of dancing. By six o'clock, the couple had left and the guests had said their goodbyes and thanks to Halley for a fabulous event, and she took a moment to sit quietly and think about what an unforgettable day it had been.

Valerie was a tall, fine-featured blonde, twenty-seven years old, and she had been dating Seth Parker for almost three years. They had met at the beginning of the pandemic, and had gotten close quickly, sheltering together in place several times. Valerie was an attorney at a firm that specialized in entertainment law, and Seth

Parker was one of their major clients, the producer of a string of hit TV series. He was thirty-nine years old, divorced, with no children, and had a massive, successful, all-consuming career, which was convenient for Valerie, since she was in no rush to have children and start a family. She was much more interested in becoming a partner at the law firm where she worked. They had offices in Los Angeles and New York and she had been commuting between the two cities for the past two years, in order to be with Seth. She had just moved to L.A., a month before the wedding. Most of the two hundred and eighty-five guests and wedding party had flown in from there, several of them on private planes.

Valerie's identical twin sister, Olivia, had moved to Los Angeles at the same time Valerie did. She was an artist and could work anywhere, and she had just signed a contract with a reputable contemporary art gallery in L.A. to represent her. The girls had given up the New York apartment they shared in Tribeca when Valerie was in town, and Olivia had given up her studio in SoHo. They were making a clean break by going to the West Coast together, which was how they had done everything all their lives. They were inseparable, had gone to school together since nursery school, and had gone to Yale because of the excellent fine arts department for Olivia. When Valerie went on to Columbia Law School in New York, Olivia was back in the city working in her studio.

Halley lived in New York on Fifth Avenue in a beautiful big apartment, where she and her daughters had lived for nineteen years, since Halley's first best-selling novel. The twins had been eight when they moved there from a much smaller, more modest apartment on the Upper West Side, which had been all Halley could afford at the time. Their current apartment still felt like home to the twins. Halley lived there alone now, but the girls visited often, and spent weekends with their mother occasionally. When they did, the three of them always had fun together.

It was going to change Halley's life dramatically not to have her daughters nearby. One or both of them had always been available for a spontaneous meal, a movie, or an afternoon of shopping when she wasn't writing. She rarely had a day without one or both of the twins in it. If Valerie was busy, Halley would drop in at Olivia's studio on her way home, to see what she was working on. Olivia had a great eye for form and color, and real talent. Halley and her daughters were extremely close and called themselves the three musketeers. Now it would all be different, with the girls living in L.A.

Valerie's fiancé, Seth, didn't mind having Olivia tag along. He enjoyed having two beautiful women with him, and teased them about it. Valerie was confident and outgoing, with determined opinions and occasionally a sharp tongue. She didn't hesitate to go after what she wanted, and was outspoken. Olivia was quieter and more retiring, she had a gentler style and her mother often found her to be the kinder, more empathetic, and compassionate of the two. Valerie was a fighter for whatever she set her sights on. Olivia was less sure of herself and could be swayed more easily. She was no match for her twin sister in an argument, and favored the underdog in most things. She was usually more sympathetic to her mother than Valerie, who had a more cut-and-dried, black-and-white view of everything, including their mother. Valerie's battles with their mother had been fierce in her teens, but had calmed down eventually. Olivia had been the peacemaker.

Olivia was worried about her mother now that she'd be alone in New York. Valerie said she'd be fine and dismissed her twin's concerns. She was busy setting up the spectacular house Seth had just bought for them in Bel Air. Olivia was renting a small, modest 1930s Spanish-style house with a pool, nearby in Beverly Hills, but Valerie had set up a room for her in their house too, so Olivia could stay with them whenever she wanted. They had shared a room for their entire lives until Valerie got married. Valerie tried to include her twin in everything she did. Olivia was the person Valerie loved most in the world, even more than Seth or their mother. It was the nature of twins, and a relationship like no other, for both of them.

Halley had brought the girls up on her own, in somewhat unusual circumstances. She was twenty-two when they were born, and forty-nine now. She was turning fifty in December, which was a landmark she wasn't looking forward to. It made her feel old, although she wasn't, and she looked younger than her age. She was facing an empty nest for the first time. The three of them often took trips together. Now she'd have to wait for them to visit from L.A. She didn't want to intrude on them, particularly Valerie in her new life. It was all going to be very different. Halley was determined to make the best of it and fill her own life. She had a demanding writing career, which would keep her busy. She worked late into the night, and hadn't had a man in her life in three years.

Valerie's wedding had marked the end of a chapter, a big one for Halley. The twins had been the hub of her life and her whole universe for twenty-seven years. She would have to get used to being on her own now, with them living far away. Halley was still a strikingly beautiful woman, with creamy white skin, green eyes, and hair as dark as the twins' was fair. The girls looked a great deal like her, except for their coloring. Like her own mother, Halley had modeled briefly when she was at Connecticut College and after she graduated. She had done it for the extra money, but writing had been her passion. She poured her heart and soul into what she wrote, which her readers could feel in every word. There was honesty and integrity and raw emotion in her writing. She never hid from the truth and her stories touched her readers deeply.

She had started writing seriously after the twins were born. After five years of struggling with her first novel, her perseverance paid off. Her first book was published when she was twenty-seven, and she had her first bestseller three years later, at thirty. It was a dark, complicated psychological novel that had captivated reviewers and won her a loyal readership from then on. She had a deep compassion for human suffering, and clearly a profound knowledge and understanding of those who created it. There was a hungry audience for what she wrote. She struck a universal chord in her readers. For the past nineteen years, every book she'd written had been on the major bestseller lists. She had a rewarding career, which would fill her time once the twins left.

She was planning to start a new book that week, which would distract her from their absence. Valerie would be on her honeymoon, and Olivia painting in L.A. All Halley's familiar landmarks were slipping away. She tried not to dwell on it, but she felt like a ship slowly leaving port for unknown destinations. She had no idea where she was headed, without her daughters near at hand, other than writing the next book. Writing was what she knew, and it had always saved her. It was the one place where she felt safe and comfortable, and she knew that writing the book now would ground her, as it always did. She was determined to fill her time without her daughters, and have a good life on her own, whatever it took. She would have to learn to live without them.

The wedding was lavish but just restrained enough to be elegant and not overdone or pretentious. *Vogue* had covered it. The guests were exuberant in a wholesome way. They danced through the afternoon and into the evening. Seth and Valerie's friends were happy for them. In their three years together they had built a solid relationship, knew each other well, had a wide circle of friends, and always managed to include Olivia. Halley had written Valerie a letter, telling her how happy she was for her and that she was sure their union would be a success, and Valerie was touched by her mother's faith in her. Halley had given her the letter the night before the wedding.

Although Valerie rarely said it, both twins were fully aware of how much their mother had done for them, with no help from anyone. They didn't know a great deal about her childhood and youth. She seldom spoke of it, and avoided discussing the details with them. She was always reticent and discreet. Both girls had long since understood that she didn't like to talk about her past, and never explained why. But it was obvious that she had suffered more than she admitted. She preferred to live in the present, and had buried the past.

Halley was talented, modest, and enormously successful in her own right, and didn't make a fuss about it. She had no one to rely on but herself. That had always been the case. She was six years old when her mother left her and her father. It had been a blow at first, but a mixed blessing, as it made her strong and resilient and self-reliant, traits she tried to impart to her girls, even though they didn't need to be as independent as she had been as a child. They had her to comfort and protect them. She had never let them down, and they knew she never would. She was as solid as a rock and had always been there when they needed her, at every age, and even now. Whenever one of them called, she was instantly available to them, eager to listen and offer advice, if asked, or even if not. But she knew she had to let them go and let them fly now, and she had to forge a life of her own without them. Valerie's marriage and the girls' move to L.A. provided a natural break for all three of them, and a time to grow up, for Halley too. It was necessary, but nonetheless painful for her. It was a huge change.

Halley lay back in a chair on the terrace after everyone had left and she visualized the wedding again. It had been entirely made up of the couple's friends, and very few of Halley's, which was the style of weddings nowadays. Seth's mother was there, although he wasn't close to her. He and his brother, Peter, were the product of her first marriage. She'd had three husbands, and she lived in Palm

Springs with her current one. Seth and Peter had no relationship with their father and hadn't seen him in five years. He was married to his fifth wife. Halley had talked to Seth's mother at the wedding and had nothing in common with her. But Seth and his brother were close. They'd had very little parenting growing up in L.A. Seth had made a big career for himself in television production. And Peter was a tax attorney for several famous clients.

The wedding guests were attractive and successful, some of them celebrities with big careers of their own. They were impressed by Seth's dazzling success in TV. He had fallen in love with Valerie the first time he laid eyes on her, when she walked into a meeting at the law firm that represented him. He had been instantly enchanted by her and attracted to her, and fascinated when he discovered she had an identical twin, and met Olivia, who looked entirely the same, but was a completely different person. Like everyone who knew them, he had a hard time telling them apart at first. Even Halley made mistakes at times, and they had loved playing tricks on their mother, their friends, and their teachers when they were younger, and even on the boys they dated in high school and college. Olivia had never had a long-term serious boyfriend and few short-term ones. Valerie had dated many men, but Seth was the first one she fell seriously in love with. He was her soulmate.

Physically, the twins were indistinguishable, but no two women could have been more dissimilar in personality. Valerie's steely determination served her well in her law career. She was a strong woman with definite ideas, sure of her opinions and willing to defend them. Valerie had her mother's strength and perseverance.

Olivia had Halley's warmth, compassion, kindness, and artistic nature. Halley felt at times as though her traits had been equally divided between them, but not blended. She could see herself in both of them, her weaknesses and her strengths. But their history was not even remotely similar to hers. She had done everything in her power to make sure of that.

Halley had followed in her own French mother's footsteps when she modeled briefly in college and for a short time after. She had no long-term ambitions in that direction, unlike her mother. Halley only did it for the extra money. She'd been in the studio of a famous photographer, Locke Logan, who had been taken with her innocent charm when she modeled for him. She was shy and retiring, always happy to disappear into the background. He had taken an interest in her and had taken her under his wing. He loved photographing her. She had an inner beauty that shone through.

She was twenty-two at the time, and he was forty-eight. He was married and had three children. He fell in love with Halley, and took a spectacular series of nude photographs of her that became legendary. You couldn't see her face but there was an innocence and poignancy to the photographs and a vulnerability that touched him profoundly. He never had any intention of getting divorced. Halley was one of a long series of affairs. His wife was well aware of and tolerated them, and had infidelities of her own in their stormy marriage.

When Halley got pregnant, she hesitated to have an abortion, and after the first sonogram, as soon as she knew she was having twins, she couldn't do it, and decided to have them. She asked nothing of Locke. He stuck by her and helped financially to the degree Halley needed. A small trust from her grandparents gave her enough to live on modestly, and Locke's contributions made up the difference. Halley was careful and responsible, and took motherhood seriously. She put her own youth on hold to take care of the twins and be a good mother to them.

Locke saw them from time to time and was warm and playful with the twins, but fatherhood was not his long suit. By the time he got divorced a decade later, the affair with Halley was long over. He remained a figurehead in the twins' lives, and came to their birthdays and graduations. He was never on hand for their daily lives. He loved them, and Halley, in his own erratic, irresponsible way. Halley made up for it by being everything to the girls.

He had been at Valerie's wedding but Valerie had opted to walk down the aisle alone. Locke had never been a father figure to her, but she was happy to have him there. He was seventy-five years old now, still working though slowing down, and had come to the wedding with the young model he was currently dating, several years younger than the twins. She couldn't have been more than twenty. He and Halley had stayed on good terms. He never interfered, and she hadn't needed his help in nearly twenty years. Once her second book became successful, she and the twins had been secure. Halley never took her success for granted and was grateful she could do that for them.

The twins had lived a very comfortable life thanks to her. The fact that their parents had never been married posed very little problem and hadn't bothered them. And Locke showed up when it was important to them. He hadn't been a very present or strong influence in their lives, but he had been good enough and a loving though distant presence at key times. Halley supplied all the rest and was ever present, fully responsible, and always loving. She had been the mainstay of their lives, and they of hers. She had grown up quickly once she had them. Valerie had been briefly critical of her as a teenager, but once they grew up, both girls agreed that she was a terrific mother, and she had never let them down. If anything, she held on a little too tight, but their move to L.A. would change that, which all three of them recognized. Halley wasn't fighting it, she was trying to adjust and love them with open arms, and fill her time in other ways. Nothing would replace having them in her daily life, but she was choosing to view it as an opportunity to grow and to develop a new life of her own, a challenge she was determined to meet with grace, and without being a burden to her daughters.

Halley had had no family of her own from the time she was fourteen, so her decision to have the twins, unmarried at twenty-two, didn't shock anyone. There was no one to shock or to help, except the babies' father to the minimal degree he wanted to be involved. He had his hands full then with his own three children and a turbulent, failing marriage. Halley had made no demands, and figured out most of her parenting on her own. Her being busy with the twins had precluded much of a dating life, and she had virtually no serious love life for a decade, a sacrifice she had willingly made. She had a few brief minor affairs, and met the love of her life at thirty-five. Robert Baldwin was two years older than she was, and fell deeply in love with her and the twins. He was a senior editor at her publishing house, never married, with no children of his own. They had spent twelve years together, and lived together for ten of them. He had developed a brain tumor at forty-nine, almost three years before. He was in the final stages of his illness at the beginning of the pandemic, when he caught Covid. Officially, he had died of the coronavirus, but he wouldn't have lasted much longer anyway. Halley had made her peace with losing him. They would have enjoyed the years after the twins left, and filled them well, but that wasn't their destiny. She had to face that now on her own. She had nursed him until the end. He had decided not to go to the hospital when he caught Covid. He didn't want to die alone at the hospital, so he had stayed at home with her and died peacefully in her arms. And miraculously, she hadn't caught the virus from him, but she had been willing to take the risk to give him the end he wanted. They had isolated from the twins. He was a wonderful human being and the twins had loved him too. He was the reason for Valerie deciding to walk down the aisle alone. Robert had been more of a father to her than her own father was, and without Robert there, she had chosen to walk alone, in memory of him. The gesture had touched Halley to the core.

The childhood history Halley never shared with the twins, or as little as possible, had been very different from Valerie and Olivia's. Halley's mother had been French, which was one of the few details the girls knew about her. Halley's maternal grandmother, Hélène Vivier, was a young woman at the end of the war, when the Americans liberated Paris. She fell in love with a handsome boy from California and got pregnant. He intended to take her back to California and marry her there, to live and work on the farm where he grew up near Bakersfield. GI's weren't allowed to marry in France, and he was going to send for her once he got home. When they discovered that she was pregnant, they had a marriage ceremony performed by a local priest in Paris, which the Americans didn't recognize, but which gave Hélène some comfort and dignity. Both her parents had died during the war, her mother of illness and her father in the Resistance. Hélène's handsome GI was one of the last casualties in France and died before he got back to the States. She could never find his family later, and their daughter, Sabine, was born in 1946.

With no other attributes or skills other than her striking beauty, Sabine became a model in Paris in her late teens. Her mother had died from tuberculosis by then, and Sabine was on her own. She was sent to New York for a photo shoot at nineteen, and the modeling agency that had brought her over helped her use her parents' French marriage certificate to prove the paternity of her American GI father, which allowed her to obtain American citizenship so she could stay and work legally in the States. She never became a superstar, but she was a very successful model for a time, and rapidly fell in with the fast crowd of celebrities and socialites at the fashionable Stork Club, the last club of its kind, and became one of a bevy of beautiful women who danced and drank their nights away.

Sabine partied for the next six years, was frequently photographed in the press with important men. At twenty-five, she met William Holbrook IV, the black sheep scion of his aristocratic family. The family had lost the bulk of their fortune in the crash of 1929, but they had enough left for him to play, gamble, drink, and spend what remained on beautiful women and fast cars, without working, and he was most frequently seen with Sabine, who eventually got pregnant. Bill did the gentlemanly thing and married her, although neither was in love, or enthusiastic about the marriage or the child, and it didn't slow down his affairs with other women. Halley was born in 1972, when Sabine was twenty-six and Bill was forty-two. Sabine had the distinguished Holbrook name then and she blamed the child for all the ills in her life, a husband who didn't love her, the fetters of marriage to a man she didn't love either, her slowly fading beauty from the dissolute life they led, and her modeling career on the wane. She was no longer the woman everyone stopped to stare at when she walked into a room, and she blamed Halley more than Bill. If Sabine hadn't had Halley, she would never have married him. She was uneasy about abortion, so she didn't have one. She married Bill, since he was willing. And he was from an important family. But she wasn't happy about him, or the marriage.

Halley's first memory of her mother was of a severe beating when she was three. She had spilled a glass of milk at breakfast, which dripped on Sabine's navy blue suede shoes, and she beat Halley until blood dripped from her ear. Bill saw her do it and quietly left the apartment. He had an appointment with his barber and didn't want to be late. He left Sabine to deal with the child, as he always did. Halley remembered his leaving while her mother

was beating her. She remembered the sound of the front door closing as her mother landed another blow. Sabine said her shoes were
ruined.

She took Halley to the hospital to stop the bleeding, and said
she had fallen down the stairs. Halley instinctively knew not to
contradict her and remained silent when they treated her. A nice
nurse said she was lucky she hadn't broken an arm or a leg. And
just for good measure, her mother hit her again when they got
home. She said Halley had ruined her day as well as her shoes.
Halley was afraid to drink her milk at breakfast after that, and
never did again, no matter how thirsty she was. She didn't want to
risk making her mother angry again, but it was unavoidable.

That was only the beginning. Sabine unleashed her full fury on
Halley from then on, with beatings for any excuse. She had a violent temper, and hit Halley hard. A broken wrist, a beating with a
jeweled belt buckle that left cuts and marks on her back that
couldn't be explained so they were never treated and left scars, a
cut just below her eye from the ring Sabine was wearing, which
required stitches. She told the nurses at the hospital that Halley
had fallen into the corner of a table. She was four by then.

Very few memories of Halley's childhood remained, and there
were none of kindness or a gentle touch. But she remembered
each of the beatings for the rest of her life, carved in memory as
though etched in stone. A push down the stairs, a broken arm,
bruises on her arms and legs when her mother kicked her, beatings
with a hairbrush, headaches from being violently shaken when she
caught her mother doing something bad, like meeting men at their
apartment when her father was out. Her mother said she would

kill her if she told, and Halley knew she would. She never understood why her mother was so angry at her and hated her so much. She tried to be very good, but she was never good enough to satisfy her mother, who told her that nobody loved her. Halley knew that was true. Her parents demonstrated that to her every day, especially Sabine. Her mother spoke to her in French and in English. She was just as violent to Halley in either one.

The beatings got worse as she got older. The marks and the bruises were there, but usually faded away, though a few stayed. She lived in constant fear of her mother, and hid from her whenever she could. More often than not, her mother found her and beat her again for hiding. Her father never intervened. When Halley was five, Sabine found a new playground, new friends and pursuits. She became one of the first regulars at Studio 54, where she added drugs to alcohol. The marriage was almost nonexistent by then, and her modeling had dwindled to an occasional job until the agency dropped her entirely. She never showed up on time and looked ravaged when she did. Halley learned much of what was happening when she heard her parents argue, usually at night, if Sabine came home. She didn't always.

Sometimes neither of her parents would come home, and Halley was alone. It frightened her at first, but she fed herself from what was in the fridge when she got hungry. She would sit in her room and talk to her dolls and play, or watch TV in her father's study. And then one day, miraculously, Sabine left after a particularly vicious fight with Bill, and never returned. A week later, he told Halley her mother was never coming back. Halley didn't know what that meant for her and was afraid to ask. All she remembered was the enormous feeling of relief that the beatings would stop. She was six then. She could tell that her father was happy too.

Once Sabine left, her father gave parties all the time, and filled their large, comfortable Park Avenue apartment with his friends, whom Halley had never seen before. No one paid any attention to Halley for the first year, but she was cursed with her mother's dark hair, green eyes, and beautiful face. Their housekeeper was there in the daytime, and the parties went on all night.

She was seven the first time one of her father's friends put his hands on her. He began stroking her arm in a strange way, and tried to pull her into a bedroom with him, and Bill told him to stop. It was the only time he ever intervened. After that he treated her like a toy for his friends' amusement when they hugged her too tight, or sat her on their laps. Her father ignored her entirely, as though she was someone else's child. He never believed her when she complained about them, so she stopped telling him what they tried to do, and figured out ways to avoid them herself. If they were drunk enough, it was easy to run away from them and hide until they left. If they were sober, they didn't dare insist when she resisted or escaped from them.

She was almost eight when another one of her father's friends reached under her skirt, and that time no one saw. She ran away and hid in a closet until he left. There were others after that, always wanting to touch her in private places, but she was artful at avoiding them and fleeing to another part of the apartment where she could hide. She was afraid to go to bed when his friends were there. Once one of them came into her room and got into bed with her, but he was so drunk he was easy to get away from. She was small but fast, and clever at disappearing. She slept in her closet after that. Her father said they were just having fun, and meant no harm, but she didn't believe him. She knew the look in their eyes now, and what they would try to do after that. None of them ever succeeded. She didn't let it happen, and knew that only she could save herself, no one else would help her. She had no protectors or allies. The adults in her life were dangerous. She had only herself to rely on.

When she was still eight, her father told her that her mother had died of an overdose. She hadn't seen or heard from her since she'd left two years before, and no one had beaten Halley since. She wasn't sad when Bill told her that Sabine had died, but she knew she should be. She was just relieved to know her mother would never come back to hit her again. She had been afraid Sabine might come back and do that again one day, and that Bill would let her.

Halley went to the funeral with her father. They were the only ones there. Bill's parents had died by then, and they buried Sabine in the same place as his parents. She was thirty-four years old.

Halley spent the next five years avoiding her father's friends. She knew when to stay away from them. By the time she was thirteen, she had a womanly body, with small firm breasts, a tiny waist, her mother's long, graceful legs and exquisite face. Many of her father's friends tried to take advantage of her, and Bill turned a blind eye, just as he had to the beatings. But she was an expert at avoiding them. She was well aware that she was a burden to her father—he made that clear. He had housekeepers take care of her in the daytime, but they never stayed long. In light of the debauchery they knew went on there, they always quit. Halley didn't care. They were no protection for her anyway.

When she was thirteen, her father stepped over the line himself, one evening before he went out. The housekeeper had already left for the day. They were alone in the apartment, and he'd been drinking all day with his friends and had come home to change, as he often did. He walked into her room while she was studying at her desk, and she turned when she heard him come in. He was naked and very drunk and invited her to take a bath with him. She was shaking as she kept her eyes on his face, and wouldn't let herself look any lower. Knowing she had to get out of the room she pushed her way past him, mumbling some excuse, and he staggered when he tried to follow her. Then he didn't try to find her, and went to his bathroom alone. She couldn't forget the way he had looked at her, and she hid in a closet until she heard the apartment door close behind him. She never trusted him again, and locked her bedroom and bathroom doors after that whenever he was in the apartment. She had no illusions about him. He was just like his friends. She lived in enemy territory, with no one to protect her, no one she could turn to or ask for help. She had no friends at school because she couldn't bring them home. And her father's family name, background, and social status protected him from all suspicion. No one would have believed her if she told them, and she wouldn't have dared. She rarely met his girlfriends. They didn't look like nice women. They treated her like an annoyance.

When she was fourteen, one afternoon after she came home

from school, two policemen came to the apartment to tell her that her father had been killed in a car accident. He was fifty-six years old. She sat in the living room and talked to them like an adult, which she was by then, because of the life she had lived. She had no living relatives. The officers took her with them to stay in a children's shelter.

Her father's lawyer came to talk to her there the next day. He explained that there was a trust for her education and related expenses when she turned eighteen, and a small second trust from her paternal grandparents when she turned twenty-one, but no funds were available until then. Her father hadn't expected to die so young and had made no provision for her until she reached eighteen. He had spent most of his money. There was very little left, barely enough to pay his debts. The apartment would be sold and the proceeds added to her trust, with no access to it until she turned eighteen, no money until then, and no one to take care of her. She had four years ahead of her with no means of support. She was sent from the shelter to a state orphanage on the Lower East Side in Manhattan. There was no funeral for her father and she wouldn't have gone anyway. His lawyer arranged for him to be cremated, according to his wishes, with no religious service, and buried in the family plot with Halley's mother and grandparents. He had wanted no funeral, and had said he was an atheist. His lawyer took care of everything. He offered to take Halley to the burial and she refused.

The other children at the orphanage were from poor families and younger than she was. They had no trusts to look forward to at eighteen, but they might be adopted. She was told by the superintendent of the orphanage that at fourteen it was unlikely that anyone would want to adopt her. Two families tried her out as foster parents, and said that she hid all the time, refused to engage, barely spoke to them, was closed off and uncommunicative, and they returned her to the orphanage. She preferred it there anyway. She didn't trust the fathers in the two homes she was sent to. She knew what men were capable of. It never even occurred to her to want a family that would love her. She couldn't conceive of it, having never been loved by her own family. She couldn't even imagine what that felt like.

Halley spent the four years in the orphanage without complaint, until her eighteenth birthday. She felt safe there. She helped out in the office, to have something to do after school. She attended public high school a few blocks away, made no friends because she was too ashamed of where she lived, and was reticent with the teachers. Her own home had been far worse than the orphanage. She had time to study there and the counselors and teachers were kind to her. She was a good student, and a school counselor had helped her apply to college. She remained shy and unengaged. She enrolled at Connecticut College, and was released from the orphanage like a prisoner who had served her time when she turned eighteen. Her counselors had helped her get her high school diploma six months early, and she left as soon as she got it, with no fanfare and a few discreet goodbyes. She had formed no close relationships, and didn't want any. In four years she hadn't opened up to anyone. The funds from the trust were waiting for her in a bank account.

She rented a room near the college in New London, Connecticut, and got a job at a bookstore until classes started in the fall. She moved into the dorms in August. It was a small, picturesque college with two thousand students, on seven hundred and fifty acres of land overlooking Long Island Sound, with the quaint seaport town of Mystic a few miles away. It was a gentle place for her to reenter the world.

Halley spent peaceful years there, and got excellent grades, particularly in her creative writing classes. She made a few friends and had a few dates, and no serious romances. She didn't share her history with anyone, or tell anyone she had spent her high school years in a state orphanage. She wanted to disappear into the crowd and was afraid to attach to anyone. She focused on her classes and kept to herself. She took a heavy class load and graduated in three years, when she was twenty-one. She went back to New York when she graduated, rented a studio apartment with the money from her grandparents, which was available to her by then, and still had some of her father's money left. She worked as a model to earn some extra money, and met Locke Logan. Locke was gentle and protective and he was the first person she had ever told about the abuse she had endured as a child. He asked her about it, when he saw the scars on her body, which upset him for her. He airbrushed them after he photographed her. Even with the scars she was stunningly beautiful. There was a gentle aura about her, and something magical about her from within. Listening to her history, Locke knew that Halley was a remarkable person, more than he could cope with, or deserved. She was like a survivor of a terrible war, with scars so deep he had no idea how to help her heal them. She had endured so much and was incredibly strong.

And what struck him was that there was a light in her that nothing she had experienced had extinguished. She still burned brightly with kindness and hope. Her mother had beaten her body, but hadn't killed her spirit.

The first time Halley opened her heart and fell deeply in love was with the twins she gave birth to. She gave them all the love she had pent up for years and didn't even know was in her. All her forgiveness and love and compassion went into her mothering. She never told them the story of her childhood and youth. She didn't want them to know, and only said it had been difficult, and offered no details. She was afraid they might blame her for it, as her parents had, as though it had been her fault. She was grateful that she had an unlimited supply of love to give the twins, all the more because of what she had been through herself.

Once she met Robert, she told him her secrets over time, and eventually had told him all of it. He had guessed some of it from her writing, where she exposed herself and her deepest feelings. It made his heart ache for her as he came to understand and know about her past. He was awed by her fortitude and endurance, and that there was anything left of her at all. He thought she was more human because of it, deeper and stronger, and more loving, not less. Before she met Robert, she knew she could love a child, but didn't know if she could love a man. He loved her with such gentleness and compassion that she blossomed and thrived. She was able to open up to him as she never had before, physically and emotionally. She admitted to him guiltily that she had never forgiven her parents, and he didn't see how she could. He hated them on her behalf, for everything they had done to her, but she didn't expect him to. He loved her even more, knowing her history. She had no bitterness or anger. She had survived, and that was enough. And she was able to love, which was a miracle in itself.

Robert was the first man she had ever trusted and loved. Their relationship was whole and clean, with no lingering trace of the damage that had been done to her. She had buried the past in a dark, secret place and moved on. She had left the past behind, with no desire to unearth it. Loving the twins, and being the kind of mother she'd never had, had healed her deepest wounds. And Robert was her reward for surviving.

Halley lived in the sunlight of the present, not the dark shadows of the past. She loved Robert purely and simply, as she did the twins, and he had unlimited love to give her. Losing him when he died was the first real loss she regretted in her life. The evil people in her past no longer mattered. Robert and the twins had amply made up for them and had healed her injuries. He had helped her to erase the past. She never thought of it. It felt like someone else's life, and she never spoke of it. The stories were too brutal to tell.

She thought of Robert as she sat in the quiet corner of the terrace where Valerie had gotten married. She wished he could have seen it, but maybe he had from wherever he was now. She still missed him but the years they had shared had been an immeasurable gift, enough to make up for everything else. She had no burden of hatred to carry. She was fueled and motivated by love. It filled her soul, poured through her writing, and soothed the pain of the past.

She had let it all go through her writing, and her love for Robert and the twins.

Valerie's wedding marked the end of an era. The twins moving to L.A. was a major loss for Halley. But she had survived much harder things, her parents, the orphanage, the years alone before the twins were born, when she had no one to love and to love her. What she and the twins had shared would give her the strength now to make a new life for herself, without them in it every day.

She never knew why she had survived her childhood. The scars were there to remind her, but they had faded and seemed unreal now, like part of someone else's life. There were no longer scars on her heart. Robert and the twins had healed them. Halley was a whole human being and radiated goodness and hope. The poison of her youth had never touched her. It had only made her stronger. She knew she could survive anything, and already had.

She had volunteered anonymously for years at various shelters and facilities for abused women and children, to show them that they could survive, no matter how violent the past. It didn't have to color their future or keep them from leading a good life. She had found her voice and healing through her writing. The abuse she had survived was not a death sentence, it was a challenge to face and overcome. There could be a good life afterward, you had to reach out and grab it, and Halley had, with Robert's help, and her girls. They had been the bridge to health and sanity for her, the way back.

A little while later, as it got dark, she gathered up her things, thanked the still busy wedding coordinator, took a last look around, and drove back to New York. She had a peaceful feeling of accomplishment as she did. All her minute attention to detail had paid off. Valerie's wedding had been a success. The twins were off to their own life in California. All she had to do now was start to fill her own life again. She had done it before. It was a mountain she knew she could climb. She had the courage and the strength, and enough love stored up in her to carry her through. Nothing could diminish her love for her daughters, and the deep love and respect she and Robert had shared. The ghosts of the past were gone forever and could never hurt her again. She had found peace, and the wounds were healed.

Chapter 2

Halley had an unexpected treat the day after the wedding. She was going through her research for her next book, putting it in order so she could see what was still missing. She had a man who did research for her on a variety of subjects. He was a young writer, trying to get his career off the ground, and for the past four years, he'd been grateful for the work from Halley. He said it allowed him to keep eating, which was a worthy cause, and he did good solid work and always gave her the material promptly. He was reliable and thorough, and didn't waste her time or clutter things up, giving her things she didn't ask for and didn't need for the book, just because he got fascinated by the subject and didn't know when to stop. Terence was British and Halley liked working with him. There were a few more pieces of information she still needed, and she sent him an email with precise questions. She had just hit the send button, when Olivia called her.

"Hi, darling," Halley said breezily, happy to hear from her. She'd woken up a little sad that the wedding was over. There was nothing left to plan, nothing to look forward to until the girls came home for Thanksgiving, which was almost seven weeks away. Halley was planning to dive into her new book, which should keep her occupied with the first draft until Seth, Valerie, and Olivia arrived from California for the holiday. "Everything fine in L.A.?" Olivia had been planning to fly back to California the night before, after the wedding.

"I'm in New York," Olivia said, and she sounded a little subdued too. The day after a big festive event like the wedding, with so much anticipation for months before, always seemed dreary and was a letdown, especially for those left behind. Seth and Valerie would be continuing to celebrate in Italy on their honeymoon, in Venice, Rome, and Portofino, while everyone else went back to real life.

"I thought you were flying back to L.A. last night," Halley said, surprised.

"I was." Olivia laughed. "It turned out to be overly ambitious. I was too tired and a little too drunk by the time I got back to the city. I'd left a mountain of stuff in Val's suite, and I couldn't get it together in time to run for the plane. I stayed in Isabelle Winter's room at the hotel after I got back, and got my stuff out of Val's, and I decided I don't need to go to California till tomorrow. I've got a meeting at my new gallery on Wednesday, about the show they want to give me in March. Can I stay with you tonight?" she asked her mother. Olivia was always very thoughtful about asking to stay. Valerie just arrived and assumed it was fine. And it always was, either way. Halley still felt that her home was theirs too, since they had grown up there.

"Of course. You don't need to ask me, you know. This is your home too." The twins had keys to the apartment, and Halley had an open-door policy with them. They were always welcome, and she was delighted that Olivia was still in town and wanted to spend the night. "Do you want to go out for dinner?"

Olivia paused for a moment, mulling it over. "I have an awful hangover," she confessed. "I don't think I've ever had so many martinis or so much champagne. And I think I had a margarita before I left." The wedding of her twin was a big deal to her. She would have to share Valerie now, with Seth. She had for the past three years, but Seth and Valerie weren't always in the same city, and when they weren't, Valerie and Olivia lived together. Olivia liked Seth a lot, and he was perfect for her sister, and spoiled her rotten, but now it was official, which was an adjustment for Olivia. She was still getting used to the idea, although Seth had been really welcoming to her, and had understood early on how much the two women meant to each other, and what a special relationship being a twin was. He hadn't tried to fight it at all, and had chosen the much wiser course of including Olivia in everything they could. But not on the honeymoon, of course. They were planning to be in Italy for three weeks, and Olivia already missed Valerie. They had never been apart for that long.

"We'll eat at home then," Halley said. "I'll pick something up this afternoon." Cooking wasn't part of Halley's skill set. She knew how, she just didn't enjoy it, and it wasn't what she did best. The girls ordered in whenever they were home. Halley had cooked for them when they were little, but she'd had no other choice then, before her books were a big success. Now she had other options, and all the best restaurants in town did takeout, especially since the pandemic. Ordering takeout had become a way of life in the twins' age group. Most millennials didn't cook.

"I'll pick something up and surprise you," Olivia volunteered. She loved the idea of spending a night with her mother. They could gossip about the wedding, and who was there. There were several TV and movie stars who were friends of Seth's.

"Come whenever you want," Halley said happily. "This is an unexpected treat. I was feeling sorry for myself, and sorting through my research. I'm starting a book tomorrow." She sounded happy at the prospect, as she always did when she started a book, with a little quiver of nervous excitement. The suffering would come later, and the fatigue, as it ground along, day after day, for weeks and sometimes months on a first draft, like the one she was starting.

"I won't interrupt you, Mom. I'll just dump my stuff in my room. I'm going to leave my maid of honor dress with you in my closet, I won't wear it in L.A. or probably ever again." It was a beautiful Oscar de la Renta gown of beige lace. Valerie's dress was made of antique ivory lace. The bridesmaids had worn a champagne color, and Halley had worn taupe taffeta, which she thought was suitably discreet for the mother of the bride. Halley didn't want to steal any thunder from her daughter's show. This was Valerie's big moment.

Halley had never married. Locke, the twins' father, was already married when they met. And by the time he got divorced, they were happier as friends. And she and Robert had talked about marriage in their twelve years together and never got around to it. They were afraid to upset the balance of the relationship that worked so well. He had never wanted children, as it turned out, and the twins were enough for them. The relationship they had was perfect as it was. Halley had made a point of sidestepping the bouquet at Valerie's wedding when it flew past her, in the direction of a flock of women who wanted it desperately. Valerie had aimed it at her twin sister, who reached up and caught it, and looked delighted. There had been so many details to coordinate at the wedding, right down to the garter Valerie tossed at the men.

Halley felt a little startled that it was all over. Months of planning had gone into making sure that every detail would be perfect and the way Valerie wanted it. Seeing it all happen on Saturday, just the way she'd dreamed and Halley had envisioned for her, was like watching a movie. Olivia felt a little dazed on Sunday too. She and her twin had never been away from each other for three weeks before, and Olivia was uneasy about it. Valerie had promised to call her every day. Whenever they were apart, the first one to wake up called the other. Olivia wasn't sure how Seth would feel about it on their honeymoon, but Valerie didn't care. She needed to talk to her sister. The connection between them was very strong. It wasn't something they planned or had ever agreed to, it was just the way they were since their birth. They had cried when Halley tried to put them in separate cribs, and they had chosen to share a room all their lives growing up.

"She looked beautiful, didn't she?" Halley said wistfully. "And so did you. You looked spectacular. And her dress came out perfectly, just as she said she wanted it."

"Maybe we should have switched and given everyone a surprise at the altar," Olivia said with a mischievous laugh.

"Thank God, you didn't. Poor Seth. I was afraid you might, I didn't even dare mention it, so as not to inspire you." The twins had switched often, as little girls and teenagers, just for the fun of it.

"Actually, Val suggested it once, but I said I thought you'd be pissed if we did," Olivia said.

"Nothing surprises me with you two." But in the end the twins had agreed that switching places on Valerie's wedding day would have broken the spell and seriousness of the moment, so they hadn't. And Valerie hadn't wanted to upset Seth.

"If I ever get married, maybe we will," Olivia said, thinking about it. "I'm more like you. I'm not so sure all that traditional stuff and legality is necessary. It seems a little oppressive to me. I think Val did it because Seth wanted to. I saw the prenup they signed, it was forty pages long. I got a headache just looking at it, but Valerie is a lawyer so it seemed fine to her. You never got married, so I don't see why I would need to," Olivia said thoughtfully, but there was no one she wanted to marry anyway. She had never been deeply in love, as Valerie was with Seth.

"It wasn't a political decision in my case, it was a practical one," her mother said. "Your father was married to someone else and by the time he wasn't, you were ten years old, and none of us cared." It had only come up once or twice for the girls in school, where someone made a comment. And by the time they got to high school, most of their friends' parents were divorced. So what would have been the point anyway? Halley's only regret was not marrying Robert before he died. She would have liked to be his wife and they thought they had time and had relegated the plan to "one day." And Robert thought he would get better, and didn't want to get married while he was sick. So it never happened in the end. It had taken Halley years to warm up to the idea. What she had seen of her parents' marriage, though only a dim memory, had made her leery of the concept. But her parents didn't love each other. She and Robert did. Her mother had always made it clear that she and Halley's father *had* to get married, and it was all her fault. Halley had paid a high price for it.

"What time are you coming by?" Halley asked her.

"Maybe in an hour. I'll throw my things in a bag and come over." It was an unexpected gift that Olivia had stayed in town for an extra day, and would spend the night at the apartment with her.

Olivia arrived at the apartment on Fifth Avenue an hour later, her long blond hair held up in a clip. She was wearing jeans and a Yale sweatshirt with paint splattered on it, like almost everything she owned. Halley had enjoyed seeing her meticulously put together the day before, and impeccably groomed, although there had been a little blue smear of paint on the inside of one wrist. She was wearing ballet flats when she got to the apartment, and carrying a big, battered Hermès red alligator bag that had been Halley's. It had a few paint specks on it too. After Halley hugged her they went to the kitchen and had a cup of coffee, happy to see each other. And then Halley went back to her desk to do some work and

Olivia went to her old room to put the bridesmaid dress away in the pristine white satin garment bag it had come in. Halley had promised to store Valerie's wedding dress for her too, and have her bridal bouquet preserved. The wedding planner was taking care of it. The bouquet Valerie had thrown was a smaller symbolic one.

They met in the kitchen again for lunch, and commented that Valerie and Seth would be halfway to Italy by then, since they had left that morning.

They were going to Rome first, then driving north to Venice, the perfect honeymoon spot, and from there to Portofino, a charming little port, with fancy shops, delicious cozy restaurants, and a harbor full of enormous yachts.

They talked about Olivia's new gallery in L.A. over lunch. She liked it better than the one she'd been with in New York, and she thought her show in March would be exciting.

"Will you come out for it, Mom?" Olivia asked her, looking young and innocent. Halley still couldn't believe how fast they had grown up, how quickly they had become adults, their early years over. She wished she could play that part of the film again, to savor every moment. She had been so busy when they were young.

"I'll come out if you want me to," Halley said, as they put their dishes in the sink for the housekeeper to take care of, and Olivia stared at her.

"Of course I want you to." She had never had a gallery show of her work without her mother and sister present. She said they were her lucky charms. Halley felt that way about both of them too. "What are you going to do to keep busy, like on the weekends?" Olivia asked her. She worried about her mother being lonely without them. Valerie said she'd be fine, when Olivia talked to her about it. Olivia wasn't so sure. Her mother had had a busy life with Robert, doing the things they loved to do, and they had had the literary world in common. But without him or the girls, Olivia knew it wouldn't be easy for her, although Halley hadn't complained once about their moving to L.A. She wanted them to be happy, and do what they wanted to do. She just had to figure out her own life now, after she wrote the book. Her writing came first, it had to be the priority or she wouldn't get it done.

Olivia went to meet a friend that afternoon, to visit a gallery she wanted to see, and Halley went back to the mountain of research on her desk. She was starting to make good headway, organizing it, when Olivia came back. It was after six o'clock, and Olivia had brought Indian food home with her. It smelled delicious as they unpacked it together. They both loved Indian food, while Valerie hated it. Olivia had gotten a text from her while she was out. They had arrived safely in Rome, had checked into the hotel, and were strolling down the Via Condotti, admiring the shops, where they stopped at an outdoor café for a glass of wine. The twins agreed to talk the next morning, before Olivia boarded her flight to L.A. It would be afternoon for Valerie in Rome by then. The time difference would be easier to manage from California. Valerie said she was having fun. She texted a photo of Seth, at the table, with a glass of wine in his hand. Just texting made Olivia miss her sister. She was happy to see her mother when she got home.

They had dinner in the kitchen, and Olivia told Halley about the gallery she'd visited that afternoon, and her new house she'd rented in L.A. She was going to paint in the big kitchen. The rent was a fraction of what her studio and the twins' apartment had cost Halley in New York.

"I'm going to have to work hard to be ready for the show in March," Olivia said, as they ate the lamb curry she'd brought home. They both liked it hot. Halley loved hearing how excited she was about her show. They talked about the L.A. art market and how it compared to New York's. Valerie had already commissioned her to do two paintings for their new home. She loved the work her sister did, and Seth did too. And as they finished the meal, Halley told Olivia about her new book. She was eager to get started, and Olivia liked hearing her mother tell the stories. She had only read a few of them, as she wasn't a big reader, and Valerie was always working and didn't have time. They were proud of Halley, but rarely read her books. They each had their very different jobs, and worked hard. Halley had taught them the importance of that while they were growing up, and they had taken it to heart. She was proud of both of them, and happy they had careers they loved.

Halley was hoping to finish the first draft of her book by the time they came home for Thanksgiving, which was a little less than two months away. The girls hadn't figured out Christmas yet, but she assumed they'd be coming home. The holidays were important to all three of them, and Halley had particularly loved Christmas ever since they were born. The girls had changed everything for her. Holidays that she had dreaded in her childhood and that were bad memories had become magical with the twins. They baked cookies and decorated the tree together, even now as adults. Halley took pride in cooking Thanksgiving dinner herself, and had a chef who came on Christmas. Seth had joined them the year before, once he and Valerie got engaged. They had spent a cozy evening together on Christmas Eve, and he had taken the twins skiing in Vermont for New Year, and had rented a fabulous chalet. They hadn't decided what to do this year. All their energy had been focused on the wedding, and now they could finally get back to other things, like Halley's book, and real life. The wedding had been all-consuming for Valerie for months, while her mother organized it all with the wedding planner, who had done a good job.

Halley and Olivia went to bed early. They were both tired from the wedding. Olivia looked at the clock in her room before she went to bed. It was four in the morning in Italy, and Valerie would be asleep. They each liked to keep track of what the other was doing.

Halley was in bed with her computer, checking emails, and there was a sweet one from Valerie, thanking her for the beautiful wedding. She said it was the most perfect one she'd ever seen. Halley smiled at the memory of how exquisite she had looked as a bride. Locke had taken some pictures of her, but they had also hired one of the best wedding photographers in New York. Halley couldn't wait to see the proofs, and hoped she'd have them to show the girls on Thanksgiving so they could look at them together. She had told the photographer she wanted them by then.

Thanksgiving was only seven weeks away. She knew the time would fly while she was writing. She lost track of time and the days. Robert had always been very understanding about it, and kept himself occupied while she was writing. He had worked until the last month of his illness, until he couldn't get to the office anymore. She had spent his final days sitting quietly with him while he slept. He would wake up and smile when he saw her there, and they talked for hours. Sometimes she got into bed with him and held him, and then he'd drift off to sleep, as she'd try to wish the angel of death away. She didn't want to lose him, and could no longer imagine life without him. On his last night, she had fallen asleep holding him, and when she woke up in the morning, the sun was streaming into the room and he was gone. He had breathed his last breath peacefully during the night, in her arms.

She put the computer away finally, turned off the lights, and lay in bed thinking about him. They had had so much fun together when the girls were young. He said he'd arrived for the best time, when they were old enough to be interesting and fun to be with, and good company, and all the messy part was done. They were twelve when Halley met him, and fourteen when he moved in. They had called him their Step-Fabulous and Step-Wonderful, and he took an interest in everything they did. He had encouraged Olivia to start painting and took her to the Art Students League, and helped her with her homework. He suggested law school to Valerie and she fell in love with the idea. He helped her prep for her LSATs and she had passed with high scores, which she said was thanks to him. The twins had been as heartbroken as Halley when they lost him. He was such a good person, and it seemed so unfair to all three of them.

They had wanted him to adopt them, but he thought it would be disrespectful to their father. Locke was erratic and often inattentive when he had a new woman in his life, but he loved them, and Robert had the best of them anyway. Sometimes they pretended he was their father to their friends, or people who didn't know them well.

Halley drifted off to sleep, thinking about him as she did. The dreams she had of him now were always peaceful. They didn't have that terrible raw ache she'd had in the beginning, when she thought she wouldn't survive losing him. But somehow she had. The last three years had been lonely without him at times. She wrote more to fill the void, and there was an empty space in her heart that she knew no one else would ever fill, and she didn't want to try.

When Olivia left for the airport in the morning, it was in a mad rush. She was always late for planes if Valerie wasn't with her to get her up and out of the house on time. She flew into the kitchen, drank a quick cup of coffee, hugged her mother, grabbed her bags, and ran out the door.

"See you on Thanksgiving," she called over her shoulder as the elevator came.

"I love you," Halley called after her, as the elevator doors closed. She heard Olivia's answer and smiled as she closed the front door. She was happy they'd had the extra day together after the wedding. She liked having time alone with each of the twins. They still shared their hopes and dreams with her.

She walked into her study and sat down at her desk then, in her bathrobe. She glanced at the outline she had been working on for months, on a big yellow pad. The story was all laid out and the research was in good order, as she picked up a pen and began to write on a fresh legal pad. It was exciting starting a book. She loved the smell of the new pad. She had written twenty-six books by then. This was going to be twenty-seven. Within half an hour, she was lost in the story, as she wrote line after line and page after page, laying the groundwork, sharing her characters' histories, and by the end of the first chapter that afternoon, the characters were real to her. Until the book was finished, they would be closer to her than anyone she knew.

She didn't bother to stop for lunch, not wanting to interrupt the flow. She grabbed an apple from a bowl in the kitchen, some crackers, and a cup of coffee, and she kept writing until it was dark outside. She helped herself to some of the leftover curry at dinnertime, took the plate back to her desk, and ate there, as the characters she wrote became flesh-and-blood people on the page.

She fell into bed, smiling, at midnight. It had been a very good first day, and she hoped that it would be a good book. Robert used to read the pages sometimes before she finished. She had never let anyone else do that, but he was so unobtrusive, offering few but helpful comments, that at first she thought she wouldn't be able to write without him. But she had. Just as she had adjusted to living with him, she had adjusted to living without him, and she could still hear his voice in her head when she wrote a passage she really loved and knew was good. She could always tell from the look in his eyes if he liked the book. And even now that he was gone, she still wrote them for him, or with him in mind.

Chapter 3

With her usual determination and discipline, Halley finished the rough first draft of her book three days before Thanksgiving. It had gone more smoothly than usual, which always worried her and made her wonder if she had left something out, some vital piece of a character's history, some plot twist she'd written in the outline and had forgotten. It happened sometimes, although she was meticulous with both the outline and the draft. The books needed very little editing. They were very clean, even in first draft, which wasn't always the case with writers. Some were slapdash or careless, or panicked and anxious and needed a lot of help. Halley felt confident and sure of herself when she wrote. And after she finished the first draft, she corrected it diligently in a second draft.

She had organized Thanksgiving very thoroughly weeks before, in anticipation of starting the book, but she still had some last details to take care of. The day after she finished writing, before she even read the draft, she went out and bought what she was still missing for dinner. She ordered all the pies they loved, mince, pumpkin, apple, and pecan. She got heavy cream to whip to put on top of them, and vanilla ice cream. She had everything she needed for the three kinds of stuffing, sausage, chestnut, and plain. She'd ordered the turkey a month before, got all the vegetables, and cranberry jelly. She was going to serve good French white wine, and she had already ordered caviar and all the trimmings for the first course. None of it was complicated to cook, which allowed her to shine the one time a year she prepared a real meal for them. The girls always said it was their favorite, and Seth had never had her cooking before.

The rest of her purchases were delivered on Wednesday morning. She set the table with beautiful linens, crystal, and china, and the silver flatware she and Robert had bought at the silver vaults in London. They had loved doing things like that.

She was wearing gray slacks and a white cashmere sweater when the doorbell rang at six o'clock. She knew they had landed on time. Valerie had texted her from the car. They were staying until Sunday, Valerie and Seth in the guest room, and Olivia in the twins' bedroom they had grown up in, still full of their mementos and treasures, and photographs of them as teenagers and at college.

When Halley opened the door to them, all three were smiling and laughing. Seth had just told them a funny story about their Labrador eating the turkey on Thanksgiving morning when he and his brother were boys. They'd had Big Macs for dinner, which he'd preferred. They'd been born and raised in Pasadena, and various parts of L.A. Their father was a famous game show host, frequently married, and never an attentive father. And his mother had married several times too. Holidays and family gatherings were always fraught with tension and disappointment. So Seth was looking forward to a real traditional Thanksgiving with his new family.

Seth had TV in his blood. His brother, Peter, was a tax lawyer, and had several big-name stars among his clients. Olivia had been paired with him at the wedding, since he was Seth's best man and she was the maid of honor. Peter was six years younger than Seth. They had both gone to UC Berkeley and Peter had stayed for law school.

He had spent the entire evening of the wedding flirting with one of the bridesmaids, and they had left together. Olivia wasn't too impressed, although he was handsome, and very bright. He was obviously a player, like his father. Seth was good-looking too, although more serious and reserved, the responsible older brother in a fatherly role. Peter had always been the wild one, and still was. He was divorced, and had two young daughters. He had shown Olivia pictures of them on his phone. They were four and six years old, a redhead and a brunette. He said he had them on weekends. He'd been married for five years, and divorced for almost two. His ex-wife was an actress with a part on a daytime soap opera, and was getting remarried to one of her co-stars. Olivia felt as though she knew everything about Peter, as he took off to the dance floor with the bridesmaid of his choice. Olivia wasn't attracted to him, and he wasn't interested in her. "Too serious, too arty," he whispered to Seth, when his brother told him to dance with her. The other girl was much more fun, and had huge implants. She was almost falling out of her dress. Olivia had the same perfect figure as the bride in the elegant beige lace dress.

When Seth and the twins walked into Halley's living room, after they took off their coats, they all looked related. Seth was as blond as Valerie and Olivia. He was tall and handsome and had a faint air of Hollywood about him. Halley noticed that he was wearing matte black alligator loafers she recognized as Hermès, jeans, and a blazer. He had arrived in a down coat, and so had the girls. It was freezing and had already snowed twice in New York, and it was bitter cold the day they landed. It felt like Christmas. It was cozy inside the apartment despite the weather and Halley poured them all champagne, after Seth opened the bottle for her.

"It's nice having a man around the house," Halley said when she thanked him, and Valerie laughed.

"Don't be fooled, Mom," Valerie informed her, "he's already told me he doesn't do house repairs. He won't even change a light bulb."

"I hope you'll carve the turkey. I make a mess of it," Halley said to him, and then toasted the newlyweds. They looked happy and relaxed, and Halley noticed that Olivia had paint on her hands. She usually did, and on her clothes. "Working on a new painting?" she asked her. Olivia was the younger twin by four minutes, as Valerie always reminded her.

"I'm doing a triptych," Olivia answered proudly. "The panels are six feet tall, it's a commission for a huge house in Malibu. The gallery is really busy," she said happily.

Halley went to turn on the lights in the kitchen, and light the candles. She had set a pretty table. The elegantly set table in the dining room was for the next day. The girls liked dinner in the dining room for special occasions, but they preferred the kitchen. It was cozier and warmer.

They had fresh crab for dinner, which was one of the girls' favorite meals, Halley liked to spoil them when they came home, like with the caviar she'd ordered for the next day. It had just been delivered before the twins and Seth arrived. Everything else was there for her to fix the next day. She had everything organized, as always.

Over their champagne, Valerie told her mother about the movie she'd watched on the plane and said she would love it. It was about a woman who took in a homeless boy who was later alleged to be a murderer. He told the court that an intruder had killed his parents. He was then accused of murder, and a famous lawyer took his defense, and it turned out that the father's girlfriend had killed the parents. The boy knew about her, but didn't tell anyone that his father had had a girlfriend. He was afraid his father would kill him if he did. The girlfriend was arrested for murder at the end.

"Movies like that make me anxious," Halley said.

"Me too," Olivia said. "I watched The *Sound of Music* again on the plane and fell asleep." Halley smiled. It was so nice having them home. The casual banter continued over dinner. Seth and Valerie talked about their honeymoon in Italy, and how incredible Venice had been. They'd both been there before, but it was even more special on a honeymoon. They had stayed at the Cipriani, and had wandered all over Venice, visiting little churches and artisanal shops. And in Portofino they stayed at the Splendido. The beautiful warm fall weather had held up until they left. It was a time they would never forget. And it touched Halley to see how happy they were together.

It was a warm, cozy meal in the kitchen. Seth loved being with all three of them. Although there was no father present, they felt like a real family. His own parents had been so dysfunctional when he and Peter were growing up, too often married and more interested in themselves than their boys. Seth and Peter got along with their mother now, but their childhood memories weren't pleasant. Both parents had remarried and divorced several times, in true Hollywood style, and as a result, the holidays had been a nightmare, with Seth and Peter being pulled between warring parents and dividing their time, with stepparents who were inhospitable to them, and with stepsiblings they barely knew. The Parkers were a poor role model for their sons' relationships later on. Both Seth and Peter had been divorced. And Peter was making up for lost time, casually dating many women.

There was a peaceful atmosphere in Halley's home, where Seth felt warmly welcomed, and it was obvious that the twins had grown up with a mother who loved them profoundly, even though Valerie said a little too much so. She liked living in California now, with Olivia nearby and some breathing room from their mother, except when they wanted to see her and went to New York to do so. Olivia missed her more than Valerie did, but she was living alone. Valerie had Seth to be with.

Olivia hadn't dated in the nearly two months she'd lived there. She was too busy painting, and hadn't explored the art scene yet, or met other artists. She was planning to do that after Christmas. She had promised Valerie she would. She worried about Olivia being alone, and she and Seth were out a lot, for his business, and her own, although they spent most weekends with Olivia.

They had coffee in the living room, and Halley retired to her room. She wanted to give them space to be together. They opened another bottle of wine, and went to their rooms at midnight. The girls were going to help Halley cook the Thanksgiving meal, as was their tradition.

The apartment smelled delicious the next day. They convened for champagne at six o'clock. They were going to sit down to their Thanksgiving dinner at seven-thirty, after Seth carved the turkey. He did a masterful job of it, although he said he'd never done it before, but he enjoyed cooking, unlike his wife and her twin. Neither of them was particularly domestic, and both were more interested in their chosen professions. Their mother wasn't a great cook either. It was a family trait.

Seth had watched while Halley made the stuffing, and he and the girls helped her cook the vegetables. He made the whipped cream for dessert while Halley basted the turkey.

"I love being here," he said happily, and gave his mother-in-law a warm hug. They all went to dress for dinner then, and met for caviar in the living room just before dinner. Halley served it with both blini and small triangles of toast, with finely chopped egg and sour cream, and lemon wedges on the side. "You run a very fine restaurant, Mrs. Holbrook," Seth complimented her with another hug. He was a warm person, and grateful to be there.

"My kitchen is like Brigadoon," Halley said, smiling at him. "It only appears once a year, on Thanksgiving." And they all laughed. The dinner was as delicious as it had smelled all day while it was cooking. The table and the meal looked like a Thanksgiving spread in a magazine.

Seth had a small slice of each of the pies, smothered in the whipped cream he had made himself. The girls only had one kind of pie each. Olivia ate her favorite, pumpkin, and Valerie pecan. Halley had apple pie with vanilla ice cream, and they were all quiet and sated at the end of the meal, when Halley brought out a bottle of Château d'Yquem, a sweet Sauterne wine, which was like mixing liquid gold with candy. It was Halley's favorite, and she poured a small glass for each of them. It was the perfect end to the meal.

They put the dishes in the kitchen to deal with the next day. Seth said it was the best Thanksgiving he'd ever had, and it was Valerie's too, since he was there and they were married now. While they recovered from the meal they'd eaten, they watched a movie, and went to their rooms at midnight.

Halley lay in bed, thinking about the day. She was soaking up the joy of having them home again, and excited to know that they'd be back in a month for Christmas. She had a book to write after the holidays, and she was planning to go to California in early March and stay for a few weeks when Olivia had her show. She loved staying in the bungalows at the Beverly Hills Hotel and hadn't been there in years, not since she'd gone there with Robert.

She fell asleep making Christmas plans in her head, and drifted off with a smile. It had been a perfect Thanksgiving, and Seth was an excellent addition.

Halley got to the kitchen early and made order from chaos before the others got up. Seth came in before the twins and she poured him a cup of coffee. He was impressed when he saw how clean and tidy everything was.

"You should have told me. I would have helped you." He looked as though he meant it. He was a successful man with a big job, but he wasn't above helping her, which touched her.

"It was easy," she said, and sat down at the kitchen table with him, with an espresso, and Olivia walked in.

"Hi, baby," Seth said, smiling at his wife, and Olivia laughed at him. She loved it when that happened.

"Wrong baby. Your wife is still sound asleep." He looked startled and then grinned.

"I always think I can tell the difference and then the two of you fool me. So are we going skating today?" he asked her. She was wearing a heavy pale blue ski sweater and jeans, her hair in a braid down her back. Seth's hair was the same color as theirs, but his eyes were blue instead of green.

"I hope so, if you can get your wife out of bed. Do you want to come with us, Mom?" Olivia asked her casually, helping herself to a cup of tea.

"I think I'll stay home, I have work to do. And if I break a wrist, I won't meet my deadline for the first draft of my January book."

Halley was a good skater, and had always gone with them when they were children. She had learned when she was at Connecticut College, and had loved it. She'd never had the chance to do things like that when she was a child, or in the orphanage. It would never have occurred to her parents to take her skating or do something fun with her. There had been no joy in her childhood, only pain.

Valerie walked into the kitchen then, also in a pale blue sweater. They often did that, showed up in the same colors, without having checked with each other before. Olivia always said it was some kind of weird twin telepathy. Halley had dressed them identically when they were little, for as long as they had been willing to put up with it. Valerie was the first to object. Olivia had liked it.

The skating party left the apartment a little while later, for the rink in Central Park, and Halley sat down at her desk to check her emails. There were two from her publisher, one about ads they were placing on social media for her next book, and the other offering her a choice of cover designs. She liked keeping track of all the different facets of publishing.

Halley dressed before they came home. They had dates to meet friends that afternoon, and were going to dinner on their own that night. They were planning to go to the Museum of Modern Art on Saturday, and invited Halley to go with them.

They all enjoyed the exhibit, wandered around the museum afterward, and walked back on Fifth Avenue.

Halley made hot chocolate when they returned. They were having dinner at home that night, since Seth and the twins were leaving for California in the morning. The days had flown since they arrived, but had been perfect.

Seth noticed the photographs of Robert in the living room and asked Valerie about him. She said he was their unofficial stepfather growing up, and explained what had happened to him. Valerie had mentioned him before, but he had never seen pictures of him. He was a handsome man and Halley looked blissfully happy with his arm around her.

"She must miss him," Seth said, sad for her. "She's young to be alone." She was only ten years older than he was. Seth was twelve years older than Valerie and closer in age to her mother. "Maybe she'll meet someone now that you girls are out of the house in California," Seth said. He thought Halley was a lovely woman and as beautiful as her daughters.

"I don't think she wants to. She was madly in love with Robert. I don't think anyone else would measure up to the reality, or her memories of him."

"You never know," he said thoughtfully. "I didn't expect to meet you, and then you walked into my life." He had been determined not to marry again, until he met Valerie. They were wonderfully well suited to each other.

Valerie smiled at the memory too. "But I didn't have much to live up to." Seth's first marriage had been a bad experience, and he had no pleasant memories of his ex-wife. She wasn't an evil woman, it just wasn't a match. They had split up after two years and she moved to London. She had been cold and inattentive, a competitive and ambitious network executive. The marriage had ended five years before. They hadn't spoken since. He had found her intelligence seductive, but she had been unpleasant and critical once they were married. His brother called her the Ice Queen. And his brother had fared no better, married to a narcissistic young actress. Both brothers had made poor choices in their previous life partners. They'd had no role models for successful relationships while they were growing up. But Seth could tell that Valerie and Olivia did, with a loving mother. Their own mother had been constantly distracted and absent.

"What were your mom's parents like?" Seth asked Valerie, curious about them. He guessed that they were loving people because she was. She never talked about them, and he only knew they were dead now.

"I never met them. My mom's grandparents died in France before her mother came to America. And her mother died when she was eight. She's never said why. Her father died when she was fourteen. Her childhood is kind of a taboo subject, she doesn't talk about it," she whispered so Halley didn't hear her. "She never talked about it when we were kids, and still doesn't. She's a very private person."

"What happened to her then?" he asked, curious about the woman who was visibly so crazy about her daughters, and so warm and welcoming to him. She was such a dedicated mother that he could easily imagine her coming from a loving home. "Did she live with relatives?"

"No. She spent four years in a state orphanage in New York. That I do know, but she never talks about that either. And she was on her own after that. Her father and his family had left her some money. She went to Connecticut College and then she met our father and had us. That's about all I know. I don't think she had a happy childhood. In fact, I think it's safe to assume she didn't, or she would talk about it. She never mentions her parents, and changes the subject when we do."

"She's such a warm, loving person."

Valerie nodded, thoughtful. "I felt smothered by her when I was a kid, in my teens. Olivia didn't mind it. I did. She's all right now, though. We're the only family she has. That's a heavy weight for a kid to carry sometimes," she said, and Seth nodded, thinking about his own family, which had been so dispersed and disrupted every time his parents got divorced and married someone else. His mother had finally settled down and had been married to the same man for ten years. But Seth and Peter's childhood had been a mess.

"I always felt like I had no family, because everything changed all the time," he said. "New stepparents, boyfriends, girlfriends, stepsiblings. I couldn't figure out who they were half the time, and I didn't want to. Every time I got to know them, they all split up again. All I wanted was to get the hell out as fast as I could, and never see any of them again." She knew that his mother lived in Palm Springs with her latest husband, whom Seth described as "nice enough." And his father lived in Mexico with a woman he'd married, and Seth hadn't seen him in five years. "Families scare me, or families like mine anyway. Your mother created a real family with the two of you. My brother thinks the way we grew up was funny. I never did. But he had me as a constant in his life that he could rely on. And he's actually a good father to his own kids, in spite of the craziness we grew up with. The woman he married is ridiculous. She's an actress and only cares about herself."

Halley walked into the room then, and they made dinner together. Seth made a big bowl of pasta carbonara, from a recipe he'd gotten in Milan, which was delicious. Halley made a salad, and they put some of the leftover turkey and stuffing on the table, it was a relaxed, wonderful meal.

They were eating some of the leftover pie when Seth said something in passing about a boat and St. Bart's, and all three women looked at him.

"You got the boat?" Valerie asked him. "You didn't tell me."

"They texted me yesterday, and I forgot. I had the bank wire them the money, so it's secure," he said, looking pleased, as Valerie glanced at Olivia, who knew nothing about it. "I've chartered a very handsome yacht in the Caribbean over Christmas and New Year's. And you're all welcome, of course," he said generously, looking thrilled. "We're meeting it in St. Bart's. It has six cabins, and we want you all to come. The four of us, plus my brother, and I thought I should invite my mother and her husband. We never go to Palm Springs to see her." Halley looked paralyzed as he said it, and didn't say anything. "That leaves us one extra cabin. We could even take a friend."

"My mother gets violently seasick just looking at boats," Valerie explained in a choked voice.

"Why didn't you tell me?" He frowned at his wife.

"Because you said you didn't get it, so it didn't matter. You were on a waiting list."

"The two groups ahead of us dropped out. So I've chartered it now." He looked at Halley, who was smiling bravely, determined to be a good sport.

"It sounds like a fabulous opportunity," she said kindly. "I don't want to ruin the trip for you. I'd be sick the whole time. Robert and

I took a cruise once. I was sick the entire time, either seasick or nearly comatose on medicine. We flew home after three days."

"I feel terrible," he said, as a pall settled over the table. "Are you sure?"

She nodded vehemently. "I promise. I'll be fine here. And it will be nice for you to be with your mother and brother. You should have time with your family too," she said fairly. "That's what married people do."

"What would you do, Mom, if we're away for Christmas?" Olivia asked her, upset.

"I still have the second draft of the new book to do. It's due in January. I can work through the holidays, and have it ready early. Don't worry, I'll be fine." She sounded cheerful about it, but Olivia knew her better, and hated to leave her alone, but the trip on a yacht in the Caribbean sounded incredible.

"Would you want to stay at a hotel in St. Bart's, while we cruise around? I was thinking we could visit various islands. But at least you'd have the hotel and the beach," Seth said. It sounded even lonelier to her, in a strange place, alone at a hotel for Christmas, worse than being at home by herself. But she'd been counting on spending Christmas with them, just like Thanksgiving. It hadn't occurred to her, or the twins, that they might go away. It was costing Seth a fortune to charter a two-hundred-and-fourteen-foot yacht, and he was committed now. Seth felt bad about leaving the twins' mother, but it was too late to back out, since he'd paid.

"How long do we have it for?" Valerie asked him.

"Two weeks." At double the normal rate because of the holidays, which he didn't say. Halley was quiet for the rest of the meal, while trying not to look upset, and Valerie came to Olivia's room to talk about it while Seth got ready for bed.

"What do you think we should do?" Valerie asked her. "The charter costs a fortune, and he's committed now. We can't cancel. I know Mom won't come. Do you think she'll be okay here?"

"Okay, yes. Happy, no. That's really sad for her, to be alone for Christmas. Why didn't you say something when he told you about it?" Olivia asked her, annoyed.

"Because he talks about stuff like that all the time, safaris in Africa, swimming with the whales, the Galapagos, China, Japan, Turkey. Most of it never happens. And we were third on the waiting list. He said it would never get to us."

"But it just did," Olivia said grimly. Valerie didn't want to upset Seth, her new husband, but instead, they were abandoning their mother for the holidays. Olivia felt awful. "Maybe I should stay here with her, and you go with Seth and your in-laws. That's what people do when they get married." Olivia looked very unhappy, but couldn't see any other way.

"He never takes his mother anywhere, and I know he was thinking it would be nice for her. They're not close, and he feels guilty he doesn't see her more often. And I want you to come with us. He showed me a brochure of the yacht, and it's incredible. You have to come, Ollie." Valerie hardly ever called her that except when she really wanted something. "We'll make it up to her," Valerie said, feeling torn between her mother and her husband, and it was an enormous amount of money for him to spend for their entertainment. "Seth's brother will come. You'll have fun," Valerie promised.

"He didn't say ten words to me at your wedding, he was so busy chasing your bridesmaids."

"He's getting over his divorce. He wasn't like that before. He's really a nice guy. I can't go without you," Valerie said. "Mom will understand. She always does. She's an adult. She'll figure out something. You heard her, she said she wants us to go, it's a fabulous opportunity."

"She said that because she's a good person and she loves us and wants us to have a good time. This will be awful for her, alone on Christmas, if we go."

"She's not a hundred years old," Valerie answered. "She's turning fifty, not ninety. And if she works on her book, she won't even know what time of year it is."

"She's not senile, for heaven's sake. Everyone knows when Christmas is," Olivia said tartly, annoyed at her sister.

"Not when she's writing. She always asks me what day it is, sometimes what month, when she's deep in a book." They both knew that was true, but this was different.

"I feel like a terrible person," Olivia said. "I want to go," she admitted, "but I don't want to leave her alone."

"She can see friends. We're not leaving her alone in a strange city. She lives here."

"And her friends go away every year, to their families somewhere else, or their country houses. She never has friends here over the holidays. She just has us," Olivia reminded her, and they both knew it was true.

"I can't get out of it. I'll have to go now that he's paid for it. And I want you to come with us."

"I need to think about it, and talk to Mom," Olivia said, looking tormented. They were flying back to California in the morning. There was no time left to talk about it, except by phone, which wasn't the same. They couldn't see their mother's expression or the pain in her eyes.

Valerie scurried down the hall to the guest room, where Seth was already in bed, waiting for her. She wanted to talk to him about it, and ask his advice, but he got amorous the moment she slipped into bed next to him.

"Thank you for a beautiful Thanksgiving," he said to her. "The best one in my life," and then his words were forgotten when he kissed her, and they made love, and he was asleep five minutes later. She felt sad for him. He had wanted to do something wonderful for her, having her family and his own on a fabulous trip on a yacht, and instead, it was turning into a crisis. And Valerie wanted her sister to come. It wouldn't be nearly as much fun without her. Nothing ever was.

In her own room, Halley was thinking about it. The prospect of not being with her daughters for Christmas weighed like a stone on her heart. She didn't want to deprive them of an exceptional experience. Seth could do things for them that she could never have done. The cost of a two-hundred-and-fourteen-foot yacht in the Caribbean for two weeks was way out of her league. Only Seth could afford that, and she thought they should go. But Christmas without them was going to be incredibly hard. It suddenly reminded her of the orphanage, when she had no family, and her college years when everyone went home for the holidays, and she had no home and no family to go to. She had gone home with one of her friends once, and she had never felt more like an orphan, an outsider, looking in through a window in a place where she didn't belong with people she barely knew. She had spent Christmas alone when she was pregnant with the twins, but she was used to it then and she had something to look forward to. Once she had them, she had never been alone for the holidays again, and she had always made it wonderful for her girls. She loved spending Christmas with them. Christmas would be meaningless without them.

Now she had come full circle. After twenty-seven years of celebrating the holidays with her daughters, they had other plans, a golden opportunity, and she didn't want to keep them from it. After all these years, she was facing Christmas alone. The prospect of it was harder than she could ever have imagined. But she felt she should be gracious about their going. It seemed like the best gift she could give them this Christmas. A two-week trip on the fabulous yacht Seth had chartered in the Caribbean. How could she cheat them out of that? She couldn't. She had to let them go, and not let them know how sad she was about it. It was a sacrifice she knew she had to make, out of love for them.

Chapter 4

As always when they were about to leave, Sunday morning was hectic. At one point, Seth took refuge in the kitchen, to escape the confusion of the twins trying to figure out what to take with them and what to leave at their mother's and who was taking what, carrying armloads of clothes to each other's rooms. As soon as Seth walked into the kitchen, he found himself alone with his mother-in-law. She was standing by herself, staring out the window. It was a cold November day and it was raining, which suited her mood. After three days of the house being full again, she hated to see them go. And it would be a long time before their next visit or hers to them. She turned to look at Seth with a sad smile.

"I hate to see you all leave, it was so nice having you here. I hope you come back soon."

"We will," he reassured her, and sat down at the kitchen table with her. "You gave us a wonderful Thanksgiving," he said to her.

"The best one I've ever had. My family could never seem to get it together for holidays, or anything else. They were always in the wrong place at the wrong time, with the wrong people. I got out as soon as I could, and got married myself, and married the wrong person. I never thought I'd marry again until I met Valerie, and I knew right away that she was the right woman. You did it all right with the girls. They're both fantastic women. Sometimes I feel like I'm married to both of them." He smiled as he said it.

"Twins have a very special relationship. Nothing comes between them. Sometimes I felt like an outsider with them when they were growing up." They were both quiet for a minute, thinking about the twins and how close they were, to the exclusion of everyone else at times. Halley had gotten used to it, but it was still new to Seth. There would always be times when Valerie would be closer to her twin than her husband.

"Fortunately, in different ways, I love them both," he said after a minute, and then looked seriously at Halley. "I'm so sorry about the boat. I thought I was doing a good thing, and I didn't mean to leave you out of it. I thought you'd come along. It never occurred to me that you wouldn't. And I hate like hell to leave you here alone."

"I'm a big girl." She smiled at him. "I've been alone before. I can handle it. And I don't want Olivia to miss what sounds like a very special trip. She doesn't need to sacrifice herself for me. She'd be miserable here without her sister. I want her to go with you. If I didn't get so sick just looking at a boat, I'd come too. Although your mother deserves some time with her family, without my tagging along."

"We haven't gone on vacation with her in years. My brother suggested it, and he's probably right, but I'd rather be here with you," he said, and she smiled. "We've never had much of a relationship. My brother is more forgiving than I am." She nodded, with a distant look, thinking of her parents. There had been so much to forgive, and she knew she never had. There had been too much. She had laid the past to rest and moved on in her life. It was the best she could do, and she had made a good life for herself and the girls, without bitterness over the past. But she could never forgive what they'd done, or even understand it, once she had children of her own. It made what her parents had both done even more unimaginable.

"I want you to go on the trip and have fun. It's an off year for me, that's all. It's not a tragedy. That happens when one's children get married. They alternate years with the in-laws."

"You won't have to do that with me," he reassured her. "I think this trip with my mother will be a one-off."

"She'll probably never forget it. It's a nice thing for you to do as her son."

"What about you? Will you be all right?"

"Of course," she said bravely. It was going to be much harder than she would admit to him, but she didn't want to spoil the trip for them. She had made the decision the night before to sacrifice this Christmas for them.

"The holidays don't mean as much to me as they do to Valerie. I kind of avoid them. So I wanted to make this Christmas special for her, and you were part of the plan. As I said, it never occurred to me that you couldn't come."

"You're doing a wonderful thing for everyone, Seth. You don't need to feel guilty about it."

"You're an amazing person," he said with feeling, grateful that she was his mother-in-law, just as both girls exploded into the room. They were both wearing black jeans and black sweaters, with their hair pulled back, and black sneakers, and for an instant, he couldn't tell them apart, and neither could Halley. She recognized Olivia first, because of her expression. She looked anxious, as she always did before a trip, and in this case, sad to leave her mother, especially if they wouldn't be together for Christmas. She was angry at Valerie for not vetoing the boat the first time Seth brought it up, and now it was too late to get out of it. She was still torn between going on the yacht with them and coming to New York to be with their mother. But she could tell that her mother was going to be stubborn about sacrificing herself.

"What have you been up to in here?" Valerie asked her.

"We were waiting for you two to get organized," Halley said with a smile. Just seeing them together that way made her happy. They were gorgeous women. It was like seeing double looking at them when they dressed alike, even more so as adults. They were spectacular looking, and Seth was admiring them too.

"I'm going to be the envy of every man on the plane," he said warmly, and Halley knew it was true.

They put their coats on then and picked up their bags, and Seth hugged Halley warmly before he left.

"You can still change your mind, you know. We'll get you the best seasickness medicine on the market."

"I'd be a zombie, and you'd want to throw me overboard by the second day, if not before." She hugged the girls then, and Olivia clung to her tightly for a minute, hating to leave her.

"Be careful, Mom. Don't work too hard. I'll call you when we land in L.A."

"Fly safely," she said, as they loaded their bags into the elevator, and an instant later, the door closed and they were gone. She walked slowly back into the apartment, realizing that she didn't know when she would see them again, but with the boat trip in the Caribbean at Christmas, she knew it wouldn't be soon.

"Now I'm in love with three of you," Seth said seriously, looking out the window of the car he had hired with a driver to take them to the airport. "Your mother is a wonderful person," he said to his wife.

"Most of the time," Valerie conceded with a smile. "Actually, she's pretty good," she said, and kissed him, as Olivia stared out the window in the front seat, worried about her mother and still trying to decide what to do about the boat trip. She had less than four weeks to make up her mind. They were sailing on December 20.

She was quiet on the plane, thinking about it, and then she put her headphones on and watched a movie. She was sitting with her sister, and Seth had taken a seat with a stranger. He had work to do on his computer, and he knew the twins would rather be together, even if they didn't talk to each other.

* * *

When they landed in L.A., Seth's car and driver were there, and they dropped Olivia off at her house. She said she wanted to unpack. She'd had an idea on the plane for a new painting for her show and wanted to make some sketches, and buy some new canvases tomorrow.

The airport had been mobbed with people coming back from Thanksgiving with their families, and the highway was jammed. It took them longer than usual to get home in the traffic.

Their housekeeper was at the house in Bel Air, waiting for Valerie and Seth, and made them dinner. When they went upstairs to their bedroom, Seth put his arms around Valerie and kissed her. "It's nice having you to myself," he said softly. "I love Olivia and your mother, but I haven't been alone with you in four days." They fell into bed, without touching their suitcases, and made love in their extremely comfortable bedroom. Valerie was lying next to him naked afterward, as he admired her body and trailed a sensuous finger around her breast. They'd had a great time in New York, but he was happy to be home, and to have Valerie to himself.

Olivia was happy to be home too, as she wandered around her house, walked into the kitchen alcove that was her studio, and turned on the lights. She stood looking at the lineup of her paintings for a few minutes, thinking about her show in March. She had a lot of work to do to get ready. Then she went to make herself a cup of tea and called her mother. Halley was happy to hear her. The apartment had been dead silent all afternoon. She had started editing her first draft after they left. It was a good way to spend a winter afternoon. It was too cold to go out.

"What did you do today?" Olivia asked her.

"I did some editing on the new book," Halley replied, happy to hear her voice. She hadn't spoken to anyone all day since they left.

"I had a crazy idea on the plane," Olivia said pensively. "Why don't you go somewhere for Christmas?"

"Like where? I hate traveling alone. I'll be happier at home working."

"You can't work all the time," Olivia reminded her, but she did anyway.

"Yes, I can." Halley smiled.

"You love Paris. Why don't you go there for Christmas, or New Year's?"

The last time Halley had been there was with Robert. It had been romantic and fun, but it wouldn't be fun alone. She never even went to restaurants by herself, and didn't enjoy it.

"What are you doing this week?" her mother asked her, changing the subject.

"I have an idea for a new painting, maybe a series, I want to fool around with it tomorrow. The show is only three months away. I need to get to work."

"That sounds like fun," Halley said. Listening to Olivia made Halley miss her more. It had been so nice to have her home. They hung up after a few minutes, and Halley sat thinking about what Olivia had said about going to Paris. It was a crazy idea, and the kind of wild, spontaneous thing she never did, and she liked being at home for Christmas, but not alone. Or maybe she could spend Christmas at home, and fly to Paris after that for New Year's. It was a big trip to take by herself. But maybe that was what she needed to do. Something crazy. She was turning fifty before Christmas.

Maybe she needed to celebrate it, instead of mourning her youth. The girls had wanted to give her a party, which she didn't want. They had been planning to celebrate when they came home for Christmas, so their absence was a double loss. None of them had thought about that when Seth told them about the boat. It only occurred to Halley now.

The seed Olivia had planted was stubborn, like a weed. Halley couldn't get it out of her head. It followed her around like a stray dog for days.

Halley had hated her birthdays since her childhood. They had always been sad, painful days. She preferred not to celebrate them, even now, and to treat them as normal days.

The girls sent her three dozen roses on her birthday, and they had a beautiful bag delivered to her that she loved. They called to wish her a happy birthday and she thanked them. Then she surprised them both. She felt suddenly liberated by the landmark birthday. If she was going to be old, at least she should have some fun.

"I'm going to stay home for Christmas, and then I'm going to fly to Paris and celebrate New Year's there. It's the craziest thing I've ever done, but I think Robert would be proud of me. He always wanted me to be more spontaneous. I'll edit the book before I go, and do it again when I come back, or I can take it with me, to work on at night. I have to figure out where to stay. And if I hate being there alone, or get too lonely, I can always come back." A week or

two in Paris was hardly a jail sentence. "It will be an adventure."
She sounded excited about it.

Olivia felt relieved when their mother told them her plan, and
didn't feel quite as guilty for going to the boat and leaving her
alone for Christmas, although she still felt bad about it. But Valerie
was being so insistent, and her mother had told her to go. Seth and
Valerie had invited two couples to fill the two empty cabins. The
trip was going to be fun, there was no denying it, although Olivia
wasn't excited about spending a vacation with Seth's brother and
mother. But she knew the two couples they'd invited, and she liked
them. With her spur-of-the-moment plans, Halley had freed her
from guilt, and Olivia was starting to look forward to her trip. So
was Halley.

She booked a ticket to Paris online for the twenty-sixth of December, and called a well-known realtor in Paris to see about renting an apartment for two weeks. She didn't want to stay at a hotel.
She wanted to feel Parisian while she was there. She kept reminding herself she could come home if she had a terrible time. But
how bad could Paris be? Paris was Paris. And oddly, she always felt
an inexplicable tie to it because of her mother. Halley was half
French, a fact she hardly ever thought about. And her big adventure would start the day after Christmas, doing something so different. She felt as though she was turning a page with her landmark
birthday. What lay ahead were like blank pages in a new journal,
that she could write any way she wanted. It gave her an incredible
sense of freedom she'd never felt before.

Chapter 5

As usual, Halley's estimate of her work was accurate. She had
finished the first draft of her new book just before Thanksgiving,
and she completed the second draft, making changes and correc-
tions, at two in the morning on the same day that Seth, Valerie,
and Olivia flew to St. Bart's to meet the boat. She was nervous for
them, since the last leg of the trip was on a tiny plane and there
had been mishaps before. She didn't let herself think about that as
she finished the second draft of the book, which filled her mind, as
it always did, to the exclusion of all else.

The girls had both been busy in L.A., getting ready for their trip.
Halley had talked to them several times, and they were looking
forward to it. And Halley's trip to Paris was set. The realtor had
found her a gem of a small house in the 7th arrondissement. It was
available for three months, but she only took it for two weeks. The
owners were going to their home in Marrakesh for several months.

She had a vague thought in the back of her mind that if she was having a great time, she might stay longer, since the house was available. She was keeping it open-ended. She had nothing to rush back for, since the girls were flying straight back to L.A. and not stopping in New York. The trip to Paris, and finishing the book, were keeping her from thinking too much about being alone on Christmas Eve and Christmas Day, which hadn't happened in twenty-seven years, since the twins were born.

Finishing a draft of a book was always like returning from a trip. She let mail pile up when she was working, checked her messages once a day when she finished writing, and answered only those that were urgent and couldn't wait. She cleared her desk before she started a book, and tried to focus on nothing but writing while it was in progress. As soon as she finished a draft, she caught up on everything, as though returning from another world.

She did that the night she finished, before she went to bed. Real time didn't matter to her when she was writing. She would keep at it until she found the right time and place to take a break for a few hours to get some sleep. Sometimes she didn't stop until the sun came up, or didn't go to bed at all if she was too wide-awake to sleep in broad daylight. And sometimes, she worked straight through for another day, and then crashed for a longer stretch. Her nights, while she was working, were more like naps. And when the book was finished, in whichever draft, first, second, or final, she caught up on everything, including sleep, and sometimes slept for ten or eleven hours after she wrote the last page.

The night she finished, she checked her messages and mail. There was nothing pressing, invitations to a few Christmas parties she hadn't gone to and didn't care if she missed, Christmas cards from old friends or people she barely remembered, or had never known well. There was a message from her publisher with text proof schedules, and marketing plans for her next book, which was due out before the one she was working on. She had finished that one almost a year ago. She kept up a steady pace with her writing. The one she was working on now was due out next fall. She dealt with it all in a few hours and went to bed late, hoping the twins and Seth had arrived safely at the boat. She had a text the next morning from Olivia, assuring her they had, and Halley was relieved. Olivia had included a photo of the yacht, taken from the dock. It looked incredible. They promised to call her soon and she knew they would.

She had a lot to do that day. It was four days before Christmas, and she hadn't bothered to order a Christmas tree for the first time, since the girls wouldn't be there to see it, and she would only have it for five days before she left. It didn't seem worth it. She had sent her gifts for them to L.A. before they left, and they were taking them to the boat with them. She spent several hours picking up things she needed for her trip, all practical and nothing related to Christmas. The holiday had become a nonevent for her this year, without her girls.

She walked past a florist shop that afternoon, stopped to look at the displays in the window, and bought a small tabletop Christmas tree that would look pretty in her living room, and that she could save until next year, since it was artificial, but looked real. It was small and elegant with silver and gold decorations and sparkling lights, and she put it in her living room when she got home.

She had to hurry to dress after that. She hadn't been sure she would make it that night, but since she'd finished the book, she wanted to go. It was the one Christmas party that was important to her, at the shelter for abused women and children where she volunteered. She knew many of them well. She tried to get there once or twice a month. It was run along the same lines as Alcoholics Anonymous, with total anonymity. None of the women she spoke to knew her last name, and she didn't know theirs. They were women who had had the same violent experiences, currently or in their youth. Many of them had been abused as children, and had partnered with men of the only kind they knew. Their men were as violent as their fathers had been, and it had taken every ounce of courage they had to leave them.

It had been hard for Halley to accept at first, but many of them went back, even several times, until they were finally able to extricate themselves for good. Some, even many, never did. Some of the women she had met repeatedly had been killed. The statistics were horrifying as to how many violent, abusive men made good on their threats and eventually murdered their partners. It was a fact Halley had to accept, volunteering with them. She never gave up when she met women returning to the shelter for the seventh or eighth time. The hope was always that this would be the last time they'd gone back, and they wouldn't be pulled back in again. The uninitiated who had never experienced abuse had the uninformed view that the women must like it, or feel they deserved it, when in fact they went back wanting to prove to their abusers that they were good people, after countless accusations of how "bad" they were, or they returned to their partners naively willing to believe empty promises that things would improve, which they never did. In many cases, the more violent the men, the more convincing their remorse afterward, until they did it again. It was only a question of when the women would finally give up and have the courage to leave. It took some longer than others to get there. What usually broke the chain of abuse was when their children were abused, and they fled with their kids to protect them.

Halley had never experienced the violent physical abuse of men, only subtler forms of sexual abuse, perpetrated on a child with no one to protect her, but there were others like her, many of them children and teenagers who had been violently abused by their mothers, which was sometimes hard to believe. Halley knew it well, and she spent most of her time with them. There was always the disbelief to get through that the person they trusted most and who should have protected them was the most dangerous person in their life, as her mother had been for her. Many of their mothers were already in jail for their crimes or had abandoned them, as Halley's mother had at a much higher social level, which should have made it more incredible but didn't to Halley. The children she met with usually wound up in foster care. The system was far more aware of abusive mothers than they had been in her day. They had developed immeasurably since those days, and emergency room medical personnel and police were trained to spot the victims, who almost never denounced their abusers, and protected them. The children were far more loyal than their parents and also justifiably afraid of reprisals.

Sabine had committed her abuse entirely below the radar, and benefited from the ignorance of the day, and the dignity of her husband's distinguished name.

Halley put on jeans, red sneakers, a festive red sweater, and a warm down coat, and took a subway to Charles Barton House, the shelter on the West Side, where she was a familiar sight and they knew her well. The woman who ran it knew who she was, but no one else did, and no one had recognized her in the ten years she'd been volunteering there. The twins were in high school when she started volunteering at the facility, and she never mentioned it to them. They thought it was her "night out with the girls," a small circle of her women friends. She often came home with a heavy heart, and was quiet the next morning at breakfast, but they were busy with their own teenage lives and never questioned it. It was an isolated part of her life she chose not to share. She had told Robert about it, and he respected her desire for privacy and only discussed it with her when she brought it up, if she was particularly troubled by a child she'd seen, or an outcome, if one of the shelter's adult clients was killed, or even worse, a child. They had lost several in the past ten years, killed by either one of their parents, or a boyfriend, or someone in their severely damaged lives.

The ones who did survive and recover from the trauma had a remarkable endurance and indomitable spirit that seemingly nothing could break. Halley had seen cases like that, which sometimes reminded her of herself. It was hard to know why some children survived and others didn't. Many of them turned to drugs in their teenage years, with disastrous results, but some survived whole, and surprisingly solid, like flowers that had grown strong and beautiful in the ashes of war, and which nothing could destroy. They were the lucky ones, protected by some blessing from the universe. Halley knew she had been one of those. All she wanted was to steal the more vulnerable ones from the jaws of death.

She walked two blocks when she got out of the subway, and went up the chipped steps of the shelter. It was an old brownstone that had been donated and hadn't been renovated yet. They had room for twenty women and children to live there, and others came for the day, or as outpatients for counseling and therapy. It was entirely supported by private donations and benefactors, and Halley was a major donor.

The house had been an elegant home at the turn of the twentieth century, but had long been in poor condition. It had been rescued and donated by one of their benefactors. The house had come to life again in what was now a slowly gentrifying neighborhood, with most of the old homes turned into apartments for middle-class families. The neighborhood was finally safe again, and the interior of the building had benefited from fresh paint and donated furniture. It had a shabby look to it, but the atmosphere was warm and inviting. There was a Christmas tree in the front hall, laden with decorations the children had made, and there were raucous sounds of shouts and laughter and Christmas carols coming from the living room, and the smell of homemade cookies from the kitchen.

Halley saw countless familiar faces as she walked into the living room, and several of the children ran up to put their arms around her and shouted her name when they saw her. She had three of them in her arms at once within minutes, and they showed her the Christmas cookies they'd made that afternoon. She smiled as her eyes met their mothers', and the children who had no mother there were even happier to see her. They clung to her like barnacles, and she needed ten arms to hug them all. She had donated an amount to pay for Christmas toys for each of them, and gift certificates for the mothers to buy whatever they needed, and she had paid for the party. She knew that she was by no means the largest donor, and that others had done as much, on an ongoing basis throughout the year, as she did. The children constantly needed clothes and school supplies and everything practical. They attended a public school nearby if they lived in the house for thirty days and intended to stay. A few were placed there by the courts, arranged by social workers who knew about the shelter, but it was a small private operation, which was what Halley liked about it. It had a family atmosphere and had remained personal.

Charles Barton House had been in existence for seventeen years, and had some notable successes, particularly with the children. There was more hope for a subsequent good life for them than for their mothers. The children were more resilient, and hadn't become addicted to abuse, which often happened to the women. The goal at the shelter was to break the cycle that kept the women trapped in abusive relationships forever. The shelter's greatest success story was a teenage girl who had been a resident in its first few years of existence, had been an outstanding student, had gone to college and medical school on scholarships, became a child psychiatrist, and saw the current residents pro bono whenever possible. Halley had met her and she was an extraordinary young woman. She was blind in one eye, from bleach her mother had thrown at her, and had scars on her face and body.

Halley chatted with the counselors and some of the women, played with the children, and was one of the last to leave. She left, as she always did, with a warm feeling, and promising to come back soon. It was the real meaning of Christmas for her, and one of the things that gave her life as much substance as her writing. It was part of her life she didn't discuss with anyone, not even her children. She would have had to explain to them why she cared so much about it, and she didn't want to. She had never shared the details of her early life with them. She took a taxi home wearing an arm full of the friendship bracelets the children had made for her, and a necklace of macaroni and wooden beads. She carefully put them in a box of treasures they made for her.

And the next day she started packing for her trip.

The girls called her from the boat. They were still in St. Bart's and were planning to stay there until Christmas, and would then set sail for Pinel on St. Martin's, a rugged part of that island with no electricity. Seth had planned their route with the captain. He was Australian and the crew of eighteen was mostly from England and New Zealand, according to the broker. They were known to be one of the most accommodating, popular crews for charters, and did everything possible to make the guests comfortable and keep them happy. And the boat was one of the most beautiful available for charter.

After they talked to their mother, Valerie and Olivia went to lie on sunbeds on the upper deck. The others were still having a gargantuan breakfast in an outdoor dining area on the rear deck, served by three stewards, a man and two women.

The two girls looked at each other as they lay down, and Olivia laughed at her twin.

"You are going to get so damn spoiled, you're going to be unbearable," Olivia said to her sister. "You already were, and this is going to make you even worse."

Valerie grinned and nodded. "Yeah, I know. Seth is very good to me." She was grateful for it and didn't take it for granted.

"Good to you? He spoils you rotten. You don't deserve it, but I'm happy for you. His mother is nice, by the way." Olivia had talked to Katherine at dinner the night before, sitting next to her. She wasn't an exciting person, but she seemed like a decent woman, even if Seth said she had never been an attentive mother. And she seemed somewhat ill at ease in his extravagant life. Her husband had sold insurance and was retired, and she was in real estate in Palm Springs. They were ordinary people. As a game show host, Seth's father had been a big step up for Katherine. She had been young and pretty then. Of the three husbands she'd had since, her current one was the nicest, though also not an exciting person.

Katherine enjoyed talking to Olivia, half the time she was confused and thought she was talking to her daughter-in-law. Olivia finally stopped correcting her. It didn't matter. At least someone was talking to her. Katherine's husband, Frank, was playing liar's dice with two of the other guests. The atmosphere among all of them was relaxed and easy, although the group was very mixed in both age and lifestyle. Seth and Valerie had an eclectic, varied group of friends. One of the couples they'd invited, Ted and Marie, were lawyers at Valerie's firm. And the other, Jaclyn and Basil, were British, worked in TV, and were friends of Seth's. Basil was a sound technician, and Jaclyn was a screenwriter. Everyone got along.

"Peter is nice too." Valerie put in a good word for her brother-in-law. She wanted Olivia to like him, and she knew she wasn't impressed. He was less serious and more extroverted than Seth. He was smart, had a good career as a tax lawyer, and had a sense of humor. "What do you think?" Valerie asked her, and Olivia rolled her eyes at her twin.

"Stop pushing. He's fine. We have you and Seth in common, and that's all, and we'll see each other at your kids' birthdays and christenings. That's enough." Olivia could tell Peter was a womanizer, and seeing him in action at the wedding had turned her off.

"His kids are adorable," Valerie added as a selling point, and Olivia gave her a shove.

"I'm sure they are. And so are the fifty women he met online in the last month. He's a player, Val. I'm sure he dates hot girls in L.A. I'm an artist, I don't have breast implants, I hardly ever wear makeup, and everything I own is covered in paint, except what I bought for this trip. I'm not his style, and he's not mine. But he's perfectly good company."

"How do you know who *is* your style?" Valerie said, exasperated. "You never date. All you do is paint."

"I have a show in less than three months. And dating is too much work, and it seems so fake. I get dressed up to go out and seduce somebody, and then they get the real me and have to think

I'm adorable in overalls covered in paint, with uncombed hair. I had to buy a new hairbrush for the trip because I couldn't even find mine. I think I threw it out by mistake."

"You need to make more effort," Valerie said primly. She always looked impeccable and killer chic. Olivia didn't care what she wore.

"That's probably true, but I'm perfectly happy the way I am." The only time Olivia made an effort to look decent was when she went out with Valerie and Seth.

"You're going to wind up an old maid," Valerie warned her, as Peter arrived on the upper deck in a bathing suit with dolphins on it, ready to sunbathe, with the business sections of *The New York Times,* the London *Financial Times,* and *The Wall Street Journal,* and Olivia closed her eyes, lay in the sun, and ignored them both. Seth joined them a few minutes later, to make sure everyone was happy.

Peter asked him if there was a disco to go dancing in St. Bart's, and Seth said he'd look into it, and a few minutes later, he went back downstairs to check on the other guests, and Olivia pretended to be asleep. She didn't want to make chitchat with Peter and didn't care about the disco, and he was engrossed in his newspapers anyway. Valerie left a little while later to find Seth, and by then Olivia really was asleep in the warm sun, and snoring softly. She woke up with a start an hour later, and Peter was lying on the sunbed next to her, and smiled.

"You snore," Peter said with a look of amusement. Olivia rolled over onto her side and gave him an irritated look.

"Thank you for telling me."

"I do too. A lot of people do. Do you like to dance? I never got to dance with you at the wedding."

"You were busy."

"Jeanie and I used to date when we were in college. It was fun seeing her again," he said easily. "We both got incredibly drunk that night," he added with a grin. There was no artifice about him. He was like a big teddy bear, or a big kid. Olivia laughed sheepishly.

"I did too. I had an unbelievable hangover the next day. It was a beautiful wedding, though," she said, thinking about it. "They lead a charmed life, your brother and my sister."

"He can afford it, so why not. And he's crazy in love with your sister. He'll be good to her." He looked at Olivia intently then. "It must be weird having someone who looks exactly like you, like looking in the mirror." She smiled when he said it. "I never know which one of you I'm talking to."

"I'll give you a clue," she said, grinning. "She always looks perfect. I forget to comb my hair. Or actually, I don't bother to when I'm painting, and I always have paint all over me, somewhere."

"Good to know," he said, as they lay side-by-side on their sunbeds, chatting. "What do you paint?"

"Abstracts. Big ones."

"Do you enjoy it?"

"I love it." He rolled over on one elbow then, and took a good look at her, and looked like he was going to share something important with her.

"I usually date actresses and models. It's kind of what you do in L.A. if you're single. Most of them are looking for a husband or a boyfriend to support them so they can stop working. It's nice to meet someone who enjoys what they do."

"I take it seriously. I have a fine arts degree from Yale, and I'm not looking for a husband or a boyfriend."

He nodded. "I figured. That's probably a good thing."

"Why?" She was curious.

"The snoring, and the uncombed hair. You know, you can get special strips to wear over your nose for the snoring. My ex-wife made me wear them. They didn't work, apparently I'm a serious case, Level Three. But they give the other person the impression that you're trying to do something about it. I actually used to take them off when she went to sleep, and pretended they fell off in the night. That's probably why the marriage failed. I wasn't serious enough about the snoring. It can be a real deal-breaker. She also had me wearing glasses with little lights on them to change my sleeping patterns."

"Did they work?" Olivia asked, amused.

"Not really. I put them in the recycling bin. She told our couples counselor about it. Apparently, it showed a bad attitude on my part. Our kids are great, though, so it was all worth it. Do you want to see a picture of them?" he offered enthusiastically, reaching for his phone.

"You showed me at the wedding. They're adorable."

"Thank you. I didn't remember, sorry. I must have already been drunk by then. It was a great wedding. You never answered when I asked if you like to dance."

"It depends what, when, and with whom," she said, smiling at him. He was funny, and a little awkward.

"Well, we're related now, and I figure we're going to be at a lot of weddings over the years—my kids, Seth and Valerie's kids—and we can always dance with each other if the weddings are boring. Most weddings are a lot of people thrown together who don't know each other, all dressed up. And no one introduces them to each other, so they stand around, bored. That doesn't always make for a good party. But at least we'll have each other to talk to and dance with. We should practice tonight so we're ready, if Seth finds somewhere where we can dance. Or maybe we can just play music on the boat. This is amazing, isn't it?" She nodded. She had never seen anything as luxurious and couldn't begin to guess what it had cost Valerie's husband to charter. "My brother has always been incredibly generous," he said. "I didn't think he'd ever get married again, until he met your sister. Does she snore too, since you're identical?" Olivia laughed out loud when he said it.

"No, actually, she doesn't. But I have allergies."

"Then you're not identical," he said confidently, and then he was curious again. "Do you like being a twin?"

"We love it. We had a lot of fun with it when we were younger. And I think we're closer than most sisters. We shared an apartment and a bedroom all our life until she and Seth got married."

"I'm close to Seth, but I wouldn't want to share a bedroom with him. I need my space. But we've gone on a lot of trips together. He's the best guy I know. He's someone you can always count on. Our parents were pretty unreliable, and he was always there for me."

"Valerie and I are like that," Olivia said. "Except that our mother is super reliable. We could always count on her."

"I guess that's why you're both such nice, solid, normal people, and I mean that as a compliment. And I don't think it's a mystery why Seth and I both failed in our marriages. Our mother's a nice person, and our father is a character. But they were terrible role models for relationships. They made poor choices, and so did we, and then they screwed it up every time, after marrying the wrong person. Seth and I learned from our mistakes, but we did it the hard way. I think my mom is okay now, and her current husband is a good guy, although pretty boring. But she seems to like him, and I don't think she has the energy to get divorced again, which is a good thing. We had a revolving door on our homes while we were growing up. And you never knew who would come through them."

"Our father wasn't the best choice either," Olivia said quietly, "but our mother managed fine on her own, and was kind of mother and father to us. We had everything we needed from her emotionally. He was just a cameo appearance occasionally."

"Our whole family were guest stars who changed every season. The only constants were the two of us," Peter said, as Valerie and Seth appeared on the sundeck to check on them.

"What are you two up to?" Seth inquired, and sat down on a sunbed next to them, as Valerie slathered sunblock on him so he didn't burn, since he was so fair. Peter had brown hair and dark brown eyes, and they looked nothing alike.

"We're just covering the basics," Peter said, and turned to Valerie. "You didn't tell me that your sister snores," he said seriously, and Valerie looked mortified.

"She does *not*," she said, glancing at Olivia, who was laughing.

"Oh yes, she does. Don't lie. I heard her and she admitted it. She needs to get those little strips that Barbara made me wear, if she ever wants to find a husband." Seth started to laugh, Olivia was grinning, and Valerie wasn't sure how to react.

"Peter says I'm going to wind up an old maid if I snore," Olivia volunteered. "I want to be a spinster aunt one day."

"So are we going dancing tonight?" Peter asked his brother.

"Apparently there's a very good disco, if you're serious. The crew will drive us there."

"I think it would be good for Mom," Peter said, and Seth laughed again.

"If you pour enough champagne before we go, she might enjoy it," he said. "Lunch is in ten minutes. We came up to get you." Valerie had been nervous that Peter and Olivia would be at each other's throats by then, but they seemed very much at ease, almost like a real brother and sister, taking friendly potshots at each other, and there had been a few serious moments before their respective siblings joined them.

"We'll be down in a minute," Peter said, as Seth and Valerie disappeared down the staircase to the lower deck, where lunch was being served. "Shall we?" he asked Olivia, and she got up and wrapped a turquoise pareo around her. She was wearing a black bikini and had the same spectacular body as her twin. Peter made no comment about it, but followed her down the staircase, watching the natural sway of her hips. He was looking forward to dancing with her at the disco, and planned to make sure they went.

Chapter 6

On the morning of Christmas Eve, Halley had everything ready for her trip. The clothes she was taking were hanging on a rack in her bedroom, ready to put in her suitcase, with all the accessories laid out to go with them, bags and shoes. She was taking casual clothes, since she wasn't going to be doing anything special, just walking and exploring museums and places she had liked before, and some shopping. She was packing one simple black dress, in case she went to a nice restaurant for dinner, though she wasn't planning to. She was going to cook for herself, or go to nearby neighborhood bistros that were busy and informal enough that she wouldn't feel uncomfortable being alone. People-watching had always seemed exceptionally good to her in Paris restaurants. The combinations were always interesting, much older men with pretty, very young women, or sexy, sophisticated middle-aged or older women with handsome young men, couples who looked bored with each other and flirted with people at other tables, girls glancing coyly at men, hoping to be picked up, and men alone or in pairs more than happy to oblige them, some wearing wedding bands. To Halley's keen observer's eye, there always seemed to be an undercurrent of sex and romance in Paris. She had said that to Robert when they were there, and he had laughed, but they had made love for hours when they got back to the hotel. "Is that what you meant?" he asked her, as they had lain in bed afterward in their luxurious suite at the Ritz.

"Precisely," she said, and then they had taken a long bath together, talking and laughing and whispering. They were lovers and best friends, which was what made it so hard to lose him.

Millie, Halley's assistant for the past fifteen years, showed up midmorning, to deliver the typed version of the manuscript. She came to get the filled legal pads as Halley finished them, and typed them up neatly for her. She had come to bring her the last one, so Halley could take the whole manuscript with her and work on it during her evenings at home in Paris, of which there would be many, according to Halley. She didn't anticipate going out at night.

The manuscript was clean and impeccably tight. Millie had no trouble deciphering Halley's handwriting. She had worked for her for so long that she could read it backward and upside down, she knew what all the little abbreviations meant, and following the asterisks all over the margins was easy for her. Halley accepted the manuscript with relief and slipped it into her briefcase. Millie always had her manuscript ready on time, whatever the deadline. She also came in to help Halley in the office two or three days a week, with manuscripts and galleys to copy, bills to pay, papers to file, journalists to call. She communicated with Halley's agent and attorney, and genuinely made life easy for her. She was forty-three and had come to Halley through an editor at her publishing house, who knew Millie was looking for a job where she could work from home a good amount of the time. She wasn't a beauty but she was attractive with very fair skin, big blue eyes, and blond hair cut short. She had an easy California style, which was where she came from. She was very capable and solved all of Halley's problems on the days she was there. Her schedule was flexible. She would come in according to how much Halley needed her to do, and didn't mind staying as late as it took to get the job done. She had lived with her invalid mother until a few years before, when her mother had finally died. And now, like Halley, she was alone, and filled her days and nights with work. Halley paid her well for it, and Millie was proud to work for her.

She loved Halley's books and typing the manuscripts seemed like an honor to her. She was worried about Halley going to Paris alone. Millie never went anywhere, although she used to go to Atlantic City with her mother, because her mother loved to gamble, playing blackjack and the slot machines. Millie hadn't been back there since her mother had died. Halley's trip to Paris sounded ambitious and particularly risky to her, with a house rental offering none of the protections and security of a hotel.

They exchanged gifts. Halley had bought Millie a leather tote bag, to bring her things to work, but Millie said it was too nice and Halley was afraid she wouldn't use it. Millie gave her a cozy robe to wear when she wrote at night, and a red leather passport case for her trip, both of which Halley loved. Millie always gave her useful, thoughtful gifts. She slipped her passport into the case immediately, and put it in her purse.

"I wish you'd stay at a hotel. You loved the Ritz the last time you were there."

"Too many memories," Halley said simply. "A house will make me feel like a Parisian. There's some kind of guardian. They left the keys with him. And I'm sure the house has an alarm. Nothing's going to happen, I promise." Millie didn't look convinced.

"Let me know if you need anything, and I'll take care of it," she said, still frowning with concern. There was a warm mutual respect between them. Millie had been supportive through all of Robert's illness, and had helped Halley organize the funeral. She had common sense and good judgment, kept track of all the details of Halley's life, and reminded Halley of things she might have forgotten otherwise. The twins called her for help or advice or information sometimes too, and she had done little errands and missions for them, when she had time and didn't have a manuscript to finish. Halley's work was the priority, but she liked all three women and was grateful for the job. The girls had just been kids when she started. She lived further uptown in the East Eighties, in the apartment she had shared with her mother in the old German neighborhood that was mostly young working people now. Only a few of the old Germans still lived there.

When Millie left, Halley answered emails and then started packing. She was surprised that she needed three suitcases in order to take everything she thought she'd need. And she took a few of her monogrammed towels, in case she didn't like theirs. She was particular about good quality bed linens and towels. Halley surrounded herself with the best of everything, including efficient employees. Halley had promised to call Millie from Paris soon after she arrived.

When she finished packing, she made a salad and poured herself a glass of wine. It was Christmas Eve, and she hadn't been alone on that night since the twins were born. She tried not to think of what day it was, and of all the Christmases having dinner with the girls, dressed up and sitting at their dining table, and later, with Robert. Even though her childhood Christmases had been so painful, the ones that came later were precious memories. She felt as though she had come full circle, after all those wonderful years, and was alone again. But she was glad that Valerie and Olivia were together, sharing Valerie's new life, on the boat, with Seth's relatives, and their friends. It sounded magical. Halley stood looking out the window, as snow fell on Central Park. It looked like a Christmas card, with a dusting of snow sticking to the ground and the trees. She was glad that she was going to Paris, even by herself. It gave her something to look forward to.

The girls called her before she went to bed, and it sounded like they were having a wonderful time. There was laughter and music in the background. The girls were happy. Seth got on for a minute to wish her a merry Christmas, and apologized again for taking a vacation she couldn't join in.

"We'll plan it better next time," he promised. "We all wish you were here."

"So do I, if you were on firm ground. I'd be moaning in my cabin now, if I were there." They had left the port that night, to avoid the revelers, and were at anchor just outside the port. The boat was rocking gently, which didn't bother any of them, but would have ruined Halley's Christmas. Valerie and Olivia got back on the phone after Seth.

"We miss you, Mom," the girls said in unison on speakerphone. "Are you okay?"

"I'm fine. I miss you too, but I'm happy you're having fun. I packed today, so I'm all set. It's snowing here."

"We're going to play charades after dinner and have a dance party," Olivia told her. They sounded like children. "We're going to open our presents from you tomorrow morning when we get up, just like when we were kids." The gifts were all supposed to be from Santa Claus then, and one from her. She had always made Christmas especially wonderful for them, and Locke had turned up at some point in the day to give them each a gift. Halley too. It was always something fun that she wouldn't have bought them. She suddenly remembered the year Santa had brought them twin pink Barbie bikes, which she had spent all of Christmas Eve putting together with a wrench and diagrams, and almost didn't finish in time. She smiled at the memory as she talked to them. She had bought them each a Chanel handbag, a bikini, and a pareo. Valerie's was orange, and Olivia's shocking pink. The bags were both black, which would be useful when they got back to L.A. And she had presents from them to open the next day.

* * *

Peter turned out to be the most creative at charades, and Seth, Valerie, Peter, Olivia, and the two guest couples stayed up to dance on deck for a while after Katherine and Frank, Seth's mother and stepfather, went to bed. They danced for a while and then sat around talking about Christmas memories. Peter and Seth remembered their Christmas in Las Vegas with their mother, the third time she got married, at the Elvis Chapel.

"It was colorful," Seth said, with an arm around his wife.

"We should go to the disco again, before we leave St. Bart's," Peter suggested. They'd had fun the first time, on their second night of the trip. "It might be our last chance for a real disco," Peter said, smiling at Olivia. She'd had fun dancing with him and all the others. Peter danced with everyone, and was impressive on the dance floor. He had called his daughters that night, and Olivia noticed he looked serious afterward. She could tell that he missed them, and he went to his cabin afterward.

Halley went to bed after she talked to the girls, and when she woke up in the morning, the park was blanketed in snow, and she could see children hurrying there with their parents with brand-new sleds, and silver saucers to ride in, to try them out. It wasn't her usual Christmas, but she was leaving for Paris the next day so she didn't feel she had a right to complain. She had a wonderful life, and missing one holiday was not a tragedy. And she could guess there might be other holidays alone ahead, if Seth and Valerie had travel plans, or Olivia met someone and went away with him. They were grownups now. She couldn't hang on to them, and knew she shouldn't. It was an art, parenting adults and learning to step aside so as not to get in their way. This Christmas was a reminder of that. Other parents had to live with it when their married children alternated holidays with their in-laws. This was a first for her, but it probably wouldn't be the last, and as long as Olivia was single, and maybe even after, she would always opt to be with her sister.

She spoke to the girls again on Christmas morning on FaceTime and opened her gift from them while they were on the phone. They always got her a joint gift, and had bought her an antique gold bracelet from the 1950s at Fred Leighton. It was very chic and she loved it and put it on immediately, and they were wearing their new bikinis and pareos, which she could see on FaceTime.

Halley went for a walk in the snow, watched the children sliding down a hill in the park for a few minutes, and thought of the children at the shelter. She closed her suitcases when she got home, and was all ready to leave the next day at two P.M. She gave herself extra time because of the snow. But it was already melting by noon. Her flight was at six, and she had to check in at four. She had treated herself to a first-class ticket, with a seat that could turn into a bed with a mattress, a comforter, pillows, and a blanket, and her own TV screen to watch movies. The flight only took six hours heading east, and would arrive at six A.M. local time at Charles de Gaulle airport.

The day after Christmas, the doorman sent a porter up to help her with her bags when the driver arrived, and she came down-stairs in black suede boots and a big black down coat. She was wearing a white sweater and a white knitted cap and gloves, and carrying a big travel bag she loved that she'd bought at a fancy vintage auction. It was a big alligator Hermès Birkin that was well worn and looked seasoned, in a size they called a forty, which meant the length of the bottom of the bag was forty centimeters, or sixteen inches, and she could put everything in it and still close it. She had her passport, wallet, credit cards, cash in dollars and euros, a small pouch of makeup, her hairbrush, keys, and all the odds and ends she traveled with, and to freshen up with when she arrived, since she checked her cosmetics through in her luggage. She had put in a book that she wanted to read, a current bestseller, and the January *Vogue* to read on the plane. She always traveled with some small lucky things the girls had given her. The bag was bulging and heavy but closed when she left the apartment, and she smiled as she rode down in the elevator. It really did feel like an adventure. She suddenly couldn't wait to see Paris and the house she had rented. She hoped it lived up to the photographs the real-tor had sent her.

The snow wasn't too bad on the road, but the driver was careful, and drove slowly. The highway had been cleared by snowplows earlier and there was salt on the ground. There was a separate area for first-class passengers when she got to the airport, and an Air France ground crew member and a porter helped the driver get her bags through curbside check-in. She tipped them, thanked the driver, and walked into the terminal. They looked at her passport and all was in order. The trip was off to a smooth start. She noticed that a few passengers were wearing masks, as a cautious leftover reminder of the pandemic. Some people traveled with them now, particularly older people and travelers from Asian countries. Halley wasn't wearing a mask. She'd had the vaccine and felt comfortable traveling.

She went through security and took her laptop, iPad, and phone out of her bag and put them in a bin separately. Her boots and coat were in another one, and she placed her large, well-worn alligator bag on the moving belt. It was too big for the bin. It was a beautiful piece of craftsmanship, with a subtle patina to it that conjured up images of sheer elegance. It was unique and killer chic. She saw several women stare at it. It was hard to ignore for its size and style, an object of ancient luxury. It disappeared into the X-ray machine and lumbered out the other side, as Halley stepped through the metal detector in stocking feet and went to reclaim it. She set it down at her feet, got her boots and coat on, and tucked all her electronic devices back into the alligator bag. There was a horde of other travelers lined up around her, as it was a busy travel day, and as she stowed the bins she'd used, she bumped into a tall, good-looking man next to her, with brown hair and blue eyes, and a dusting of gray at his temples. He was traveling in jeans, after-ski boots, and a big down parka, and he smiled at her as she put her coat on, and they set off into the terminal to head for their gates.

She stopped to buy magazines and some snacks, put it all in her bag, which got noticeably heavier, and reached the gate in plenty of time to board the plane. She noticed the tall man in the black down jacket checking in for the same flight. He smiled at her again, and she nodded, and a member of the ground crew ushered Halley inside quickly as a first-class passenger. There were only four first-class seats on the 777 flight. She had reserved a single window seat, and the one on the other side of the cabin was occupied by a woman wearing dark glasses, with a Yorkshire terrier on her lap. And in the center section there were two seats together, as yet unoccupied.

A steward and a flight attendant greeted Halley and ushered her to her seat, where she set her bag down and got organized. She pulled a cashmere blanket out of her bag and dropped it on her seat, folded her coat onto the smaller seat in front of her, and got her bearings. The seat across the aisle from her was one of the two unoccupied. She sat down and took one of the magazines out of her bag and glanced through it, just as the last two passengers arrived, both men. One was older and took the middle seat on the other side of the cabin, across from the woman with the little dog, and the man she'd already seen twice in après ski gear sat down in the seat across the narrow aisle from her.

"We keep running into each other," he said pleasantly, as he removed his coat and the steward took it from him to hang in the closet. Halley noticed that he had dark brown hair with graying temples and bright blue eyes. He smiled and put a briefcase he was carrying into the overhead rack. He was tall enough to do it with ease, and then he took his seat again, put on his seatbelt, and accepted *The New York Times* from a flight attendant. He looked to be somewhere in his fifties, with an athletic body and a youthful face. He didn't speak to Halley again until after they were in flight, on schedule. He accepted the glass of champagne they offered once in the air, and Halley took the sparkling water and flipped through the movie choices with the remote, as the tall man glanced over at her.

"Do you live in Paris?" he asked her. She looked like it. Even in her wintry snow gear, she had a stylish air to her that looked French to him. He had put his paper down when he took the glass of champagne.

"No, just visiting," she said, with the remote still in her hand as she glanced over at him. Normally, she didn't speak to strangers, but he seemed friendly and relaxed, he had a respectable air to him, and there was a holiday spirit on the plane. "Are you going skiing in Europe?" she asked him. It wasn't like a pickup, they were just fellow travelers on the same flight, and there was no harm talking to him.

"No, my son works for an American law firm in Europe and lives there. They were with his wife's family over Christmas, and now I'm flying over to spend two weeks with them. He has some time off. I'm looking forward to it," he shared with her, and he looked happy. "I thought you were French when I saw you in the terminal." Her alligator bag was at her feet again. The steward had put it in the overhead bin briefly for takeoff, and had taken it down for her when they reached their cruising altitude. "Do you work in fashion?" he asked her. There was a quiet chic about her, which the oversized bag contributed to.

"No, I'm a writer," she said. She usually didn't mention that, but he was so friendly and open that she relaxed more than usual. When they didn't want to talk, they both had curtains to close off their seat area and give them privacy. Most people only closed them when they wanted to sleep, but some did it for the entire flight. It was the day after Christmas and people were friendly and more expansive than usual, and even the flight crews were more festive.

There were menus at their seats and a flight attendant took their dinner orders. Halley ordered the roast chicken and a salad, and he ordered a steak with vegetables, followed by cheese, and a dessert. He had picked a hearty meal and she a light one.

When the food came, they both paused the movies they were watching, and he glanced over at her again.

"I'm Bart Warner," he introduced himself, with his meal in front of him.

"Halley Holbrook," she said with a cautious smile, and he reacted immediately, which she hadn't expected, and usually liked to avoid. She didn't like having a fuss made over her.

"The novelist?" He looked impressed as she nodded, and he smiled broadly. "I'm a fan. I've read your work. I like it very much, beautiful character descriptions and great plots. I can't put your books down when I start them. You've kept me up till nearly dawn on many nights." He smiled at her.

"Thank you, that's nice to hear." She never knew how to respond to people, and most of the time the compliments embarrassed her, but she thanked him.

"You have a broad understanding of the human condition and emotions. And I particularly like the way you write about men and their reactions. You get into your characters' heads and the reader really sees how they got to be the way they are. I've read five or six of your books, and I keep meaning to catch up on the few I may have missed, but I haven't gotten around to it. I've been pretty busy." It felt rude to ask what kept him so busy and what kind of work he did, in the circumstances. She didn't want to be nosy, even if he was friendly and had initiated the conversation. She didn't want to abuse it. "How long have you been writing novels? I know you've written a lot of them."

"The first one was published almost twenty-three years ago. The second one really launched my career as a writer, three years later. That was twenty years ago. Not exactly an overnight success."

"But a very impressive one. I really enjoy your books," he complimented her again, and sounded sincere.

They chatted for a while longer, and then went back to their respective movies, and eventually she glanced over at him and he was asleep. One of the flight attendants drew the curtain to give him privacy, and when Halley's movie ended, she did the same, asked for her bed to be made up, turned out her light, and slept for a few hours.

It was a relatively short flight, and a steward gently touched her arm, and woke her to tell her they were starting the descent to Charles de Gaulle Airport in twenty minutes and asked if she'd like to order breakfast. She ordered croissants and coffee and went to the bathroom to brush her teeth and hair, and wash her face. She got back to her seat feeling fresh and wide awake, and saw that her neighbor's curtains were open, and he looked up and smiled at her.

"Did you get any sleep?" he asked her.

"Enough. I usually work late, and I'm fine with only a few hours."

It was hard to get much sleep on the New York–Paris flight, with a movie, a meal, and only a few hours to sleep.

"I travel a lot, and I sleep like a baby on planes." He looked rested too. Her breakfast came then, and he disappeared into the bathroom and came back looking neat and properly groomed.

The steward brought him his jacket to get ready for landing, and set it down across from him, as they came through the cloud cover over Paris and could see the airport below.

"Where are you staying?" Bart asked her.

"I've rented a house for two weeks." She smiled at him. And she suddenly felt ready for her big adventure. It was exciting. Christmas was behind her, and she no longer felt nostalgic or lonely. She felt thrilled to be landing in Paris and couldn't wait to see the house she'd rented, and hoped it was as lovely as promised.

"That's brave of you," he commented. "Through friends or an agency?"

"An agency," she answered.

"I'm staying with my son and his wife. She's French. She's very sweet and lets me stay with them when I come to town. They live in the 6th arrondissement. Where's your house?"

"In the seventh."

"We're nearly neighbors," he said, smiling, and reached into the pocket of his jacket for his wallet, pulled out a card, grabbed a pen out of his briefcase, jotted down a number, and handed the card to her. "That's my cell. Give me a call, if you need a hand with anything. My son and his wife could be very helpful."

"Thank you very much," she said, glancing at the card, and saw that he was the CEO of a major corporation. For all his relaxed, congenial ways, he was a very important man in the corporate world. Halley knew the firm by name, and that they made electronic components. He had a huge job, and Halley was impressed. And he appeared just as pleased to meet her, since he had read many of her books.

"Do you want to give me your cell number, just in case?" he asked her. "I'll put it in my phone just so I have it." Realizing what a major figure he was in the corporate world, she felt comfortable giving it to him, which she wouldn't have otherwise. She gave him her cell number and he put it in his phone. "It's been great talking to you. I really enjoyed it." He smiled warmly at her again, and she didn't have the feeling that he was picking her up, or flirting with her. He was just extremely personable, was relaxed in anticipation of seeing his son, and seemed like a nice person. She suspected he could have talked to anyone. He had excellent people skills, and had made her feel instantly at ease, even before she knew who he was, where he worked, and his status as CEO.

They landed smoothly, and were both given rides in separate cars to the main terminal, as first-class VIP passengers, and they met again at the baggage claim area and stood together, waiting for their bags. It took a while before the moving carousel was activated and the bags began to come out, as a member of the ground crew with them apologized that there were no porters at that hour. It was six-thirty A.M. and Halley's bags came out right before Bart's. He lifted them off the carousel for her and set them down. He didn't complain about how heavy they were, but she knew and felt guilty about it. He was athletic and did it with ease. The two ground crew members brought them carts. Bart's single suitcase fit on his, and it took two carts for Halley's, which she and the ground agent pushed toward the exit, with Bart right behind them with his cart and agent.

"I've got an SUV and driver waiting," he said to her. "Do you want a lift into the city?"

"That's very nice, thank you. I have a car waiting too. Really, thanks so much." Millie had arranged a car service for her stay.

They walked outside together, and their drivers were waiting, holding up signs that said "Holbrook" and "Warner," and they parted on the sidewalk outside and got into their cars. There was a Mercedes sedan Millie had booked for Halley, and an SUV for Bart.

"Have a great time in Paris," he said to her. Talking to him had made the trip more pleasant, and had made the time go faster.

"You too," she said with a smile, and no one would have suspected that neither of them had had more than three hours' sleep, if that, and had just gotten off a flight. They looked ready to start their day and tackle Paris, with all its delights and beauty.

He waved as he got into the back seat and was driven away, and two minutes later, so was Halley. She briefly envied him the family he was going to, and would have liked to do the same, but she was smiling in anticipation as her car headed toward the city. She dozed for a few minutes on the way, and woke up in time to see the impressive monument where Napoleon was buried. And behind her was the Champs-Élysées with the Arc de Triomphe at the end, and there was an enormous French flag fluttering in the breeze under the arch. She was deeply moved when she saw it, and the car rapidly headed over the Alexandre III Bridge to the

Left Bank, Saint-Germain-des-Prés, and the address of her rented house. It was on the rue Jacob, tucked in between other lovely houses. There was an entrance for carriages with tall gates and solid shiny black doors, and neatly trimmed hedges in front. It looked very chic. She had already agreed to pay the gardener for the duration of her stay. And she could see the guardian's lodge. There was a maid who would come three times a week.

Halley saw the guardian watching her as they drove in. He was standing in his open door staring at her before she could ring the bell. She walked over to him and introduced herself, and he looked as though he wanted to snarl at her, but didn't. She knew his name was Henri Laurent.

"I'm very pleased to be here and meet you," she said, as he continued to gaze at her suspiciously. "The realtor told me that you would give me the keys," she said in French. She spoke it adequately after studying it in private school before her father died and again in college. She still remembered a little from her mother, but had forgotten most of it since she was so young then. She continued to be pleasant to the guardian despite his unfriendly welcome.

"I don't know why they rented the place," he growled at her. He had a five-day beard stubble, and he didn't look clean to her. His hands were dirty, and the wool shirt he wore under a battered down jacket made him look even more unkempt. She stood there, waiting for the keys, and he reluctantly went inside to get them. She realized that he had a dog, and heard it more than saw it, but she hoped it was a good dog and would protect them. The dog came out a minute later, and Halley saw that it was a pit bull. She could never understand people who owned them. What was the point of having a dog who would terrify the residents of the house as well as strangers? It seemed to reflect his own attitude, unnecessarily aggressive.

"Is the alarm on?" she asked him over her shoulder after he handed her the keys, and he laughed.

"You don't need an alarm, and no, it's not. Medor here will keep you safe. You have no enemies in Paris. Why do you need an alarm?" She didn't answer. He stood in the doorway watching her again, as she went to the main door of the house and unlocked it with the keys. She groped for the lights in the front hall, located them and turned them on, and found herself in the elegant front hall of a small but exquisite classically decorated house. There was a black-and-white marble floor in the entrance hall, an antique Japanese screen, and handsome black lacquer chairs. She turned on the lights to explore the main floor. There were two sitting rooms which adjoined each other, and a wood-paneled library with a fireplace. Each room had one with an antique marble mantel. There was a graceful staircase which led to the upper floors. The dining room and kitchen were on the floor above, there was an elevator she didn't take, and the master suite was on the floor above that, with a large bedroom, sitting room, and dressing rooms, and two big marble bathrooms. On the top floor were four bedrooms she didn't need and wouldn't use. It would have been perfect if the twins were coming. The rooms were well proportioned with beautiful windows and curtains. It was a small house but perfectly laid out and beautifully done. She realized then that she needed the alarm code from Henri so she could use it. She knew from the realtor's information that there was a laundry room in the basement with three rooms for the help, and storage, and there was a large well-stocked wine cellar. It was a lovely house in excellent condition, and she could see easily from the furniture and art that the owners had great taste. They were at their home in Morocco for three months. She would have loved to entertain there if she knew anyone in Paris, but she didn't. She thought instantly how much Robert would have loved it, even more than the Ritz. Despite its elegance, the house had a warm inviting feeling.

She came back down the stairs to the main floor, after she checked out all three upper floors, and found Henri Laurent standing in the formal living room with the dog, which made Halley uneasy. Henri grudgingly helped her driver get her bags upstairs in the elevator. He said something under his breath she didn't understand and then left with the dog, and the driver left a few minutes later, after giving her his card so she could request a car whenever she wanted one. She had them on an on-call basis. She looked around nervously after they all left. The house was beautifully furnished, and so tastefully done. It was more space than she needed, but she smiled as she looked around her home for the next two weeks. Her Paris adventure had begun. Other than the creepy-looking, somewhat surly guardian, the house was perfect for her. It was even prettier than the photographs, and it was in a very desirable neighborhood, with antique shops and art galleries all around. She needed groceries, but other than that, she had everything she needed. The housekeeper had left her enough for breakfast. It was exactly what she'd wanted, and hoped for, and more. A little shiver of anticipation ran up her spine. She had actually done it. She had come to Paris. She felt very brave, and very lucky with the house. She couldn't ask for more. Her Paris adventure was off to a perfect start, except for an unpleasant guardian. But who cared about him? Halley didn't. She was thrilled to be in Paris and couldn't wait to go out and look around.

Chapter 7

Their last day on the boat in St. Bart's was idyllic. They'd been there for almost a week and knew their way around. They had been to the best restaurants, and had excellent meals on the boat. They ate dinner at L'Isola, the best and most elegant restaurant on the island, on the last night, and went back to the boat afterward, and the captain arranged for a van to pick them up at midnight to take them to the disco they'd been to before. There had been very fine wine at dinner, and champagne on the boat until the van came. Katherine and Frank didn't join them for the trip to the disco, and Valerie and Olivia were laughing and giggling in the back seat during the twenty-minute ride. Seth would have liked to stay on the boat with his wife, but they didn't want to be rude to their guests, so they went with them, and he ordered champagne, vodka, and tequila at the club when they got there. Alcohol was served at astonishing prices, and the bill didn't surprise him. It had been just as expensive the first time they went. Peter switched to vodka, and Olivia stuck with champagne. Everyone was in good spirits, the music was great, and they all headed to the dance floor shortly after they arrived. There were people from other boats, and some staying in villas or at the hotels. It was a racy American and European crowd of big spenders, whom the island depended on during the holidays to support their economy.

Peter claimed Olivia as a partner as soon as they got to the dance floor, and she had fun dancing with him. They had fallen into an easy friendship in the past week, and he genuinely enjoyed her company. She was smart and funny, and he was dazzled by her looks. They'd gone snorkeling together, and he admired how athletic she was. They stayed on the dance floor when the others went back to the table, and at three A.M., Seth shepherded them back to the boat after a fun evening. The crew were waiting up for them with a snack, and Seth and Valerie finally slipped away to their cabin, thrilled to fall into their bed after a long day and evening. Everyone had had fun. Their four friends stayed on deck for a quick snack, and then went to their cabins too, and Peter and Olivia were left under a star-filled sky, and relaxed slowly after a very active night, with one crew member at the bar to take care of them. Peter let him go after a few minutes and said they would help themselves, and they'd go to their cabins soon. The young crew member was relieved to be allowed to go to bed, and Peter and Olivia sat talking quietly. It was peaceful with no one else on deck.

"I haven't danced this much since college," Olivia said, lying on one of the outdoor couches under the stars. The silence of the night was a nice way to unwind, as Peter sat down next to her. "Or drunk this much," she added. She was comfortable with him now, and he had undeniable charm and endless energy. He made her laugh all the time, but there was a serious side of him she found appealing too. She liked him much better than she had expected to, and he was more relaxed than Seth, who always acted like a big brother around him, and was an attentive host to all his guests. Seth wanted everyone to be happy, his mother, their friends, his brother, his wife, and her twin.

"I like being with you, Olivia," Peter said softly, and gently stroked her leg, as Olivia let him. She was too tired to stop him and didn't want to, and when he kissed her, she responded to his touch, and the skirt she had worn to go dancing seemed to slip away of its own volition. Suddenly their bodies were entwined. The night was too inviting, and their mutual desire, enhanced by what they'd been drinking, was overwhelming. Olivia wasn't sure when it had happened, but she had begun to find him powerfully attractive after the first time they went dancing, and the feeling had gotten stronger day by day. He was easy to talk to and she was comfortable with him. There was a playful side of him which appealed to her immensely, and he had never known anyone like her. She was so honest and so real, so naturally sexy with no artifice about her. She was a good woman, and her natural kindness and compassion touched him deeply. He couldn't keep his hands off her, and neither of them wanted to stop as he made love to her under the stars. It was the most powerful wave of passion they had experienced. They felt bound to each other as they became one. It was the best sex either of them had ever had, and when it was over, she lay in his arms on the couch, and he felt like a new man.

She was what he had been looking for all his life and didn't know it.

"Oh my God, are you okay?" he whispered to her. He felt suddenly sober, and terrified she would hate him in the morning, but they had been equally unable to stop, and didn't want to.

"Yes." She smiled as she nodded and clung to him. She had never wanted any man as much, or loved one more. "How drunk are we?"

"I don't think I am. I think I'm sober, or I'm drunk on you." She kissed him when he said it.

"Let's not tell anyone. Val will think I lost my mind. Actually, I think I have. Come on, let's go down to my cabin before anyone gets up or the deckhands show up," she whispered to him, and they tiptoed downstairs like two children and slipped into her cabin, and made love again. Their feelings for each other were even more powerful the second time.

"I think you put a spell on me," he said, as they made love in the shower, and then in her bed again, and she laughed. They couldn't tear themselves away from each other, like two people who had been starving. And then she sat up next to him and laughed.

"Did I forget to tell you that Olivia and I switched places tonight? We thought it would be funny to do to Seth," she said. Peter looked as though he'd been shot as he sat bolt upright and stared at her in horror.

"Are you serious?" He leapt out of bed, and pulled the sheet around him as though it would make a difference now. He had slept with his brother's wife unknowingly, he couldn't think of a greater crime. "You and your sister are insane," he said, panicked at what they'd done.

"All right," she said, lying back on the bed again, "I'm just kidding. I'm Olivia, it just sounded funny for a minute."

"It is *not* funny, and don't you ever do that to me again. You scared the shit out of me," he said, and lay on top of her, pinning her arms down. "Swear to me you two will never pull a switch on me."

"I swear," she said innocently. "Besides, Val doesn't think we should do that anymore, except for unimportant stuff like drivers' licenses, or little things."

"This is not a little thing," he said to her seriously. "I think I'm falling in love with you. I've never felt like this in my life, or had sex with anyone the way we do. Isn't there any way to tell you two apart?"

Olivia hesitated for a long time before she answered. It was a secret she and Valerie had never told anyone, not even their mother. "Maybe," she answered vaguely, and brought a graceful foot up to where he could see it. "There," she pointed.

"Where?" Peter was still shaken by her pretending to him for a minute that the twins had switched. "What?"

She pulled two of her toes apart, and pointed. "I have a freckle Val doesn't. It's the only mark on our bodies she doesn't have. Even our beauty spots and moles are the same."

"I think you're clones," he said, staring at the smallest freckle he had ever seen, between two of her toes.

"I'm going to make you show me that every time before I make love to you. I am *not* going to sleep with my brother's wife because you think it's funny. It's not." He looked serious.

"I'm sorry, I didn't think you'd believe me when I said it. I wouldn't do that to Val either, sleep with her husband. Besides, I don't want to. I think I'm falling in love with you too, or it was the tequila. It was great, wasn't it?" Olivia grinned at him and he kissed her. "I mean the sex, not the tequila."

"I think I'm going to give up drinking so I don't get confused. I need all my faculties intact to deal with you. What are we going to say to the others?"

"Nothing. Let's keep this as our secret for now. We don't need them all watching every move we make."

"Not if tonight is any indication of the kind of moves we're capable of," Peter said, smiling again. "And I want you to meet my daughters." She looked faintly worried at the prospect of that.

"I'm better with adults than kids," she said. "What if they hate me?"

"They won't. I love you. They'll take their cues from that."

"Girls are difficult."

"They're not, they're sweet kids. They're only four and six. They're not complicated yet." Olivia nodded, thinking about it. She wanted it to work with him, and had never felt that way before either. Everything about Peter was new to her. He wasn't the kind of man she usually fell for. He wasn't an artist. He was conventional, he was a player, he had children. But she had fun with him, he was smart, he was kind, and she loved him, and sex with him was incredible, and she wanted more.

The sun had come up by then, as she looked at him. A new day had dawned, for both of them, in more ways than one. "You'd better get your ass out of here, before someone sees you when you leave, if you want to keep this a secret." They both did, they wanted time to adjust to it themselves, without dealing with gossip and opinions, which would only complicate things. She knew that Valerie would approve, which was all that mattered to her. She'd been pushing her at Peter for three years and it had finally clicked.

"Can we do this again?" he asked her, as he put his clothes on and wished that he could stay and make love to her one more time.

"I think that can be arranged," she said, smiling. She felt like a queen with him, a sex goddess, and a happy woman.

"I'll be back in an hour," he said, and she laughed. She loved the fact that he was funny and made her laugh. He didn't take life so seriously, except for his daughters. She was nervous about them.

"See you at breakfast," she said innocently, with a grin.

"I'm not even hung over," he said with a look of surprise. "You're definitely a witch. A good witch," he added, and came back to the bed to kiss her. It was a searing kiss which aroused them both again.

"Go!" She pointed at the door, and he pulled himself away from her, which took real effort, and smiled at her from the door.

"Thank you," he said, "and I'm going to demand to see that freckle between your toes before I touch you from now on." And then he slipped out the door, and Olivia lay in bed, smiling. The room looked like a tornado had hit it. They had made love on every surface possible. It had been a night she would never forget, nor would Peter. He was lying on his bed in his cabin, exhausted, smiling too. He wasn't sure what had hit him, an amazing woman, but he knew he wanted more. He could hardly wait to see her, and make love to her again. And even though her twin looked exactly like her, except for one ridiculous freckle, Olivia was unique.

Chapter 8

Valerie was already at the breakfast table outdoors when Olivia showed up, wearing dark glasses and a pink sundress over a matching bikini. Valerie was wearing a darker pink one, and smiled to see her twin. Their four friends had already eaten and gone ashore to shop before they left for their next destination. Frank, Seth and Peter's stepfather, was reading the newspaper. Peter showed up, looking jovial, while Olivia ate her oatmeal, and said a vague hello without looking at Peter, and Valerie's mother-in-law, Katherine, joined them, wanting to know more about their next location.

"Seth is talking to the captain about it now," Valerie said pleasantly. Katherine wasn't maternal, but she was a perfectly decent person, although Valerie could tell that she was self-involved, as Seth had said.

"What time do we leave here?" Katherine asked, as the steward set down a plate of waffles she'd ordered in front of her. "I want to go ashore one more time. There's a bathing suit I didn't buy yesterday, and I want it."

"They'll go with you whenever you want," Valerie promised. They were all being waited on hand and foot, it was going to be hard to go back to reality afterward.

She turned her attention to her sister then, who ate half the oatmeal, and then sat back in her chair. She felt Valerie tap her knee under the table, and she was looking at her pointedly. Olivia raised an eyebrow with a quizzical expression, and felt Valerie slip something under her napkin, and looked down to see what it was. It was the lace thong Olivia had been wearing the night before and had lost on the way back to her cabin. She had realized it while she was getting dressed in the morning, and hoped that no one would know it was hers if they found it. She glanced at Valerie, who was staring at her with a question in her eyes. Olivia slipped the black lace thong into her bag, and smiled at her sister innocently. Valerie gazed at her pointedly, and cornered her when they left the breakfast table and were alone.

"What is that about?" she asked Olivia in a whisper.

"Nothing. Tequila. No big deal. We went swimming off the boat last night after everyone went to bed."

"Naked?" Valerie asked with interest, almost sure Olivia was lying. She always knew when she was. Olivia was a terrible liar.

"Yeah, no big deal. He's seen it all before. He was so drunk, he didn't even notice."

"Oh my God, you're lying to me," Valerie said as she stared at her. "Do you like him?" She was desperate to know, and they never kept secrets from each other. "I told you he's nice." She wanted Olivia to like him. She loved the idea that she and her twin might be with brothers.

"He's fine. He's your brother-in-law. We're just being friendly and getting to know each other."

"How friendly, losing-your-thong-on-the deck friendly, midnight-swim friendly, or more?"

"Don't get excited, Val. We're not attracted to each other." Olivia felt like Pinocchio saying it to her, and Valerie would know.

"You've never lost your underwear hanging out with a guy you weren't attracted to before," Valerie said suspiciously. Olivia didn't want her hovering, or pushing her and Peter, or making more of it than it was. They didn't even know themselves yet, except that they couldn't keep their hands off each other, as demonstrated by the sexathon the night before. Peter saw them talking to each other from further down the deck and wondered what it was about, and then Seth joined them, explaining their route to Valerie, and Olivia went downstairs to get her phone. She said she had forgotten it in her cabin. Peter followed her down a crew staircase a minute later when no one was watching. He let himself into her cabin, so no one would see him at her door. Olivia looked up, startled, in her short pink sundress, and looked even more beautiful to him than she had the night before.

"What are you doing here?" she asked in surprise, whispering. "One of the maids will see you, they're doing the cabins." He quickly turned and locked the door and crossed the room to where she was standing, as a smile dawned in her eyes.

"You look incredible," he said, and kissed her, and a moment later, the sundress was on the floor, and her bikini a minute later, and she stood in all her naked glory.

"I forgot my thong on the deck last night," she said breathlessly, as he kissed her and pulled her toward the bed. "Valerie suspects. I told her we went swimming," she said and then forgot about it as he laid her down and put his head between her legs, and a few minutes later his bathing suit was off and he entered her, as she tried not to make any noise. It was over faster than they expected, and she looked up at Peter with a grin. They were having fun with their secret love affair. Peter didn't see how they could hide it for long. "We have to go," Olivia said, and they took a quick shower together and put their clothes back on. "I told Valerie I'd be right back."

He kissed her one last time and slipped out the door of her cabin, and Olivia found her sister having a cup of coffee with Seth, looking relaxed.

"What took you so long?" she asked Olivia.

"I couldn't find my phone," Olivia said blithely.

"Maybe you forgot that on deck too," Valerie said with a raised eyebrow that Seth didn't notice.

"Very funny. I left it in the purse I wore last night. Ready for some sun?" Valerie kissed Seth, and the two sisters went to the top deck to the sunbeds and stretched out.

"Do you think we should call Mom now?" Valerie asked her.

"She just arrived in Paris this morning. Give her time to settle in. You know how she is when she arrives anywhere. She likes to get everything put away immediately, and she won't have her bearings yet. I hope the house is decent."

"She should have stayed at a hotel anyway," Valerie said. "She can always move if she needs to, or go home. I still think it's crazy, her being there alone, not knowing anyone, in a strange house for two weeks. I don't know why you suggested it to her. She'll be miserable and lonely."

"I suggested it because it's too depressing for her to just sit there at home without us. Maybe this is what she needs, something new and different. She hasn't gone anywhere since Robert died, and she never travels now, or goes away alone, even for a weekend. She's fifty, for God's sake, not eighty, and now we're gone. Who knows, maybe she'll meet a handsome Frenchman," Olivia said, lying on the sunbed with her eyes closed, talking to her sister, and thinking of Peter.

"Don't be ridiculous. That's not Mom's style. What would she do? Pick him up on the street?" Valerie snapped at her.

"Destiny intervenes sometimes," Olivia said mysteriously.

"You watch too many series on TV. And on those shows the hot guy always kills the woman, or tries to."

"There's a cheering thought." Olivia smiled.

"We should call her later. She's going to be lonely in a strange house. After two days of shopping she'll go home. I'll bet you she's in New York by New Year's Day, and back at her desk."

"I hope not," Olivia said. "That would be sad for her. I hope she stays."

"Well, just don't lose your thong again. You're going to give Peter the wrong impression, and that's not fair."

"I'll try to remember," Olivia said chastely, grateful that her sister's eyes were closed and she couldn't see the grin on her twin's face.

Halley unpacked all her hanging clothes, after she made a cup of coffee and had another look around the house. It was beautiful and the owners had fabulous taste. She was surprised that they were renting it for three months while they were away. It wasn't the kind of house people usually rented to strangers, but it was through a very high-end realtor, and even two weeks was expensive. But she had decided to follow Olivia's advice and do something crazy and fun and out of character, and she had a feeling that Robert would have approved. Being alone for the holidays, once she knew the girls weren't coming home, was just too depressing. It reminded her of her lonely youth with no family to spend it with. She was alone now, but being in Paris made it special.

The house had a warm, inviting feeling. It didn't seem scary or ominous, other than the creepy-looking guardian, but she didn't need to interact with him. The housekeeper had left her croissants and orange juice for breakfast, and salami, cheese, and a baguette for a snack, and some macarons.

She finished unpacking in the master dressing room, had some of the salami and cheese for lunch, and thought about calling the girls, but it was still early for them, so she sent them both a text, and one to Millie, to say that she had arrived safely and the house was lovely. She had even noticed Porthault sheets on the bed, and felt silly for having brought some of her own towels with her. The house was luxuriously appointed, impeccably neat, and well stocked. It was better than the Ritz, and well worth what she'd paid for it. This wasn't camping, it was heavenly extravagance, and the treat she had hoped it would be.

After lunch, she decided to walk through the Tuileries Garden, which she always liked, and from there to the Faubourg St.-Honoré, where a lot of the best shops were. She walked along, window-shopping, feeling very sophisticated and glamorous, in Paris for the holidays. She was glad that her solitary Christmas was behind her, it had too many echoes of the distant past, which her daughters didn't know about. She only had New Year's Eve to get through now. It had never meant much to her, and she and Robert liked to stay home on New Year's Eve. They toasted each other and watched movies on TV. That was festive enough for her, and cozier than getting all dressed up and going out to a party, which was never as much fun as one hoped. She didn't feel cheated being alone on New Year's Eve. Christmas was another story, but that was over now, and she'd made it through, and kept busy, getting ready for her trip.

The Christmas decorations on the Faubourg St.-Honoré were still up, and beautiful, as they were on the Champs-Élysées, all lit up with red lights and electrical falling stars. It was only two days after Christmas, and her driver had told her that the decorations on the Avenue Montaigne were particularly elegant this year. She didn't call him for her window-shopping on the Faubourg. She wanted to walk, and enjoy the feeling of being in Paris. It was a car service the realtor had recommended to her, which she intended to use when she needed to, if she went farther afield, or when the weather was bad. But it was a sunny winter day, and she loved being out on her own.

She came back to the house after a few hours, as it started to get dark, and as she approached, she saw the guardian standing at his window. Their eyes met for a second and he glowered at her. He was clearly unhappy that she was there, and wanted her to know it. She understood but she didn't care. That was between him and the owners of the house, his bosses. She was an innocent, uninvolved party who had rented the house and intended to enjoy it, whether he liked it or not.

She had no way of knowing how long he had worked there, and if he felt proprietary about strangers in the house, but she intended to take good care of it. With her in residence, there would be no wild parties, drunken gatherings, or damage for him to deal with. She was a trouble-free tenant for two weeks and he could glare at her all he wanted or stare at her from his apartment. He seemed harmless but strange, an angry person, bitter about his life. She couldn't guess how old he was, maybe somewhere in his late forties or fifties. He was thin, and she could see that he had powerful arms when he helped with the luggage. There was a noticeable tension about him. Maybe he was mentally deranged, but she wasn't afraid of him. It took more than that to frighten her. She had given him a tip when he helped with the bags and he didn't thank her, so he was rude as well, and ungrateful. Maybe he had a grudge against Americans, or women in general. In any case, he wasn't a problem, in his own apartment, and she was safe in the house.

The twins called her that night and she told them all about the house and how much she loved it. The neighborhood was perfect and lively. It was easy to get to all her favorite places on foot. The house was comfortable and warm and cozy. It was even prettier than in the photographs, and the girls were reassured when they hung up.

"See, I told you it would be good for her," Olivia said smugly, and Valerie looked unconvinced. She hated to be wrong.

"This is the honeymoon phase, she just got there. If anything goes wrong, she'll freak out and be on the first plane home, and have wasted the time and the money."

"Nothing's going to go wrong," Olivia said firmly. She wanted it to be a success for her mother, and happy memories in the making, to replace the sad ones of losing Robert. Halley had been so subdued for the last three years, and Olivia knew she was upset about her birthday. "What could go wrong?" she said to Valerie.

"Anything. A broken tooth, the flu, a cold. She could trip on the sidewalk and hurt herself. A leak in the house, no heating, rodents. I don't know, but things happen and there's no one to help her deal with it."

"She said there's a caretaker. Don't be so negative." Valerie's litany of possible disasters annoyed her. She refused to be happy about her mother's little adventure, and expected everything to go wrong. Olivia wanted it to be perfect for her, and at first report it sounded like it was, and Olivia was thrilled, and refused to let her sister put a damper on it.

* * *

The second day in Paris started out even better than the first. It was another glorious sunny winter day. It was cold but there was no wind. Halley went for a long walk, all the way from the house to the Avenue Montaigne, where the rest of the luxury brand shops were. Chanel, Dior, Celine, Prada, Fendi, Bottega Veneta, Valentino, and others. She went on foot again, and stopped at all the shops she liked best. She lingered at each of them, tried on some things, sweaters, a pale blue wool Chanel jacket and perfect jeans, some ballet flats, a hat at Dior. She inched her way along, bought a gray cashmere sweater at Celine and tried on a duffel coat and patent leather boots. It was like playing dress-up, and she loved it. She missed the girls, but after the first few shops, she realized that no one was telling her what she couldn't buy, what looked too young, what wasn't the right look for a woman her age. They were harsh critics at times, especially Valerie, who didn't wear playful clothes herself. Olivia always accused her twin of dressing like a lawyer, and Valerie expected Halley to dress like a mother. Halley chose a wild shocking pink sweater at Gucci with butterflies all over it. She wasn't sure where she'd wear it or with whom, but it made her happy, so she bought it, and flowered sneakers to go with it. Halley smiled when she paid for them, and compensated with a very chic black Chanel jacket that was more her style. It was nice to feel free and young, and be doing something different for a change. She wasn't editing a manuscript, or meeting a deadline, or buying what her daughters said she should and already had ten of in her closet. This was her moment, and she was enjoying it fully. Sometimes, no matter how much she loved them, she needed not to be a mother, and to just be herself. It was a new experience for her. She had been on full-time-mom duty for twenty-seven years, and was serious about it. She never took a day off, had her cell phone on every night in case they had a problem and needed her. Valerie had Seth now, but Olivia was alone. And if she had an emergency, who would she call? Halley had been mother and father to them all their lives, and that hadn't changed now that they'd grown up.

Sometimes, they needed her more than ever. She was always at the ready to help, on call, like the reserves in case there was a war. But for this one brief moment in Paris, Halley was doing something for herself. She felt mildly guilty about it, but was enjoying it anyway. Her only regret was that she had brought her big Hermès alligator Birkin bag out shopping with her, because it had everything she might need, credit cards, passport, wallet, cash, her hairbrush if she tried on a sweater and messed up her hair, the keys to the house, the realtor's folder that she kept in her bag in case she needed his number. She'd forgotten to take her magazines out, and the bag weighed a ton as she walked along, but she didn't want to just slip a credit card into her pocket to go shopping. What if she lost it? And she'd brought her passport in case she needed ID.

She walked past a busy restaurant halfway down the Avenue Montaigne. She still had more shops she wanted to see, of brands she liked. She was hungry, but more than that she was thirsty. There were women having lunch on the terrace of the restaurant, and men having business lunches, tables for two with couples, a few bigger groups of young people wearing extreme fashion, and several young women wearing heavy makeup and miniskirts with brightly colored alligator Birkins on their arm. Halley didn't know how they'd paid for them, but she could guess. There was a small empty table on the terrace that beckoned to her, and she decided that she wouldn't be conspicuous as a single older woman. She didn't want to look desperate, and she looked chic enough in a black coat, black jeans, and heels, with her big vintage Birkin. She had a New York look about her, and blended right in as she approached the maître d' and pointed to the table in the sunshine. A man came up behind her wearing a stylish black suit and turtleneck with a black coat over his arm. He asked for a table, but she had gotten there first, so the maître d' escorted her to one, and settled the man nearby. He looked at Halley admiringly, and she ignored him, putting on her dark glasses. She'd had the glasses forever and loved them, a brand that no longer existed. They made her look glamorous as she sat on the terrace, enjoying the warmth of the sun.

She ordered crab salad and a virgin Bloody Mary, and almost giggled as she sat there. She wished that the girls could have seen her. Olivia would have been proud of her, going to a trendy restaurant alone in Paris. This was what she had come to Paris for, a little glamour, not just to revisit the Louvre. She put her shopping bags with her morning's purchases under the table, which left barely enough room for her alligator Birkin. She took time eating lunch, she had the whole day to herself, with no reason to rush. The stores would be open until seven, and she had hours more to shop. She ordered an espresso after lunch, with a dollop of whipped cream on top, which tasted sinful, and sat sipping it slowly.

The man who had arrived at the restaurant right after her, who was seated at a table nearby, finished his lunch before she did, and walked past her when he left. He wended his way through the crowd of people arriving and leaving. Halley saw someone bump into him, and he dropped his coat for an instant, picked it up gracefully, apologized for standing too close and smiled at her, and then made his way out of the restaurant and left. It was such a beautiful day that he didn't bother to put his coat on, and he disappeared into a cab. He was attractive and well dressed, and had smiled at her admiringly.

Halley was having fun checking out what the women were wearing, old and young, fashionable and flashy, trendy, long blond hair, jet black hair with gelled spikes, the men in leathers and suedes, in very expensive motorcycle boots, most in designer sneakers, and alligator shoes. She had a second espresso and asked for the check. She didn't expect it to be a cheap lunch, and it wasn't, but it was worth it for the show as well as the delicious crab salad. She reached down for her bag to get out her wallet with the credit cards. She groped under the table, and all she found were the shopping bags with her morning purchases. Her Birkin had obviously slipped behind them. She finally looked under the table to locate it and didn't see it. She pushed the shopping bags aside, and still couldn't find it. She got up, walked around the table, moved the tablecloth aside for a better view. Her bag wasn't there. She felt her breath catch. She thought someone must have moved it, and looked around to see if it was on a chair at a nearby table, but still didn't see it. She panicked for a minute. She had never lost a bag before, but she knew there had to be a reasonable explanation. A bag that size and that unusual didn't just disappear. She would have seen it if someone walked out with it. And everyone in the restaurant, or close to her, was wearing Birkin bags, newer and flashier than hers. She felt totally lost and the maître d' came over to her to see what was wrong. She was standing next to her table with a confused expression.

"Is there a problem, madame? May I help you?" he asked her in English. And in the stress of the moment, she forgot her college French, and answered him in English.

"My bag . . . I can't find it . . . this is crazy. It has to be here somewhere . . ." She was turning in circles, and felt like a crazy person looking for her lost bag. He caught the eye of a nearby server in a tight short black leather skirt, with dyed black hair piled on her head, in thigh-high boots, and told her in rapid French what had happened. He asked her several questions and she shook her head. She hadn't seen anything unusual happen. He handed her Halley's shopping bags, and took a small flashlight out of his pocket with a powerful beam. He looked under all the neighboring tables as Halley watched him. She felt sick as he looked at her and shook his head. He took her arm then, and spoke to her in a low voice.

"Look closely as we walk around. If you see your bag, tell me. Sometimes we have customers we don't know, though we know most of them, and women take bags they want sometimes. It has happened before. Your bag was alligator, yes?" She nodded. She felt like she was in a bad movie, a French thriller, and she followed him throughout the restaurant, looking under tables with his torch, and scrutinizing every customer and handbag. When they had finished, he turned to her with a dismayed expression. "I believe your bag has been stolen, madame." It obviously had been but that made no sense to Halley.

"But I didn't see anything, or feel anything. The bag is huge, I would have seen someone walk out of the restaurant with it." She thought of the few minutes when she had closed her eyes and turned her face to the sun, it could have happened then, but the thief would have had to be lightning quick to get the bag and run out of the restaurant with it, and people would have seen him or her do it.

"These are professionals who do these things, madame. They are not amateurs, and they are very good at it. We see it in this neighborhood all the time. This is where they come for the expensive merchandise they steal, and sell all over Europe and in Asia. Your bag will disappear very quickly." He wasn't reassuring.

"What do I do?" Halley felt suddenly helpless, as though someone had stolen her most precious possession, and she had no recourse. And in the bag she had her passport, money, credit cards, and a million little trinkets and treasures she had just thrown in. The keys to the house she was renting, and the address, and the realtor's folder. Within seconds, if he rifled through the bag, the thief would know where she lived and have access to the house.

"You must go to the police immediately. I will have someone take you. But first we will look at our security video. Perhaps we will see something." He was being very helpful, and the waitstaff were chattering among themselves and nodding, telling each other what had occurred. It wasn't the first time. But it was always unpleasant. They felt sorry for the American it had happened to. She looked shocked and disoriented. Some women screamed and had hysterics. One customer had lost an alligator tote bag her Chihuahua had been asleep in. Fortunately, the thief had abandoned the dog on the sidewalk and kept the bag, and the woman had nearly fainted, and screamed when they brought the dog back. She never saw the bag again and didn't care.

Halley followed the maître d' to the back office, while someone else took his place at the entrance to the restaurant. She followed him in, and they sat down at a monitor on a desk. He entered a code, entered the approximate time they were guessing it had happened, and the video started as Halley entered the restaurant, was led to her table and sat down. And the man who had come in right behind her was taken to his. The maître d' sped up the video then, and they saw the same man pay, stand up, leave his table, and approach her to pass her table and leave the restaurant. Halley was paying no attention and drinking her coffee, as someone appeared to bump into him. If she looked closely, she could see that the man in the black suit and turtleneck had dropped his coat artfully next to Halley's table, stooped quickly to pick up the coat, just a fraction of a second longer than it should have taken, gathered up his voluminous coat over his arm, and headed straight out of the restaurant after a brief smile at Halley. He hailed a cab on the street the minute he was clear of the restaurant and disappeared.

"Was it him?" she asked after seeing the video. You couldn't see her bag on the screen.

"It was when he dropped the coat," the maître d' said knowingly. He had seen it done before. "He scooped up your bag under it. The coat was only a device to hide whatever he stole today. It could have been you or any woman in the restaurant." There must have been forty or fifty Birkin bags there that day, and he chose hers. It was totally rotten luck for her. "The bag was under the coat on his arm when he left." He took the tape out of the machine to show the police, but the ruse wouldn't be new to them either. It was standard procedure, and the pros knew exactly what kind of restaurant to go to, and with the outdoor terrace and the good weather, there was more activity and chaos than usual right after Christmas. It had worked to the thief's advantage. And he'd even had lunch while deciding which bag to steal. He was very well dressed, like all the other diners, in order to blend in. There was nothing remarkable or ominous about him. He had looked very relaxed while he ate and chose his prey. "He must have seen your bag when he walked in behind you," the maître d' suggested.

"It's an unusually large size," she said, sorry she had worn it that day.

"He'll get an excellent price for it, in Spain or Italy or Germany. There's a market for them in Liechtenstein, I've been told, and a big market in Asia and Africa. It will be out of the country by tomorrow," the maître d' told her, and her heart sank. "You should go to the police now." He spoke to a waiter who had been watching the security film from a little distance. He told him to take her to the police station, and one of the servers called a cab.

"Oh my God," Halley said, suddenly mortified, "I can't pay for lunch. I have no money."

"Your lunch is complimentary, madame. We are very sorry this happened here. It does happen a great deal in this neighborhood, to tourists and to Parisians. These thieves are very good at what they do. Your passport?" he asked her.

"It was in the bag. Everything I have with me is in that bag." She felt overwhelmed by a wave of panic as she thought of everything in the bag, and she was fighting back tears. Nothing like it had ever happened to her. It was a terrible feeling of helplessness and vulnerability, which wasn't like her. She felt violated and afraid.

"He may throw the contents away on the street, and someone will return your passport to the embassy. You must cancel your credit cards right away." She nodded and then her eyes widened again.

"My phone!"

"He will probably sell that. Do you have an application to locate the phone?" he asked hopefully. She shook her head.

"I didn't think I'd ever need it. I've never lost a phone. My daughters have. I never do. Until now." She felt as though she had been stripped naked of every essential element she needed, especially while abroad, and her identity.

"Would you like to make a call or send a text on my phone?" the maître d' offered kindly.

"Yes, I'm so sorry . . . if you don't mind." She sent a single text to Millie, her assistant. "It's Halley. Bag stolen, please cancel credit cards immediately. Going to police now. Don't tell girls. Will buy new phone. Love, H." She was normally so efficient, she wasn't careless, and she hated dramas and helpless women. But she felt like one now. The thief had stolen everything she needed to function normally in Paris or anywhere. She had no money to pay for anything, no credit cards, no passport, and no phone. She couldn't even get on a plane and go home without a passport. And the thief had the keys and address of the house. He could rob it while she was out.

She felt dazed as she walked out of the restaurant. The servers handed Halley her shopping bags and apologized again, as she and one of the waiters got in a cab to go to the nearest *commissariat de police,* or police station.

Two of the servers and the maître d' watched her leave and wished her luck. She apologized again for not being able to pay for her lunch, and they sympathized with her over the loss of her bag.

She sat in the cab, fighting back tears, trying to be brave. She didn't ask where they were going. She didn't care, and aside from everything else the thief had taken with it, she loved the bag, and she knew the maître d' was right. She would never see it again. She felt small and violated and scared, and hadn't felt that way in years. It was a familiar feeling and the hallmark of her childhood. She was shocked by how quickly that sensation surfaced from the past. She felt helpless and stripped of her identity as they drove to the police station, with no one to help her, in a foreign country and a language she didn't speak well. And she suddenly felt like a lost child in a dangerous world where she was alone. The feeling was one she had forgotten and it came back in a rush now, and was every bit as vivid and terrifying as it had been when she was a defenseless child.

Chapter 9

The cab stopped just outside the Grand Palais, a splendid antique glass structure she recognized immediately. She had gone to an exhibit of photographs there with Robert. It was near the river, and the Petit Palais, where she'd been to art exhibits of the work of famous artists, was across the street. The waiter who had come with her pointed to the building. He spoke halting English. She saw that there was a small police station on the street level of the Grand Palais. There was a line of people waiting outside. It was in a good neighborhood and the people on line were a respectable-looking group. She heard a cluster of three women speaking in American English. Halley gestured to the waiter with her that she wanted to go inside. She walked past the people on line, and into the single door that led into the station, and there was a group of uniformed police officers watching as a man was led away in handcuffs. There was a counter with a window above it, and an officer in charge, speaking to people through the window in rapid-fire French she couldn't understand. She understood more if people spoke slowly. A few minutes later, it was her turn at the little grille the officer was speaking through, and she approached, feeling overwhelmed. Her French was not good enough to explain what had happened, which made her feel even more helpless.

"Do you speak English?" she asked him, and the officer looked annoyed and shook his head. The waiter came forward instantly, and stood next to her to explain the situation. The officer listened and then pointed to the door and answered the waiter. The police officer looked bored, and the waiter translated to Halley.

"He says we have to wait outside, for our turn. They'll take a report and you sign it."

"And then what?" she asked, still feeling dazed.

"Nothing much. They try to find your bag, and they notify you if they do," which they both knew was never going to happen, but she knew she would need a police report to file a claim on her insurance, for the value of the bag. She had no idea what it was worth, since she'd bought it long ago at auction, and she didn't know the original price. It had been expensive at auction because it was a custom order, but it was so beautiful and unusual, she thought it was worth it. She wondered what the thief would sell it for. It made her sick to think about it.

They went back outside and stood on line, and she realized that they looked like a motley couple. The waiter in his apron, and Halley old enough to be his mother. He looked to be about the twins' age. The three American women were further up the line by then.

She could hear them talking, and gleaned that two of them had had their cell phones stolen. They were from Chicago.

There was nothing to do while they waited like sheep for it to be their turn, and everyone had to wait in line. There was no avoiding it. With the waiter keeping her place for her, she walked down the street a few times, and once to the river. She stood on the bridge watching the water swirl past, with a serious expression, wondering why she hadn't kept the bag closer to her, or set it down right next to her at the restaurant, instead of under the table where she couldn't see it. It had never occurred to her it might get stolen at a fancy restaurant.

They waited two hours on the street, and then finally it was their turn to enter the police station. A female police officer in a bulletproof vest directed them to one of two tiny cubicles, which was why it had taken so long for the line to move.

Halley and the waiter sat down on two dirty-looking battered chairs, and waited another fifteen minutes for an officer to join them. The room was so small, there was barely enough space for the desk, two chairs, and the file cabinets that were in it, and there was a computer on the desk. When the officer finally came through the door, he looked like a football player. He sucked the last remaining air and space out of the room, went to the desk, sat down, and looked at Halley.

"You're American?" His senior officer had told him and he spoke passable English so they had assigned him to take the report. He was a very junior officer.

"Yes," she said, feeling breathless. She normally felt so in control of every situation, but not this one. She felt naked and young and frightened, vulnerable and exposed. A stranger had taken her most basic and essential possessions and all the little personal things she loved that she carried with her.

"Your passport," he said, writing something on a form. He spoke very adequate English.

"That's why I'm here. It was stolen." He looked immediately irritated, and put his pen down.

"You need to go to your embassy to report a stolen passport. Someone will probably turn it in." He thought that was the end of it, as he prepared to stand up, and she corrected him.

"My bag was stolen, and everything in it," she said, feeling desperate. He stopped in his tracks and sat down again, and picked up the pen with a sigh.

"What did the bag look like, can you describe it?" She did, and there was a glimmer of something in his eyes when she said "alligator," and he looked her over more carefully. That was different. "Cash in the bag?"

"Five thousand euros, and a thousand U.S. dollars. I'm traveling. I'm here for two weeks. And all my credit cards." She went down the list of contents, as closely as she could remember.

"Value of the bag?" he said, and she hesitated. She hated to tell him what she paid for it, and didn't know how much it was worth now. Hermès bags multiplied in value as they got older. And it was embarrassing to tell a normal working person what it had cost her. She could have rented an apartment for that in a great neighborhood, or paid a child's school tuition, but she worked for her money too. Halley had a good sense for the value of money.

"It was expensive. It's from a store called Hermès." He looked vaguely insulted.

"I know Hermès, madame, we have people here all the time whose bags have been stolen. It happens."

"My wallet and credit card case were Hermès too." She thought of Millie's sweet gift of the red leather passport case, also gone. "And my iPhone was in the bag." She still hadn't told him how much the bag cost her, and he gave her a pointed look. "I bought it at an auction in London fifteen years ago, for fifteen thousand dollars, and the auction charges on top of that, which were close to four thousand dollars. So it cost me about twenty thousand dollars. It would be worth a lot more today, but I'm not sure how much. I can check. It was originally a special order, and it's an unusual, very large size. I suppose it could be worth twice what I paid for it," she said apologetically, probably more than his salary in a year. He nodded, and she gave him her home address in New York, her phone number, and her address in Paris. "The thief got my keys to the house here, and I had some papers in my bag with the house address on it." He looked at her sternly then.

"That means he can enter your house whenever he wants, until you have the locks changed. You may find that you've been burglarized now when you go back to the house, or he could show up tonight, tie you up, and rob you, or something much worse. You must be very careful. Are you living alone?"

She nodded. "But there's a guardian in a lodge at the front gate."

"That won't help you if he climbs in a bedroom window when you're sleeping." The thought of what the thief could do then literally made her hands shake. "If the house has an alarm, use it. Thieves like this are usually not violent and they don't want to confront the owners of what they stole. They are the least prone to violence of all the criminals we see, but that doesn't mean it can never happen. You must protect yourself," he said severely. "We get lots of reports of burglaries committed with stolen keys when they know the address." It was a warning she didn't like hearing, and made her feel even worse. For a fraction of a second, she thought of going home to New York, and then realized she couldn't. She had no passport with which to return to the United States. She was stuck here until she got a new passport, and God knew when she'd get it, here in France. She had to stay now, and face whatever happened next.

It took two hours to get the details down, as he typed them, and then the waiter from the restaurant handed the young police officer the security tape from the restaurant, and explained to him in French what it was. The officer turned his computer toward them so they could see too. He played it, and stopped it several times when the image of the thief came on. Seeing it again, a little after the crime, she could focus on it better, and once she knew what had happened, it was shocking to see how smoothly he'd done it, and he was as well dressed as any other client at the restaurant. He looked to be about Halley's age. One would never have suspected him of being a thief. The officer looked slightly more interested then. He had an idea.

"We have cameras in Paris, surveillance cameras, to detect criminal acts. I think we have one in that location," he said to Halley in

English. He looked at a list on his computer, and nodded. "There are two outside the restaurant. We catch people who steal from luxury stores in that neighborhood." He entered a code, and a minute later there were images on the screen. He hit play, and there from two different angles they saw an even more precise account of the theft, and in one of them, you could see that the man in the black suit had some kind of large, cumbersome object under the coat over his arm. "We'll put his face into the computer and see if he's wanted for any other crimes. Some of these guys make a very good living stealing and selling high-priced items like that. And they know where to sell them. There's a booming market for stolen goods. Particularly Hermès. You won't see that bag again," he said with utter conviction. She felt stupid because it was just an object and she had bought it for herself. But she loved the bag, and all the more because there was only one of them in the world. It made her really sad that he had taken it. She was overcome with a feeling of loss and sorrow as she sat there. She felt defeated.

The officer had noted the license plate on the cab the thief took, but that wasn't enough of a clue to catch him. But he explained that they would call the cab company to find out where the driver had taken him. They needed to know where he lived, or where he hung out in order to find him and arrest him. Every minute or so, she remembered something else that was in the missing bag, and felt a little worse.

The young officer printed the report and had Halley sign it, and then she and the waiter were free to go. Nothing the officer had said to her gave Halley the faintest hope that they would find her bag or even try very hard. It was a very banal crime, except for the value of the bag. He accepted it as a fact that the bag was gone forever, and that they'd never find it, although he said they would try through resale sources, dealers they knew of stolen goods, and online. She was sure they wouldn't find it, though, and the waiter who had accompanied her confirmed it, when they thanked the officer, picked up her shopping bags, and went back to the street.

"It happens so much in Paris, and big cities all over Europe, that it's a common occurrence to them," the waiter said softly. He felt sorry for her. She looked devastated. "Like cell phones. Hundreds get stolen every day. They sell those too." Halley asked to borrow his phone then and called the car service. She got the number from information, and they promised to send a car and driver for her within twenty minutes, so she told the waiter he could leave her. He hesitated, it didn't seem right to him. He felt bad for her, and she looked very pale and sad.

"Don't worry, François. I'm fine, a car is coming for me now. Thank you for being such a big help. I would have been lost here without you." She wanted to give him a big tip to thank him, but couldn't even do that. She was planning to go back to the restaurant as soon as she had some cash again, to pay for her lunch. She wanted to tip the maître d' too. They had all been very kind. François left her to take the metro back to the restaurant, and ten minutes later a car showed up for her, with a different driver from the one who had picked her up at the airport the day before. It felt like a lifetime ago now. It was hard to believe she had been in Paris for less than two days. It felt more like weeks or years after the day she'd just had.

When she got in the car, she asked the driver to take her to the nearest store where she could buy a phone. He said there was one nearby, and she looked profoundly embarrassed when she asked him if he could buy it with a company credit card, and put it on her bill, along with a big tip for him.

"I lost all my credit cards and money, and my phone. My purse was stolen today. I can wait for everything else, but not my phone. My children will try to call me, and they'll worry if I don't answer." He smiled at her. She looked as though she had been through the wringer, and she felt as though she had.

"I'll explain it to the owner," he said gently, and handed her his gas card that belonged to the company. She looked like a decent person, and he could see how upset she was. Her hand was shaking when she took the card.

She disappeared into the phone store and was gone for half an hour. They deactivated her old phone, listed it as stolen, and activated her new phone, with her same number. Almost the instant she turned it on, it rang. It was Millie.

"What happened? I got your text. I canceled all your cards and ordered new ones, and reported your checkbook, driver's license, and passport stolen. You'll have to go to the embassy yourself tomorrow for a new passport. Have you reported it to the police?"

"I've been there for hours. I just left. They say the bag will be sold in Europe or Asia. It's gone forever." She felt even sadder as she said it. Telling Millie made it even more real.

"That's so awful," she said sympathetically, "I'm really sorry, Halley."

"Yeah, me too." She felt stupid admitting it, and it was just a bag, but she felt so depressed over it. It didn't make sense, but she felt as though a scab had been ripped off an old wound. She felt vulnerable and sad. On the way back to the house in the car, she remembered an incident at the orphanage that she had long forgotten. A new girl who had been a runaway on the streets had jimmied her way into Halley's locker with a screwdriver. She was only eleven, but she'd had more experience of a bad life than most adults. She had stolen Halley's only good sweater, some money she had saved up from doing extra chores, and a charm bracelet Halley loved with Disney characters on it. The bracelet wasn't real gold but Halley had saved for it for months, and had been so proud of it. They caught the girl red-handed, stealing from someone else, and she went to juvenile hall, but she must have taken the bracelet with her, or sold it, because they never found it. Halley had so little of her own then, and the girl had taken her most treasured possessions, and showed no remorse when they caught her. Halley wondered if the bag thief was like that, unremorseful and indifferent to the pain he had caused. For him, it was just business. For Halley, it was deep and personal, leaving her feeling violated and awakening the ghosts of the past that had been dormant for years. She was an abuse victim again. You couldn't kill those ghosts or excise them entirely. You could only hope they would remain dormant forever. Hers were waking up from the theft of her bag. It was traumatic for her.

The driver took Halley home after she got her phone, and with some trepidation, she rang the guardian's doorbell, to ask him for a spare set of keys. He took forever to answer, and she could hear him rustling around inside and banging things. He finally came to the door, yanked it open, and glared at her, his evil-looking dog at his side.

"What do *you* want?" he asked her, instantly surly. She felt like a naughty child, having to tell him she had lost the keys, though through no fault of her own. She was a grown woman and suddenly felt like a bad child, just as she had always been told she was. It was familiar to her.

"Sorry, Henri," she said politely, "my bag was stolen, I need another set of keys, and the police said we have to change the locks." She was apologetic and polite, intimidated by him, and trying not to be. She had to remind herself that he was not her parent. And she was not a child. She was an adult, and he was an employee.

"How could you be so careless? You've been here for two days, and you're already causing trouble. Do you have any idea how expensive it is to change the locks? And no one will come to change them now until after the New Year. It will serve you right if the thief comes and ties you up like a sausage and steals everything you brought in all those suitcases. I told the owners that renters would be a headache!" He left her standing in the doorway then, and went to get another set of keys. He was back with them a minute later, and handed them to her with utter disgust. She made an effort not to react to what he said and ignore it.

"Will you keep an ear out at night, in case someone does show up? That wouldn't be fun for either of us." She gave him a pointed look.

"Just keep the door locked and the alarm on," he said. The locked door would make no difference since the bag thief had the keys, but the alarm would.

"I will, thank you," she said, still jangled by everything that had happened, and he added to it.

"I'll call the locksmith tomorrow," he growled, and slammed the door, and she could hear him banging pots and slamming things even more loudly inside his apartment, as she walked to the front door of the house. She had that same uneasy feeling in the pit of her stomach she'd had as a child, when she knew she was in trouble and going to be punished, and she hadn't done anything wrong, but she got beaten anyway. It was a terrible feeling, and she didn't know why she felt that way. She had been the victim of a crime, not committed one. It didn't compute in her head, but awoke feelings in her she hadn't felt in years.

She was nervous entering the house, but all was quiet and in order. Henri had not volunteered to check it out with her, and she didn't ask him. She had a cup of tea after she looked around. She double-locked all the doors from inside and turned on the alarm. She knew she would be safe that way, but the idea that someone might try to get in was terrifying. She checked all the windows to be sure they were secure, and they were.

She was just starting to unwind when the girls called her, and Olivia picked up on something immediately.

"What's wrong, Mom?" she asked. "You sound stressed." Olivia always picked it up, it was uncanny.

"Do I? No, I'm fine. Great, actually, I went shopping today on the Avenue Montaigne. I missed you." She wasn't going to tell them about the stolen bag, they'd worry about her, especially if they knew the thief had the keys. Olivia had heard it in her voice, though. She told them about the things she saw shopping, and after they hung up, Olivia looked at her twin.

"Something's wrong with Mom," she said, frowning.

"Oh, stop it. She's fine, she sounded great. She's not a child, and she's having fun. She went shopping."

"She had that catch in her voice she gets when she's really worried about something, or scared."

"How many times have you seen our mother scared in our lifetime? She's not afraid of anything. She's the calmest person I know. And that's how she sounded."

"She's faking it, Val, I'm telling you, she was upset about something."

"Maybe she has jet lag," Valerie said blithely. "Go have a margarita and relax. Where's Peter?"

"He's talking to his daughters on the phone." Valerie had noticed that Olivia and Peter were together a lot, which could have been purely coincidental on the boat, but she didn't think so, and the forgotten thong on deck hadn't slipped her mind. She wondered if they were having a fling, but if so, they were being very discreet, and Olivia looked totally blasé whenever she was with him with everyone around. Maybe even a little too much so. But Valerie didn't want to say anything and scare Olivia off. She knew how skittish she was about relationships, and how private about her life. Valerie had thought they were perfect for each other from the moment she met him, and it had taken three years to trap them in ideal circumstances for them to get to know each other. She noticed them swimming together off the boat, all the way to nearby beaches sometimes. And they'd gone out on the dinghy together alone the day before. Peter said they went fishing, which sounded even more unlikely to Valerie.

Olivia had teased him one more time the previous night about switching with her twin. But it was when they were playing cards, and Valerie had gone along with it. They had confused him for the entire game, and Seth laughed at his younger brother.

"You have to watch out for those two," he warned him, "they've done it to me a hundred times. Too bad we're not twins so we could get even."

"So who would we both look like?" Peter asked, musing about it. "You're taller, but I'm more handsome . . . on the other hand, you have more hair."

"They love being twins," Seth said.

"I can see that," Peter said. "It must be fun."

"Or weird. So what's going on with you two?" Seth asked, trying to sound casual in a brief moment alone.

"When I have something to tell you, I will. Nothing earth-shattering to report for the moment," Peter said coolly. So far, no one on the boat thought they were involved, which was a major victory. He and Olivia liked sharing a secret. It brought them closer together.

The night Halley's bag was stolen, she had a bath and tried to relax. She lit candles and put on music, and then turned it off. She wanted to be sure that she could hear an intruder if one arrived.

She checked the windows again, and all were locked, and the alarm was on. She was wide-awake at midnight, and turned on the TV, but all she could get was CNN in English, and French TV. But there hadn't been a sound anywhere in the house. She was beginning to think she was perfectly safe and worried for nothing, when she thought she heard the back door being rattled, and she said loudly in French, "Oh, go away!" And the noise stopped. Her heart pounded for half an hour.

She left the lights on in her bedroom that night, and felt better that way. If something did happen during the night, she wanted to be wide awake and able to see what she was doing, not stumbling around in the dark in an unfamiliar house. She finally fell asleep sitting up in bed at three A.M., and woke up at ten in the morning, when her cellphone rang.

She was surprised to hear an unfamiliar male voice on her new cellphone. It was Bart Warner, the man she'd met on the plane.

"Did I wake you?" he asked apologetically.

"Not at all, I was just having a lazy morning," she said politely.

"How did the house turn out? Is it a good one?" he asked pleasantly.

"It's lovely," she said, smiling. It was nice to hear from him, although she was exhausted by the day before.

"I just thought I'd check on you, and make sure that you're okay on your big adventure. You're brave to be here all alone. It's different staying with my son, and having family here. I'm not sure I'd have the guts to just go to a city on my own during the holidays. I admire you for that. Actually, I was wondering if you'd like to have lunch. I'm sorry to be so rude, and call you on such short notice. Are you free for lunch today?" he asked hopefully. She was startled by the invitation. He had really surprised her, but she wasn't busy, and he made it sound relaxed and appealing. It was nice hearing from him, especially after the trauma of the day before.

"Yes, I'd love that," she said. She wanted to go to the embassy for her new passport, but other than that, she had nothing to do, and she had no money until her new credit cards arrived. She'd been thinking about going to some galleries, all in walking distance of the house. She was calmer than the night before, after the bag theft, the police station for many hours, and worrying about intruders all night who might have the keys and succeed in entering, despite the alarm.

"That's wonderful." He sounded delighted. "Shall I pick you up?"

"I can meet you, I might be out doing errands before lunch," like the embassy, or she could go after lunch.

"Great. Meet me at the Ritz, at the Bar Vendôme. We can have lunch in the garden under the glass dome." It sounded very elegant and fun. She hadn't expected to meet a man and have a date in Paris. She felt a little rusty. She hadn't had a date since she met Robert, and not since he'd died either. She saw friends socially, but hadn't felt ready for more than that. She wasn't sure if she was now, but lunch sounded just perfect, and very appealing. Bart Warner was a pleasant, upbeat person. And the normalcy of it was a relief after the traumatic day before.

They agreed on one o'clock, and she got ready and called the car service. She didn't have money or credit cards to pay for anything, and was lucky the driver had let her use the limo service's credit card to buy her phone. Beyond that, she couldn't have paid for a cup of coffee or an ice cream if she'd wanted one. She pulled out a handbag to go with what she was wearing and realized she had nothing to put in it. All she would normally have carried was gone with the thief. And when she was about to brush her hair, she realized that her only hairbrush was gone too, along with her favorite lipstick, her compact, and a photograph of her girls that she always carried in her bag. Everything practical or sentimental was gone, as well as the little leather address book she had carried for years, with all the phone numbers in it, and all those numbers in her phone. Gone. She threw a handkerchief and a brand-new spare lipstick into the purse she was going to wear and felt ridiculous. She changed to a little clutch bag she tucked under her arm when she left the house. She set the alarm and locked the door carefully. The car was waiting for her outside at twenty to one, and she saw Henri Laurent peeking at her from behind his curtains. He watched her comings and goings carefully, which made no sense. She assumed he was just nosey as well as disagreeable. She told the driver, another new one, that she was going to the Ritz and sat back against the seat. And she explained to him that she needed to put the charge on her ongoing bill, as she had the day before, and he agreed. She was wearing a very chic casual black-and-white tweed coat she'd brought as a spare, with a black Chanel suit jacket, a black denim skirt, and high heels, and the little alligator clutch under her arm. Her shining dark hair was pulled back in a sleek bun. She was ready for Bart Warner, at what felt like a very grownup lunch.

He saw her get out of the car in front of the hotel, and was wait-ing for her at the top of the front steps with a red carpet coming down the marble steps. He smiled as soon as he saw her, and she hurried her pace to meet him.

"You look beautiful, Halley," he said, admiring her, and he fol-lowed her through the revolving door and into the sumptuous lobby, with five-foot-tall flower arrangements on every table which enhanced the atmosphere of luxury. She tried to resist the memo-ries of staying there with Robert, and focused on Bart. The maî-tre d' greeted them solemnly in the Bar Vendôme and led them to a table outside, with the protective glass roof overhead. It was a beautiful day of winter sun. The black Chanel jacket was perfect for the Ritz, as were the diamond studs in her ears. Every inch of her was impeccable and elegant. Bart ordered champagne, and they took their time with the menu. Once they'd ordered a salad for Halley, and filet mignon for Bart, they smiled at each other. He was even more handsome than she remembered from the plane. He had an aura of power about him. It was easy to guess that he was someone important—he had a relaxed air of command about him. He asked Halley about her books over lunch.

She told him about how she had started to make notes for her first book while she was pregnant, and had started writing after the twins were born.

"What did your husband do?" he asked, curious. She hesitated for a fraction of a second, and smiled at him. She decided to be honest.

"Their father is Locke Logan, the photographer," she said simply.

Almost everyone in the world knew him. "We never married. I was very young, and had no family, so it wasn't as scandalous as it might have been otherwise. The twins filled my life. They were a blessing and still are. They're identical twins, which is fun."

"It must be," he said, admiring her in the winter sunlight. It gave her face a gentle glow. Bart had a perfect haircut, and bright blue eyes which took in every detail around him. He was attentive and focused on her.

"Their father wasn't very involved, but he showed up for them when it mattered. My daughter Valerie got married in October, and he was there. I did double duty as mother and father while they were growing up."

"And you never wanted to marry him?" He was intrigued by her. On the one hand, he could guess that she was a strong woman, but there was a gentleness to her, a vulnerability that touched him. She was very feminine and had enormous charm. There was nothing hard or tough about her.

"I didn't marry him because he already was married," she said quietly, "and by the time he divorced, ten years later, I was happy with my girls, and he and I were no longer involved. I suppose it was a rather unconventional life, but as a writer, it was never an issue whether I was married or not. My parents got married because of me and it didn't turn out well, so I was hesitant to do the same thing, and repeat history, even once we could. Their father and I are much better as friends. It was never a major love affair, the twins were an accident," she said. "A fortuitous one, as it turned out."

"I was in the same position," Bart said, feeling unusually open with her. "I dated a girl in college, but it wasn't the right fit for either of us. Classic story. She discovered she was pregnant after we broke up. We debated. I was twenty-two, she was twenty-one. Our parents had a fit, so we got married. It was over in two years, and it was pretty unpleasant for both of us. It never worked and was never right. She was as unhappy as I was, we were both children ourselves. We got divorced when I went to business school. She has a big career now too. She's the president of a bank. And the nice thing is that we're both crazy about our son. He works at the Paris office of an international law firm. He married a French girl, and they're very happy. They're moving to New York in a year. It will be nice to have him home. He's been here for four years. He loves it. Who wouldn't?"

"One of my daughters is an attorney too, entertainment law. Both my daughters just moved to L.A. They're in St. Bart's for Christmas, so here I am. It's been my first Christmas alone since they were born," she said ruefully. "So I came to Paris as a treat for me. You never remarried?" she asked him.

"No," he said, looking a little sheepish. "My first attempt cured me. I've been in several long relationships, but marriage never felt like the right option." They had both had their children at the same age, twenty-two. But Bart was older than Halley. He was fifty-six, and a very attractive man. "What does your other daughter do?"

"She's an artist. They're very different, although they look identical."

"It must be fun to have twins." He smiled at her. "Double trouble."

"Definitely. We've had a great time together. I'm going out to visit them in March. The artist is having her first show in L.A. I promised to go. I wouldn't miss it." She seemed happy when she spoke of her girls, and he noticed it. He felt the same way about his only son.

He liked how open and honest she was, how comfortable and at peace with herself. She didn't seem to be looking for anything, and wasn't manipulative. She was just a very nice person. She wasn't angry or bitter, didn't have an ex-husband she hated, or have an agenda. A lot of the women he met did. He avoided them whenever possible, but Halley had an aura of peace around her that drew him nearer, and made him feel comfortable with her. She was very appealing.

"So what have you been doing in the three days you've been here? I love walking in this city," he said.

"Art galleries, shopping, and I spent yesterday at the police station." He looked surprised.

"You got arrested?" he teased her.

"Not yet. I treated myself to lunch at a very nice restaurant, and my handbag got stolen," she said seriously. "It was kind of an epic event, that's never happened to me before. Everything I need was in it, and I loved the bag. It was a very nice one I've had for a long time. I was very upset." She shrugged with a small smile, not wanting to make too much of it. "The police said I'll never see my bag again. It's on its way to Asia or Liechtenstein or somewhere by now. There are big markets for stolen high-end bags."

"Was it the big black alligator one you were carrying on the plane?" She nodded. "I picked it up to put it on the luggage cart for you. I thought you had a bowling ball in it." He smiled at her.

"I did. My favorite one. Not to mention my hairbrush, favorite lipstick, passport, and credit cards. It was a clean sweep. Apparently the thief was a professional. The police have it on video, and so did the restaurant. They're looking for him. But they say they won't find the bag."

"I'm so sorry." He looked sympathetic and then thought of something. "Did you have money in your bag?"

"I did, all my money for the trip."

"How have you managed since yesterday, with no credit cards and no cash?"

She grinned, feeling a little foolish. "The drivers from the car service lent me a company card to buy a new phone. And they let me charge the ride home yesterday and to here today. Other than that, I'm penniless." She tried to make light of it, but it had been a deeply upsetting experience. She didn't want to share how upset she was. "And I have to get the locks changed, since the keys and the address of the house were in the bag, which was stupid of me."

"Oh, Halley, that's awful, I'm so sorry." He pulled his wallet out of his pocket then, and put five hundred-euro bills on the table, and a credit card. "Keep the card as long as you need it," he said generously. He was deeply sympathetic to her.

"I have new cards on the way," she assured him. "I'm fine. Really." She was embarrassed to take money from him, and a credit card. He barely knew her, and she was touched by the kind gesture.

"You can't go around with no money," he said, "that's not safe. We can square accounts later. Your having my credit card gives me an excuse to see you again." He looked pleased to have an excuse. He had thoroughly enjoyed having lunch with her. "Speaking of which," he said, feeling a little shy for an instant, "my son and daughter-in-law are staying home on New Year's Eve. We're going to have dinner together, very informally at their apartment. It's the day after tomorrow, would you like to join us? I don't like going out on that night, everyone tries too hard. It's nicer to be at home."

"That's so nice of you, thank you, I'd like that very much." It was providential the way something to do had just materialized. It sounded like a perfect evening, and she liked him. He seemed to be a kind, straightforward person. They'd both had a good time at lunch.

When they got up to leave, his credit card and the five-hundred-euro bills were still on the table. She felt awkward taking them.

"Bart, I can't . . . really . . ." She felt shy for a minute.

"You can and you will. I'll worry about you if you're running around Paris with no money." He folded the bills around the card and slipped them into the pocket of her coat.

"I promise I'll give it back," she said earnestly, and he smiled at her.

"I am terribly worried about it. I won't be able to sleep at night until you do, with interest," he teased her, and they walked out of the hotel together. There were well-dressed people strolling into the lobby, and a few tourists. Halley noticed the vitrines full of beautiful jewels, and they went back through the revolving door and down the red-carpeted steps to her car, waiting in the Place Vendôme. They had both had a wonderful time. As first dates went, it was remarkable, elegant, and fun, and they were so comfortable with each other. "I'll come and pick you up on New Year's Eve," he said as they stood next to her car. "It's not a good night to be out alone. Try to stay out of any police stations in the meantime." She smiled.

"I'm going to the embassy now to get a new passport."

"That doesn't sound like fun. Go shopping afterward, use the credit card. It will do you good. Are you safe at the house if the thief has the keys, and your address?" He looked serious as he asked. That worried him more than the money and credit cards.

"I put the alarm on last night, and there's a guardian. He's kind of a creep, but at least he's there. He has an apartment at the front gate."

"Call me if you need me. I'm not far from you. I'm serious, Halley." He looked into her eyes. "If you're scared or anything else happens, just call me. Or if you need more money."

"You're the first man who ever said that to me," she said, and he laughed. "I'll take good care of the credit card, I promise. Mine should be here in a few days."

"I'm very worried about it," he teased her again, and then grew more serious. "Take care of yourself. See you Saturday." It was only two days away.

She got in the car, and he waved as she was driven away, and then he walked across the Place Vendôme. He had really enjoyed spending time with her. He'd been debating about calling her. He didn't want her to think he went around picking up strangers everywhere. He had said something to his son, Ryan, and he had encouraged his father to call her. He hadn't had a serious girlfriend for a while, and Ryan felt sorry for him. He was so successful, but so alone, and Ryan wanted his father to be happy. He had reminded him that one had to seize the moments and the opportunities when they happened. And as Bart walked down the rue de Castiglione to the Tuileries Garden, thinking of her, he was glad he had.

Chapter 10

It took Halley an hour at the embassy to fill out the forms to cancel her stolen passport and order a new one. Millie sent copies of her last passport and driver's license to her new phone, so at least she had some form of ID. No one had turned in her stolen passport at the embassy. And then she went back to the house. She'd had a really nice time with Bart. He was good company, and he loved his job as CEO of one of the country's leading corporations in electronics. He seemed to have a great relationship with his son. He had told her he never saw his ex-wife anymore. She lived in Florida, but they were on pleasant terms, and had even danced together at their son's wedding. She had been remarried for twenty-five years, and had chosen well that time. She had no other children and neither did Bart. He said Ryan was enough, and he was proud of him.

Halley was happy when she got to the house. She answered some emails, and called the girls. They were out swimming. The doorbell rang as she hung up, and a messenger delivered a huge pink hat box from Fauchon, with all kinds of treats to eat, and a card from Bart. "Please don't starve. Use the card. Bart." He was fun and gentlemanly and a little bit old-school, and she liked that. He was smart, kind, respectable, and had a huge job. And why not go out with him? She was alone in Paris. She thought Robert would understand and want her to be happy. She had mourned him for three years.

She put the alarm on, and as the night wore on she got more nervous, knowing the thief had her keys. She slept with the lights on again, and in the morning, her cellphone rang, and a male French voice sounded very serious and identified himself as Major Augustin Leopold. He sounded very official.

"Madame 'Olbrook?" He dropped the H in her name, but the caller spoke English fluently, despite his accent.

"Yes?" She couldn't imagine who it was.

"I am an inspector of the Sûreté Territoriale, of the police. We are a special branch for the investigation of high and VIP crimes on our territory. We have your dossier now. It has been turned over to us by the commissariat at the Grand Palais to pursue the stealing of your bag, because of its high value. We are working on it now. Would you be so kind as to come to my office, to complete further questions?"

"Yes, of course." He sounded so solemn that it made her smile. But she was glad they were taking it seriously and had referred it to a special department of the police. At least they hadn't brushed it off.

"Will you have time today?" he asked her.

"Yes."

"At noon?"

"Fine." He gave her the address, and she called the car service and got dressed.

The special branch for high-end thefts against individuals was in a small innocuous building in a quiet neighborhood and was very discreet. She was stopped as soon as she walked in by a tough-looking police officer who asked for her ID.

She showed him the copies on her phone and explained that the originals had been stolen. "That's why I'm here to see Major Leopold." The officer told her to wait, made a call, and then smiled at Halley, pointed the way to the elevator, and told her where to go.

His name was on the door when she got there, and she knocked and walked in cautiously. A very large man stood up, very tall, with broad shoulders and a paunch. He had a mustache, and reminded her of a walrus. He was somewhere in his late fifties, and seemed military in his bearing as he greeted her.

"Madame 'Olbrook?" She nodded, slightly intimidated by his size if nothing else. The office was very spare, but there were a few photographs of the major with celebrities, including one of the French president pinning a medal on the major's chest. Her case was in good hands.

He invited her to sit down in the narrow metal chair across his desk. The office wasn't luxurious, by any means. Major Leopold was wearing slacks and a tweed jacket, had reddish brown hair, and looked more Anglo-Saxon than French. Two uniformed police in bulletproof vests walked in and out when they saw he was busy.

"Your bag upsets me," he said, as she sat at attention. She felt a little bit like a schoolgirl in the headmaster's office. "This should not happen to visitors in Paris. And your bag is very valuable. On the form, you said you paid fifteen thousand U.S. dollars for it."

"Yes, I did."

"Do you know what it's worth now?" She shook her head. "That bag was a special order. It has a small stamp on it to indicate that. One of my men went to Hermès yesterday, and they showed him a similar stamp. That bag, in that size, today would sell for seventy-five thousand dollars. For a special order, you must add thirty percent more, so another twenty or twenty-five thousand U.S., and there was only one made in that size, so it is safe to assume it is worth one hundred thousand dollars, and in the right hands, for a person desperate to own such a bag, you could possibly sell it for two hundred thousand dollars. But very certainly it is worth one hundred thousand now, if they could even replicate it. Hermès told my officer that it would be nearly impossible to find so many similar skins today for a bag that size. That is an object of great value, and extremely rare, which entirely changes the nature of the crime, and the punishment. When we catch the man who stole it, he will with absolute certainty go to prison." She was impressed, and Major Leopold made it sound like the thief had stolen a valuable work of art. She was surprised that he didn't scold her for being wasteful or for having spent too much money on herself, even at a lower price, and that he treated the value of the bag, and its origins, with great respect. He handed her a photograph of a pleasant-looking man in his forties, clean-shaven, good haircut, ordinary face, possibly an Italian suit, and wearing a large gold watch. She recognized the man from the security video at the restaurant.

"The watch is worth five hundred thousand dollars. He stole it a year ago, in the south of France. We have been looking for him ever since. He stole your bag. His brother is in the drug trade, he is in luxury goods. They're Colombian. They are high-end professionals. He is very elusive and clever. I want to find him. We have contacted all of our informants. I want to bring him to justice and send him to prison," he said with determination.

"I don't suppose you can track down my bag," she said, feeling nostalgic for a minute and shocked by its current value. She wouldn't have used it as a travel bag if she had known what it was worth today. And now she'd lost it. She was sad because she loved it, it was such a beautiful piece, with a bright red interior.

Leopold handed her the list of the contents of the bag she'd filled out at the Grand Palais station, and he asked her to make sure she hadn't forgotten anything. She read it and said she hadn't, as he nodded at her.

"You know, in this office, with the kind of objects and people we deal with, anything is possible. If people steal a cellphone, an ordinary purse, something small, it disappears. They throw it away, give it to a friend, sell it for a few euros. But at this level, with this kind of merchandise, it's complicated. If they sell it, they can make a lot of money, but not as much as you would get selling it in a reputable way, like an auction. But a bag like this is not so easy to place. It's recognizable, there is only one. It is very high quality. He may have sold it already, or maybe not. Or he might give it to his mother or his girlfriend. I'm not promising we will get it back, but we have a chance. And I will do everything in my power to return it to you." She was touched by how intense he was, and they had done some very good research already. They even had a photo of the bag from the Hermès archives. It made her sad to see it. She wanted her bag back, which she knew was unlikely, and it seemed foolish to be so attached to a bag.

Major Leopold handed her another list then. They were charges on her credit cards that the Colombian thief had made.

"Do you know any of these stores?" he asked her. "Have you purchased anything there?" She read it carefully, shook her head and handed it back to him. "These charges were all made after the bag was stolen, in one area of Paris, perhaps where he lives."

"My assistant in New York canceled my cards within an hour after the theft, when she got my text."

"Some stores don't check. American Express notified us of the activity on the stolen card. You will not be billed, but these will be added to the charges against him. His name is Tomás Maduro, but he uses many names. We know a great deal about him. Now we have to find him. He blends in well, which is how he steals where he does. He fits right in. He eats in the restaurant and steals a bag. He goes to a theater or the opera, and he steals a bracelet, and the woman wearing it never feels it leave her wrist. Very professional. He and his brother are pros. We will find him, Madame 'Olbrook. I don't know when, but we will." He stood up and thanked her for coming, and assured her he would be in touch, even after she went back to New York.

He had her escorted to the front door by one of the police officers in the bulletproof vests, and they locked the door behind her. She was fascinated by the department, and especially by Major

Augustin Leopold. Meeting him had been an experience. She was no closer to getting her bag back, but at least she knew now that a team of highly skilled, specialized detectives were working on it.

She went to Hermès herself after that, and looked around. She was still in shock over the value of her bag. It was worth more than some of her jewelry.

The next day, on New Year's Eve, she talked to the girls. They were throwing a New Year's Eve party on the boat that night, for just their little group. They were in Antigua and they were planning to stay aboard. There was too much activity in the port, and none of them wanted to go out that night. They felt safer on the boat. And there were mega yachts like theirs all around them. The trip had been wonderful so far. They had three days left on the boat, and then they were flying home. They all agreed it had been the best vacation of their lives, and everyone got along. Olivia was still sad their mother hadn't been able to join them. But she would have been sick if she'd come. They'd had a few choppy nights, which didn't bother any of them, but Halley would have been miserable. She was better off in Paris.

Halley put on the one simple black dress she had brought. She hadn't worn it yet, she had no reason to, but it seemed appropriate for a sedate New Year's Eve with Bart and his son and daughter-in-law. She wore her hair up again, and the dress showed off her legs.

She wore a pair of black suede heels that the girls had given her. They always picked beautiful shoes for her with dizzyingly high heels.

Halley had invited Bart to come up for a drink when he came to pick her up, so he could see the house. It looked pretty and festive. She had bought flowers that afternoon. They were bright red and were reminiscent of the holidays. She had been in Paris for four days by then, and still had ten days left in her trip. Bart was staying as long as she was, which was convenient, and he and Ryan were going skiing in Switzerland the following weekend, while Halley was still there.

She showed him around the house, and he liked it as much as she did. It was chic and neat, he commented on the beautiful furniture and art and the owner's great taste. The atmosphere of the house was warm, personal, and inviting. She already felt at home there. The only problem she'd had was the theft of the bag, and knowing that the thief had the keys and the address. And Henri Laurent had been a problem, but he didn't seem dangerous, just rude and annoying, and a little eccentric. She had accepted the fact that he hated her. He was irritating, but not a big deal.

They each had one glass of champagne and then went to Bart's son's apartment. It had a perfect view of the Eiffel Tower, with a terrace that overlooked the Seine, and Halley could see the Grand Palais in the background, as she stood on the terrace with Bart. There were stars in the sky, the Eiffel Tower was sparkling, and the setting was incredibly romantic. She hardly knew him, but she was very attracted to him. She recognized the signs. She could easily have fallen for him, but she didn't want to be too hasty. This was only their second date. But she could tell that he felt the same attraction, and Paris was a magical setting.

They walked back into the apartment after their brief moment on the terrace, and sat down to a delicious meal of leg of lamb and haricots verts, string beans, both with garlic. Bart's daughter-in-law had gotten the meal delivered by a caterer, and they all thought it was delicious.

The dinner was totally congenial. Bart told them about the stolen bag, and Halley told them about the major, and the somewhat secret special branch of the theft detail.

"Do you think you'll get your bag back?" Ryan asked her. He was an extremely personable, bright young man. He had gone to Princeton, then gotten his law degree at Harvard. Véronique had a master's in finance from HEC, one of the most distinguished business schools in France, and worked for a consulting firm. Ryan liked Halley and he could see that his father did too. He hadn't seen him glow like that in a long time. They seemed so at ease with each other, and had fun. They were getting to know each other, and discovering things they liked and had in common. Ryan and Véronique left them alone on the terrace for a little while after dinner, just to sit outside and talk.

"Your son is wonderful," Halley said to him, as they sat in the chilly star-filled night. Bart put a blanket around her, and sat close to her. "I like Véronique too. She's very bright, and a nice person. I'd love to introduce them to my girls. My son-in-law is a good man. They're all hardworking, kind, dedicated people, like Ryan and Véro."

Eventually, Ryan and Véro came out to join Bart and Halley on the terrace. The Eiffel Tower sparkled right on the hour of midnight like a giant decoration. Ryan put his arms around his wife and kissed her, and Bart kissed Halley a little more passionately than he'd planned. She didn't stop him, and she looked shy afterward, knowing Bart's son and daughter-in-law had seen them, but she didn't want Bart to stop. They held hands afterward, sharing a lounge chair, with blankets over them, and when the young couple went inside, Bart kissed her again, gently this time. He had surprised himself, but he felt so drawn to Halley. He didn't understand it, he hardly knew her but he felt as though he had for a long time. It was so easy being with her, and she was such a warm person. She felt peaceful that night, and as though she was in the right place, with the right people. She leaned her head against Bart's shoulder and they didn't speak for a little while. It was nice just being there together. It was so strange that she had met him coming to Paris for her big adventure. The trip had gotten off to a rough start with the stolen bag. But she was surprised how safe she felt with Bart.

She stayed until one-thirty, and Bart wouldn't let her go home alone. She thanked Ryan and Véronique for a wonderful New Year's Eve, and wished them a happy year ahead.

"I think it will be," Ryan said, looking tenderly at Véro, and they obviously had a secret they didn't want to share yet. Halley had a feeling she knew what it was, but didn't say anything to Bart. She saw them kiss, as she and Bart were leaving to take her home. She was thinking as they left that despite her mistakes, and Bart's, with his forced marriage and her decision to have the twins out of wedlock at such an early age, their children had done things right, and had chosen the partners that truly suited them, and were together because they wanted to be, not because they had to be, pregnant at the wrong time with the wrong person. Halley had no regrets and the twins had been the joy of her life, but Locke had played such a small part in her life and the girls', and Bart had married a woman he didn't love, and it had only lasted for a couple of years. They had both chosen the wrong partners, but had lovely children anyway. And as a result of their youthful mistakes, neither she nor Bart had ever married or remarried.

"You did a great job with Ryan," she said as they walked to find a cab. There were horns honking and people laughing and shouting in the street to celebrate the new year.

"I can't take all the credit for that. My ex-wife was a good mother, even though she was just a kid herself. We weren't suited to each other, but she was always there for him, and he has a good relationship with both of us. Sometimes I think that's more to his credit than ours. He's a good guy. Did your daughters suffer from not having a father around all the time?"

"Not really," she said, thinking about it. "They never had that, so they didn't miss it. Maybe they did in theory, but in reality they were happy children, and they got extra attention from me. They never went through a divorce or a sense of loss about their father. He came around from time to time, like a big playmate. He was like a child himself. And when they were thirteen, I met a wonderful man, who was more of a father to them than their own."

"What happened to him? Is he still in their life?"

"No," she said softly. "He died three years ago. That was the hardest thing my daughters and I had ever been through. Robert and I lived together for ten years, and I'm grateful we all had those years with him. It was an added gift in their lives, and mine."

"And now?" Bart asked her, wondering if there was someone in her life at home. He didn't think so, but he wanted to be sure before he made a fool of himself, or did something she didn't want. He was so drawn to her, he wanted to be sure that the attraction was mutual and he hadn't misread it, but she didn't seem like the kind of woman who would kiss him if she had a man waiting for her at home.

"It took me a long time to get over losing him, but I feel peaceful about it now. One day you wake up and realize you're ready to go on. Robert wasn't a sad person, and he was a very generous man. I don't think he would have wanted me to be alone forever," she said quietly. They stopped walking, and Bart gently put his arms around her and kissed her, and afterward, they kept walking in the direction of her house.

"I'm not sure I've ever really been in love," Bart said. "I put all my energy and feelings into my work and Ryan. I never wanted to get tied down to the wrong person again. And I never met the right one." He wanted to add "until now," but it was too soon to know that for sure. It felt that way, and he wanted time to get to know her so he didn't make another mistake. But she seemed like a very special person.

When they reached her house, he waited while she unlocked the door. He walked her inside and kissed her again. He was gentle and tender, and he made it easy for her to come back from where she'd been for the past three years.

He left after a few minutes, waiting outside until she set the alarm and signaled to him from the window, and he smiled and waved, and walked back to Ryan's apartment, thinking what sweet times he and Halley had ahead of them if everything they were discovering about each other turned out to be true in time. It was too soon to know, but he loved being with her. She was an honorable woman, and everything about it felt right. He had only seen her three times, but he felt wonderful when he was with her.

The boat stayed at anchor off Antigua on New Year's Eve. It sounded more festive and fun to celebrate on the boat, among good friends. The chef prepared an exquisite meal. They had crab and lobster that had been flown in for them, and pasta with caviar. They laughed a lot at dinner, and danced on deck afterward. There was a constant friendly banter between all of them, some more than others. They had turned out to be the perfect group to travel with, and had made memories they would never forget.

It was Seth and Valerie's first married Christmas, and at midnight Peter kissed Olivia with all the passion that had brought them closer every day, and the others smiled at them.

After he had kissed her, he whispered to her, "If you tell me that you and Valerie switched tonight, I'm going to throw you overboard," and she laughed.

"That might be fun," she taunted him, and he advanced on her, picked her up, and threw her into the water. He took off his clothes and joined her, and Seth and Valerie followed a few minutes later. The others watched them from the upper deck. The water was warm and soothing, and the lights from the underside of the boat cast a bright light into the water and they could see schools of small fish scurrying past them. The crew had put gardenias with candles on them on the water. It was an incredible vision, seeing the flowers in the candlelight floating around them. It had been the best New Year's Eve of their lives.

Chapter 11

The morning of New Year's Day was quiet on the boat. Most of the guests remained in their cabins until nearly noon. Valerie was an early riser so she came up for coffee and toast while Seth was still asleep. It had been fun the night before, and the end of a beautiful trip. They would be motoring a short distance the next day, and stopping for a last day of swimming and snorkeling. Seth and Peter liked to race each other on the Jet Skis, their old spirit of competition with each other in evidence. One was stronger, one was older, and both had been daredevils in their youth. Seth had settled down with time, and fatherhood had only taken the edge off Peter a little. He had greater responsibilities now but they hadn't dampened his thirst for life, passion, and sense of fun.

They were planning to have an early night on the boat on New Year's Day after another day of water sports. Valerie was sorry to see it come to an end, it had been a wonderful trip. Different from their honeymoon in October, but almost as much fun. She had enjoyed spending time with Olivia, her brother-in-law, Seth's mother, and their friends.

Olivia wandered up in a bikini and a shirt, and smiled as she sat down next to her sister. A steward set a cup of coffee in front of her seconds later, just the way she liked it, with a dash of milk, no sugar.

"That was great last night," she commented to Valerie. "I'm going to feel like Cinderella after the ball when I go home. This is a very nice way to live."

Valerie smiled and nodded in response. "I was thinking that too. We all got a little crazy last night. The gardenias in the water looked gorgeous. It was like fairyland."

"I think Seth should buy the boat," Olivia said, enjoying the coffee.

"I'll tell him. And by the way, I don't mean to intrude—"

"That usually means you're about to," Olivia interrupted with a grin. "What now?"

"I saw Peter kiss you at midnight. I don't know who was kissing who, but it looked like more than a midnight kiss on New Year's Eve. Seth didn't kiss me like that at midnight."

"That's because you're married now, he doesn't have to impress you," Olivia said lightly, not sure how much she wanted to say, even to her twin. She felt very private about her relationship with Peter. She didn't know where it was going, and it was all so new.

"Did something major happen on the trip?" Valerie hadn't forgotten Olivia's thong that she had found under the table on the deck. And she knew her sister. She didn't sleep with men casually, only when she cared about them, and usually not too quickly. If something had happened with Peter, she was sure Olivia would have told her, but she'd had a feeling that Olivia was keeping something from her for the entire trip. She and Peter had spent a lot of time together, which Olivia had said was just getting to know him since they were family now.

"I don't know if it's major," Olivia said, staring into space for a minute. "I like him a lot. We had a good time." It had been a lot more than that, but she wasn't sure she was ready to admit that to herself yet, or to her twin, which was why she had asked Peter to be discreet about it, and they had been. He had been sneaking in and out of her cabin for the past week, at any time of day or night. They hadn't been found out. But she knew that Valerie would sense it, and she had. "Maybe it was just the sun and the stars at night, a shipboard romance."

"How romantic was it?" Valerie asked, dying to know. Olivia laughed.

"Quite a lot. I don't know, Val. He's got kids. He has a serious life when he's not riding around on a Jet Ski off a yacht in the Caribbean. How real can that be? And he dates a lot of women. I could get hurt if I take it seriously, and then it would be awkward as hell when we're with you and Seth. It just kind of happened while we were here, but with our regular lives looming when we go back to L.A. tomorrow, maybe it was just a crazy moment, and it'll end here. He's kind of a big package deal with two very young children. I don't believe in marriage the way you do, or happily ever after. I'm more like Mom. I'm not as traditional or linear as you are. You have a big job, you dated Seth for three years, you got married, now you'll have kids. I'm more free-form."

"Mom was very traditional once she met Robert. And she was right not to marry our father when he was available. He would have married her then, he told me so. She didn't want to. And by then even we knew he was a mess, he always was, totally irresponsible, and she was with Robert, who suited her a lot better. You just haven't met the right guy. Until now. You two seem good together." She was serious and Olivia was pensive.

"I know. Maybe that's what scares me. He's an attorney, a tax attorney. I'm an artist. How would that work?"

"You could get your taxes done for free," Valerie teased her, and Olivia rolled her eyes.

"He's not an accountant. He manages huge amounts of money and estates for movie stars. I don't know. These were the best two weeks of my life. Being here with you, on this incredible dream boat, and having fun with him. So do they live happily ever after, or do they turn into pumpkins and white mice when the ship docks?"

"I vote for Option One, happily ever after. Don't make any dramatic decisions. See what happens when you both get home."

"He wants me to meet his kids," Olivia said glumly.

"That's nice, and normal. They're very sweet. You'll like them, and he's good with them. They're not brats."

"He has them half the time, that's a lot. I need to paint. That's my priority, just like your job is yours."

"I still manage to have time for Seth. Think of what I'd have missed if all I had was my work. I love him, and we have a wonderful life together. You deserve something like that too."

"We'll see. Maybe he'll forget me as soon as we get home, and go back to online dating. I don't think he wants to settle down either. He was miserable in his marriage. A week of hot sex on a yacht does not guarantee a solid relationship or a rosy future," Olivia said cynically, and Valerie laughed.

"I'm happy to know the sex was good. Only you can turn that into a doomed relationship. You can be such a gloom ball sometimes."

Olivia smiled at the expression. "I'm an artist. I'm sensitive."

"No, you're a coward about relationships. Give him a chance, Ollie. What if he turns out to be the best thing that ever happened to you?"

"Then I'd probably die of a heart attack having sex with him when I'm ninety, or break a hip or something."

"It might be worth it," Valerie commented, as Peter appeared on deck and came to sit down with them.

"What might be worth it?" he asked them, as his cappuccino magically appeared in front of him.

"Olivia wants Seth to buy the boat," Valerie answered.

"I second that." Peter grinned, and stole a glance at Olivia, and she smiled at him. "Is he considering it?"

"No, but Olivia thinks he should."

"Excellent idea, as long as I get squatter's rights and he pays for it." All three of them laughed as Seth joined them, and they shared the idea with him.

"Fine, if my tax attorney says I can afford it," he said, glancing at his brother.

"You can if you sell your new house, and get a night job to increase your income."

"I'll think about it," Seth said, and leaned over to kiss Valerie. The others joined them shortly after, and the day got off to a good start.

Peter and Olivia got dropped off at a small nearby beach that looked deserted. One of the deckhands took them in the dinghy and promised to pick them up in an hour.

They lay side by side on the white sand, drying off after they swam. "You look serious today," Peter said to her, and she rolled over on her side to look at him.

"I'm sad to go home in two days." They wouldn't be able to meet in her cabin at any time of day, or spend the nights together, although he lived on the hills above West Hollywood, not far from her. But he had his kids half the time, or close to it.

"I am too," he admitted. He'd been thinking about it for the last few days. "What happens now? We go back to our own lives, or do we try to build on what we started here?" It was the question he had wanted to ask her for days and was afraid to. What if it was just a fling for her? He wanted it to be more. "I vote for keeping it going when we go home." He gently touched her face with a finger, brushed some sand away near her eyes, and kissed her, hoping that would convince her.

"Can we do that? What about your girls?"

"What about them? They're with their mother half the time, and you could spend time with us, like normal people, when I have them. And when she has them, we can hang off the chandeliers and do whatever we want." He grinned at her and she smiled. "It's not that complicated, Olivia. It can work if we want it to. The question is, do you . . . want it to work?"

"I think I do," she said softly.

"That's not good enough," he said. "We have to know we want to. Because there are going to be times that are hard, or we fight, or the kids are a problem, or my ex-wife, or something isn't working for you, or we disappoint each other. But there could be great times too. I want to try to make it work, Olivia. My wife and I both made a mess of my first marriage. I learned a lot from it. I want to do it right with you, and really try." He was so earnest as he said it that she put her arms around him and kissed him, and she was smiling when they stopped.

"I'm in. I want to give it a try and make it work too."

They were lying on their sides, talking and kissing.

"I have the girls for a week when I get home. You could meet them then. Dinner or ice cream, or Disneyland or something." Olivia smiled thinking about it. It was a whole new world for her. "I'll miss you every night. I'm picking them up as soon as we land, and I want to give them a few days to settle in. This will be a change for them too, they've never met the women I've dated before. So it's a little bit of a big deal for them. Can you manage for a few days?" He looked worried.

"I think so. I may have withdrawal at first. And I have a lot of work to do for my show in March."

The deckhand arrived with the dinghy to take them back to the boat then. They swam out to it, and sat wet and smiling on the way back to the yacht. They had made an important decision on the beautiful little beach. And as soon as they were back on the yacht, Peter followed Olivia to her cabin and locked the door behind him.

"Welcome to my life, Olivia Holbrook," he said softly, as he took off her bikini top, dropped it to the floor and kissed her.

"I thought maybe it was just a shipboard romance," she said in a hoarse voice.

"That too," he said, as her bikini bottoms landed on the floor with his wet swimming trunks, "and that's not over yet." He kissed her, and they made it to her bed to celebrate what they had decided that morning. This was the beginning, not the end after all. The new year was off to a great start.

Bart and Halley went for a walk in the Bois de Boulogne on New Year's Day. They watched the children playing, families on bicycles, people walking their dogs, lovers kissing, old men playing pétanque. It was another beautiful day, and they walked for a long time before they sat down on a bench. There were peacocks walking past them, and they had seen swans on a lake.

"Everything always looks beautiful in Paris," Bart commented. "And there is always an underlying feeling of romance to it, and a quality of life you don't feel in the States. France is all about beauty and history, and family, and people kissing." He smiled at her as he said it, and leaned over and kissed her, since he had dared to kiss her the night before, and she kissed him back. "I'm lucky to have met you on the plane," he said happily, and she smiled in answer.

"So am I. I thought I was just going to go to my favorite shops and the Louvre. I wasn't expecting to meet anyone. It was my daughter's idea that I should come. She suggested it."

"I'm glad she did. I want to see you when we go back to New York, Halley, if that appeals to you. We both have busy work lives, but I want to make time to see you. What do you like to do?"

She smiled as she thought about it. "For years, all I did was take care of my kids and write. I didn't make time for much else. With Robert, we traveled when we had time. We put a lot of things off for the future when we wouldn't be so busy, and we never got to do them. I don't want to make that mistake again. I ride, I love going to the movies, I love books and art, going to the theater, dinner with friends, or just two of us. I volunteer at a center for abused women and children. I've been very involved with that for a long time, and it's important to me. I like spending time with the kids there, and helping them see that they can have a good future, even though some pretty awful things happened to them in the past. Some of them come to us very damaged physically, with others the damage is all inside. It's easier to help the children than the women. The damage they suffer is so pervasive, and it's a cycle a lot of them can't escape." He looked interested as she said it. They were sitting on a bench and he held her hand.

"How did you get involved with that, instead of something else? I support an entrepreneurial program for underprivileged young people entering the work force, trying to expand their vision and show them a bigger world of opportunities. It's kind of the same idea. But I meet them after they've managed to get an education and have gotten through college. It's to help them take off the limits other people may try to put on them. The program is called Limitless, and we've had some real success stories. It's my way of sharing what I've learned. Their horizons are so much broader than they realize. If they're bright, they can do anything they have the courage to do."

"That is a little bit like what I do, except that the kids I work with have been damaged by the people who should protect them and love them most. But once we get them to a safe place, they can make it to a good life. To answer your question, I had a difficult childhood, and I want to help them find their way out of theirs, and show them that they can. With the little kids, it's just about loving them and making them feel safe. Most of them have been in danger since they were born."

They talked about it for a while and then walked on, still holding hands, like two children. Halley didn't explain what her "difficult childhood" entailed, and she didn't know if she ever would. It was all she wanted to say for now. The rest was buried in a walled garden she didn't visit anymore. She preferred to live in the sun and bright daylight of the present, not the shadows of the past.

"Ryan and Véro shared some good news with me this morning," Bart said to her as he drove her home. "They're expecting a baby in July. That's very exciting. I think they're going to be wonderful parents."

"I think so too." She smiled at him. "How do you feel about being a grandfather?" she asked, and he laughed. She kept noticing how handsome he was, he didn't look like a grandfather to her.

"A little bit outraged and a little bit scared, and very happy for them. I wasn't ready for that image of myself."

"You don't look the part, and you're barely old enough to be one. I wouldn't worry about it too much."

"It's nice that they're so happy about it. They went to have lunch with her parents today, to tell them. They invited me to come, but I wanted to see you. Her parents don't speak English, and they'll have a better time without having to translate for me. Do you think your daughter who got married will start having children soon?"

"Not for a while. She's only twenty-seven and more interested in her career for now. And I'm not sure how keen her husband is on having kids. He didn't have any in his first marriage. He's thirty-nine and he has a very big job as a producer in television. He loves his work. So does she."

"They all have babies later now. Ryan and Véro have been married for three years. You and I got an early start." He smiled at her. "We grew up with our kids."

"They were the best thing that ever happened to me. They were the only family I had. My mother died when I was eight, and my father when I was fourteen. I was alone for a long time before I had them." It was his first glimpse of the difficult childhood she had mentioned lightly, and he didn't want to pry.

"You must have been very strong as a child to come through that, losing your parents so young." She didn't tell him it had been a mercy for her.

"Children are stronger and more resilient than most people realize. They survive wars without their parents, and terrible lives, and some of them come out of it whole." He could sense that whatever had happened to her, she was a survivor and had been one of those who remained whole. But one paid a price for surviving, and he suspected she had.

She invited him in for a cup of tea when they got to her house, and he said he should really get back, but agreed to come in briefly. Ryan and Véro would be home from her parents' by then, after delivering the good news.

Halley and Bart sat in her cozy kitchen and drank their tea. They were both happy and relaxed. He said he was planning to come back when the baby was born in July, and maybe a time or two before then.

"Maybe I'll go down to the south of France for a couple of weeks afterward. I love it there." He talked about a house he had rented once in St.-Paul-de-Vence, and said he would love to go back. He seemed to have a very pleasant life, and worked hard too. He wanted to read more of her books now that he'd met her. He had read most of them, which touched her, but had missed a few. And then he left, promising to call to take her to lunch and dinner, when he'd know his son's plans.

She pulled out her manuscript to edit that night and did a little work. She wasn't really in the mood, but thought she should. It was a peaceful night. She took a bath and was going to bed when the phone rang. She assumed it was the girls, since it was earlier in the Caribbean. It was almost midnight, and no one else would call her at that hour on New Year's Day.

The caller I.D. showed a blocked number, but she thought maybe they were calling from a phone on the boat. She answered and there was no sound, but the line hadn't disconnected, and then after a minute it did. Halley thought it must have been a wrong number, or a poor connection from the boat. She got into bed and turned off the light, and then the phone rang again, and she took it out of the charger and answered, and the same thing happened. It didn't disconnect for at least a minute, and it sounded like there was someone on the other end, but they never spoke and then the call ended.

She was almost asleep half an hour later when it rang again. She almost didn't answer, but with both her daughters far away, and she being the only person for them to call in an emergency, she always left her phone on at night and never turned it off. And she answered every call.

"Hello?" she answered, wondering if it would cut off again. But this time she was startled when a deep male voice answered her.

"'Ello, were you sleeping?" he asked in a silky voice. He had an accent, but he spoke English and she couldn't tell if the accent was French or Spanish or something else.

"No, who is this?"

"I know who you are, and I know where you are. You do not know me. And if I wanted to come to you now, I could, and you couldn't stop me. I have control of you now." It was a frightening thing to say, and she was shaking as she sat up in bed. She wanted to hang up, but she didn't, waiting to see what else he would say.

"You do *not* have control of me. And I assume you have my bag. I'd like it back, and my papers, and my passport." She was surprised herself by what she said, but she was suddenly furious that he was calling her and obviously trying to frighten her, and he had.

"You're a very rich woman, maybe I will sell it back to you, but not yet. We can discuss it when I call you again," and then he hung up. She sat in her bed, shaking. The call was creepy. She checked all the doors and windows again on the ground floor and made sure they were locked, and they were. She checked the alarm to be certain it was on. He had the keys and she had no way of stopping him if he used them, which was a terrifying thought. The lock-smith was coming in the morning, as the locks hadn't been changed yet, because of the holiday. But the alarm would go off, and hope-fully Henri the guardian would come and call the police if some-one entered.

She tried to find something she could defend herself with, and found a set of golf clubs in a guest room closet. She selected a sturdy-looking one, and stood it up, leaning against her night table. It wouldn't be much use if he had a gun, but maybe she could stave him off. She locked the bedroom door then, and re-mained sitting upright in bed, so she wouldn't fall into a deep sleep and would wake up if he got in. She kept thinking about what he'd said, and remembered every word. She never heard from the girls that night and wouldn't have told them anyway. They didn't know the bag had been stolen and she didn't intend to tell them until she got home, so as not to upset them. But she was terrified as she sat in bed, with the lights on, and the golf club next to her. It was an awful night of terror.

She finally gave up on sleep, and showered and dressed at seven. She put on jeans and a sweater and stayed in her locked bedroom. But once it was daylight, she didn't think he'd try to get in, and she went to the kitchen to make a cup of coffee. She was still sitting at the kitchen table feeling dazed and exhausted, when the doorbell rang at nine. She looked through the peephole, and saw Henri Laurent and another man, and she was still holding the golf club when she opened the door to them. Henri look incensed when he saw it.

"You cannot make sports in the house, you will break something, a lamp, or a painting. *Américains sauvages,*" he muttered under his breath, calling her a savage, as he led the locksmith in, and rattled off a torrent of French, complaining about her, which was perfectly clear to Halley. The locksmith kept glancing at her, and then responding to Henri.

He examined the locks at all the outer doors of the house, and then Henri explained the situation to her.

"It will take him all day. These are very expensive locks installed by the owner. He can replace them. It will be six thousand euros, and you will only get four keys. The owner normally has eight sets of keys. So you will pay extra for four additional keys, which will be another sixteen hundred euros, and since it is your fault, you must pay. Do you agree?" She didn't have much choice, given the situation, and the threatening call the night before.

"I don't agree in principle, and I'll discuss it with the realtor for reimbursement. And I will pay him today, but all my credit cards were . . ." She was about to say "stolen," and suddenly remembered the card Bart had given her. She could use that. "Never mind. I have a credit card."

"Good. I will not use my employer's money to pay for your stupid mistake."

"I didn't make a mistake," she said, seething. "My bag was stolen, I didn't lose it. Please supervise this man while he changes the locks today. I have work to do."

"I do not need to supervise him, he is my friend. We went to school together."

"That's very nice. I am the tenant here, and I am asking you, telling you, that I want him supervised. You may know him, but I don't." It was a reasonable request, and there was another torrent of French from Henri to the locksmith, who just nodded and said okay. She was going to be paying the equivalent of nine thousand dollars to change the locks, which seemed insane to her, but she had no choice. It had to be done as soon as possible, so the bag thief couldn't get in.

She went back to the kitchen then, and called Major Leopold on her cell phone. He answered on the second ring, and she told him about the call the night before, verbatim. She had a good memory and the caller's words had been unforgettable, and his tone.

"I don't like this at all," the major said, almost growling with displeasure. "The profile of this kind of thief is usually to have no contact with their victim, and no interest in them. He wants no contact, no recognition. They are looking for merchandise to sell, and once they have it, they sell it, make their profit, and disappear. There is a new breed, mostly from the Eastern European countries, where they use the keys to get in, if they got any, and they rob the house. If they find someone in the house, like a maid, they tie them up and put them in a closet, then they take what they want and leave. Mostly small objects, as big ones are too inconvenient, and that group are very clever at breaking open safes, even the most secure, that are usually full of cash. But I don't think I have ever had a case where the thief calls and bargains with the victim, or taunts her and threatens her. Maybe he has been able to verify the value of the bag with someone more knowledgeable, and he may fear it will be hard to sell, or will lead to his being caught if it's too distinctive, so he'd rather sell it back to you. But it's most unusual.

"I don't like how bold he was with you, or the things he said to you. Unfortunately, you will hear from him again. I think he may be afraid to get caught if he puts your bag on the internet, or on the market, selling it to a store. It's a very distinctive bag, and it was a special order. Hermès has an archive of it, with photographs, which is useful for us. They only made one of your bag. So it's even more valuable than you thought. They think it could sell for as much as two hundred thousand dollars at auction. But the thief won't have access to those resources, without the bill of sale. He's smart. His best bet may be to sell it back to you. You want it more than anyone else, but I don't know how much you're willing to pay for it, and he probably wants to know that. And it would be very dangerous for you to meet him, even with our protection. He will definitely contact you again, I'm sorry to say. I regret that you have to go through this. Call me when you hear from him again. I'm sure you will. I think he is calling to taunt you, to make you willing to buy your bag back. I don't think he'll actually show up. He's just scaring you."

The call wasn't reassuring, and she wasn't looking forward to hearing from the thief again. She didn't want to meet him, although she wanted her bag back. But not at just any price.

She worked on her manuscript all day, while the locksmith went from door to door, making a mess everywhere he went, and leaving black fingerprints on all the doors. Halley couldn't get much done. She was too unnerved by the call the night before, and too distracted after talking to Major Leopold.

The locksmith finished the job at five o'clock, and Henri was standing next to him when he handed the four sets of keys to him.

Henri gave one set to Halley, and said he'd give a set to the house-keeper, and kept two sets for himself and the owners. The lock-smith told him that the other four sets of keys for the owner would be ready in three to four weeks. They were slow and expensive.

Henri was muttering under his breath about having wasted an entire day when they left together, and Halley sat down on a couch in the library. She hadn't gotten anything done all day, and felt exhausted.

Bart called her half an hour later.

"How was your day?" he asked cheerfully.

"Not a lot of fun," she admitted. "I spent it with the locksmith, with the guardian glaring at me. At least the thief can't just walk in now."

"Hopefully, he won't try."

Halley hesitated, and decided to tell him. "I heard from him last night," she said, and Bart wasn't pleased to hear it.

"He called you?"

"Around midnight, he hung up twice, and spoke to me the third time."

"What did he want?"

"He talked about how rich I am, said he now controls me, which gave me chills, and hinted about selling me back the bag. It was all scary and weird. I called the major and he said it was very un-usual, and this kind of thief normally wants no contact with their victims. The caller was frightening. He had a sinister voice."

"Why didn't you call me?" Bart sounded as upset as she was.

"It was too late, I didn't want to bother you at midnight. And I'm so sorry. I used your credit card by the way. I had to pay for the locks. Seven thousand six hundred euros. It's extortionate. I'll write you a check when I have them, and I'm sorry I had to use the card. I'm grateful that I had it, thanks to you."

"I thought you might need it. Don't worry about it. You should keep it till you get your own new credit cards. You can write me a check then. You might need it again. And I think it's so disturbing that the thief called you. It sounds like he wants to show off."

"And scare me. He said he can get into my house whenever he wants. But he doesn't know about the alarm and the new locks."

"You should be safe now, Halley," he said gently. "I'm having dinner with the kids. Do you want me to come over after that?" He didn't like her being alone, with the thief possibly watching her or the house.

"I don't want to bother you with my problems."

"You're not bothering me. Why don't I just drop by after dinner? I won't stay long, but if he is watching you, it might be good for him to see some activity coming and going. Why don't I call you when we finish dinner and see if you want me to come by?"

"I'd love to see you," she said in a tired voice. Her stolen bag and the bag thief and the aftermath were wearing her out. "I'll be here, I'll be editing a book," she said.

"Try not to worry too much. The locks are changed, and you have an alarm. You're safe. And the police seem to be on top of it. Let's have dinner one night this week. You need a change of scenery."

"I think I do. I might even let you use your credit card," she said, and he laughed.

"See you later." He was excited at the prospect of seeing her, and she was still smiling after the call. And he was right, the thief couldn't hurt her. But she was tempted to buy back her bag, at a reasonable price, not a hundred thousand dollars.

She decided to take a bath and change for when Bart would come by. It was something to look forward to.

All the guests were leaving the boat by noon the next day. Seth, Valerie, Peter, and Olivia were all on the same flight to L.A. Seth and Peter's mother and her husband were on a different airline, connecting to a flight to Palm Springs. And the two couples who had been with them on the boat were flying to Orange County. They had been a totally compatible group, and had gotten along for the entire time. They had a drink at the Hotel du Cap that night and came back to the boat for an early dinner. They had all loved the boat and the crew, and were sorry to leave.

"Did I miss something on the trip?" Seth said to Valerie when she was packing that night. "I mean about your sister and my brother." He had noticed them holding hands at dinner.

"I think so," Valerie said mysteriously. "I'm not sure what's going to happen when they get back to L.A., but I think they're off to a good start." After trying to get them interested in each other for three years, it had finally happened.

"She'd be perfect for him, instead of all the bimbos and crazies he goes out with that he meets online. I hope he's ready for a good one." Valerie nodded agreement, and leaned over and kissed him. "Good work," he complimented her.

"Thank you for the best trip of my life," she said.

"This is only the beginning," he said, and smiled as he put an arm around her. They'd had a great time, but he was happy to be going home, and more in love with Valerie than ever. He hoped his brother would be as smart and as lucky as he had been.

Chapter 12

The Warners had dinner at the Fontaine de Mars, Ryan's favorite restaurant. It was a high-end typical French bistro, with delicious food, which Bart always enjoyed too when he visited. They skipped dessert and finished early, because Véro wasn't feeling well. She had just started having morning sickness at odd times, mostly in the evening, for the past week. They decided to walk home to get some air, and Bart said he was going to visit Halley. He hailed a cab outside the restaurant, and would be at her house in ten minutes. He called her from the cab.

"We ended dinner early, Véronique wasn't feeling well."

"Oh, I'm sorry. Nothing serious, I hope?"

"Pretty standard stuff, I think, but she wanted to go home. Are you up for a visit, or too tired?" It was only nine o'clock, but she had hardly slept the night before, after the midnight call from the thief, or whoever it was. It was most likely him.

"Actually, I'm wide awake. I've been snooping. I found some

photo albums in the library, and there are photographs of my landlords' home in Marrakesh. It looks like a palace."

"A lot of the French go there, and I think there are some spectacular homes."

"And yes, I would love to see you," she said, answering his question.

"I'll be there in five minutes." He was pleased that she wanted to see him. He had thought of her all day, and of how little he knew about her. The things she said were intriguing, passing mentions of her childhood, her history with her daughters' father, and the love of her life who had died of a brain tumor. She didn't say much about it, but he had the feeling that she had been through a lot. She wasn't bitter, and she had a positive outlook, but reading her books, he had always felt that she was a woman with deep feelings, a rich life experience, and compassionate nature. And compassion often came from suffering. Meeting her had confirmed it. She had a deep well of feelings that she kept carefully hidden. He wanted to slowly unravel the protective layers, and get to know her better. And he had a feeling that much of her writing came from her own experience.

He rang the outer bell when he got there, which buzzed in the house. She answered through an intercom and let him in, and when he entered the inner courtyard, he saw her waiting for him in the doorway, smiling to welcome him. Out of the corner of his eye, he saw a surly-looking man watching him from behind a curtain in the lodging near the outer door, and he guessed that it was the guardian she had mentioned and didn't like. It was easy to see why. He looked unpleasant and menacing. Bart paid no attention to him, walking swiftly toward Halley, and they went into the house and closed and locked the door.

As he had before, he found the house warm and inviting, and she led him into the library and offered him a glass of wine. It was cozy being with her in the handsome room, lined with leather-bound books. "I love this place," he said, looking around and admiring it again.

"So do I. And the owners' palace in Morocco looks amazing in the photographs." She pulled out the big leather album and showed it to him. Their home in Marrakesh was enormous and spectacular, the interior filled with Asian art, and the décor had a faintly Moorish look to it. It was very exotic.

"They must be interesting people," he said, intrigued.

"He's a famous architect, I discovered, reading about them online. And she's an interior designer." The Paris house was beautifully done in classic French style, with some magnificent antiques and a few modern pieces and paintings that blended well.

Halley and Bart talked about a variety of topics, jumping from one subject to the next, favorite books, favorite cities, favorite vacation places, their college days. He had gone to Harvard, and went to business school there for his MBA after he got his undergraduate degree. "And where did you go to school?" he asked her.

"Connecticut College. It's not an Ivy, but I got a good education, and was happy there," she said modestly. He had to remind himself sometimes that she was a major best-selling author. She was so discreet that she never played the star or acted like a diva.

"Who did you live with after your father died when you were fourteen, or would you rather not talk about it?" he asked thoughtfully. She hesitated and then told him the truth.

"I didn't live with anybody. He died in a car accident, in his fifties. And his will provided for me after the age of eighteen. He didn't expect to die so young. He had no living relatives, and neither did my mother, who was dead by then too. So I was sent to a state orphanage in New York City for four years." He looked shocked when she said it. He hadn't expected that. She looked as though she had always been comfortably brought up in the lap of luxury, but that was only true until she turned fourteen. "I'm sorry, I know that sounds awful. But it wasn't so bad really. I was safe. I was the oldest girl there for most of the time. The girls were very nice and a lot younger. The younger ones always went to foster homes, or got adopted. I was too old for anyone to want to adopt me. They tried me out at two foster homes, but I didn't fit in, so I got sent back. I preferred it really, the two foster families were complicated, and they wanted someone younger. I wasn't really unhappy at the orphanage. In a lot of ways it was better than living with my parents." That said volumes about what her family had been like, and touched him, and she said it very simply. She wasn't pathetic, and seemed strong to him.

"I led a very banal early life," Bart said. "I had adoring older parents, and an easy existence. They got along, they didn't get divorced. They weren't unusual, they were very conservative and old-fashioned, which is why they made such a fuss when Ryan's mother got pregnant. They thought I should marry her, but they didn't like her. But they expected me to do the 'honorable' thing anyway. They had a long list of concerns about her, and it turned out that they were right. It was all pretty standard stuff. But your being sent to an orphanage when your father died sounds like something out of a novel."

"It wasn't what I expected. I was shocked at first, like a prison sentence, but I tried to make the best of it, and it showed me another side of life. There was nowhere else for me to go. I left the orphanage when I turned eighteen. I had graduated from high school early, and the trust my father left for me kicked in. It wasn't much, but it was enough to live on, and provided for my college education, so I took advantage of it, and put it to good use." She seemed very peaceful as she said it. She seemed to have no bitterness about the situation her father left her in. She was matter-of-fact about it.

They talked for two hours, and then he put down his glass. The red wine she had served him was an excellent French wine that she had bought herself. She wasn't emptying her landlords' cellar, she purchased her own. It struck him how resilient she had had to be to survive in a state-run orphanage. It couldn't have been as easy as she made it sound. But she had definitely made her peace with it. He heard no resentment in her tone, and she didn't criticize her father for landing her in that situation. It showed remarkable generosity on her part.

She walked him to the front door when he left, they stopped talking, and he kissed her gently and held her for a minute. She loved the feeling of being in his arms. It comforted her after the aggravations of her day.

"Will you call me if anything happens, Halley? I mean it. I don't want you scared all night again. I can come over and sleep on the couch."

"I'll be fine now that the locks are changed," she reassured him, and she looked happy and peaceful after chatting with him. Once again, they had covered a lot of ground.

She locked the door behind him and turned on the alarm, put their glasses in the kitchen, and went upstairs to her bedroom. It was a pretty room. She sat on the bed and opened her computer. She had no emails from the girls. They were still on the boat until the next day. She was checking her other emails when the phone rang. She didn't look to see, but she thought it might be Bart, thanking her for the evening. She picked her phone up with a smile.

"I know you're home. I saw your friend leave," the same deep foreign voice said, the one she had heard the night before. He was watching her house, maybe right outside. "You won't escape me. I know you want your bag back. You'll have to pay me for it. I know what it's worth. You're just like all rich people, you think you can cheat the poor and use them. You want to poison people's minds with your trashy books."

"I don't know what you want. If you return my bag, the police will stop looking for you. That must be worth something to you," she said very directly, trying to sound calmer than she felt. Her hand was shaking again as she held the phone but her voice was steady.

"It's worth nothing. The police are fools. They won't catch me, they never have before." As she listened to him, she determined that the accent wasn't French. Spanish maybe, since the police said he was Colombian. "If you call the police, I'll kill you," he said, and a chill ran through her. It was as though he were watching her, standing in the room. "Don't forget, I have the keys to the house where you are staying. I can walk in anytime I want. But you have to get me the money first. All you had were five thousand euros in your bag. I need more than that. When I'm ready, I'll tell you how much I want. Sleep well, 'Alley." And then he hung up. For a moment she couldn't breathe, his voice had been so oppressive and his words so frightening. He sounded cold-blooded, and she had every intention of calling Major Leopold in the morning. But she had to get through another night first. At least he didn't seem to know that the locks had been changed. But he had seen Bart leave, so he had been right outside, watching the house. And all kinds of information about her was in her bag. She had another thought then. She picked up her computer, and typed her name into the search line. Her bio came up immediately with her age and the number of books she'd published, and a guess about her net worth was in the first line. He had obviously read it too, and thought she was infinitely richer than she was. She made a very healthy living from her books, but she didn't have anything like the fortune they claimed. And all it did was spur someone like him on. She hated the kind of information that floated around the internet, which incited criminals and creeps.

She wrote down what he'd said as she remembered it, to tell the major the next day. She didn't get undressed. She just lay on her bed, with the golf club near at hand, wondering what they would do about him. Major Leopold admitted that they had never been able to catch him, and had tried for years. She wondered if he had stalked and threatened his other victims, or only her. Something about what he'd found in her bag provoked him, maybe just the value of the bag itself. Even she had to admit that it was outrageous. In some places you could buy a house with what the bag was worth now. She felt guilty about that at times, but she worked hard to earn a living. And she couldn't go home to get away from him. Without a passport, she was trapped in France until she got the new one. Eventually, she could go home and escape him, but without her bag, and she would love to have it back, not for its monetary value, but because it was a familiar object she loved, and it was hers.

She felt breathless periodically throughout the night, when she thought about him. She hated the fact that he wanted to frighten her and he had succeeded. And more than anything, she hated the word "victim." She had grown up as one, her mother's victim, her father's, his friends'. She had vowed never to be a victim again, and now she was. Tears filled her eyes as she thought about it. She wanted not to be afraid of him, but she was. He was stealing her peace of mind from her, her feeling of safety, which was worse than the theft of the bag.

Several times during the night, she thought she couldn't breathe and would faint. Her heart was pounding, and she dozed off at six in the morning, and then woke up with a start two hours later. She helped herself to a cup of coffee in the kitchen. She tried to read the paper online, but she couldn't concentrate.

She called Major Leopold at nine o'clock sharp, and he answered on the first ring this time. She read the thief's words to him exactly as she had written them down.

"He's a really bad guy. He's trying to terrorize you. I loathe men like that, who victimize women," he said with feeling.

"I'm not a victim," she said in a harsh tone, reacting to it viscerally. "He committed a crime against me, but I'm not a victim," she repeated, to convince herself. "He has no right to do this to me." It was a reign of terror to control her by fear so she would give him what he wanted. It was all about money for him. For her it was about something much more important. He was dragging her back into a world of helplessness and fear, and jeopardizing her recovery that had been solid for years.

"You answered the phone," Leopold reminded her.

"He was watching my house, right here. I had a friend visiting, the caller saw him leave."

"He wants to frighten you into paying what he wants, for your own bag. It's blackmail. He rules by terror."

"Very effectively," she added. "Should I hire a bodyguard?" she asked him.

"I don't think you need one. I think he just wants to scare you into paying some crazy price. If I was worried, we could assign a policeman outside, but I don't think it's necessary." The bag's real price was crazy enough. In the right auction it was worth a fortune. But she didn't want to sell it, or buy it. She wanted it back. It was rightfully hers. Just like her safety and peace of mind. "We will find him this time. I have too many people working on it not to. We can track his every move through our cameras and informants. Sooner or later, he'll make some stupid mistake, and we'll catch him. Until then, you're safe at home, and with a car service and driver, you'll be fine." She didn't feel fine, though. She was terrified, again.

She called Bart after talking to the detective, who was championing her case, and diligent about it.

"Peaceful night, I hope?" Bart said when he answered.

"Not exactly." She read him her note of the conversation too. It gave him chills, just as it had her.

"Halley, you can't go on like this. He's stalking you. I have an idea. Maybe it's crazy. You told me the inspector said they've been trying to catch him for years, and they haven't been able to."

"He said they're closer than they've ever been. They have all their informants looking for him."

"I have a friend in Washington in the FBI. I know there's an FBI office here. I'd like to call him and ask if the office here could lend a hand, or at least talk to the French operatives, and see if the local agents on the ground here want help to find this guy. Do you want to move to a hotel?" The idea suddenly occurred to him.

"I'd have less protection there, with maids in and out of the room, room service waiters. Here, at least I can lock myself up with the alarm on. At a hotel, he could walk into my room dressed as a bellman, and I wouldn't know it's him."

"He wants money from you. I don't think he'll hurt you before he gets it. He wants to scare you enough so you'll pay him anything to get your bag back and get rid of him."

"It's working," she said with a wintry smile.

"Will you let me call my friend?"

She hesitated, but nothing else was helping. And she had nothing to lose. The thief had stolen the bag six days before. It wasn't long in real time to catch a felon, especially a smart one, but it felt like an eternity to Bart and to Halley. Her new passport hadn't come yet, and she didn't want to leave. She was still hoping that by some miracle they would catch the thief and find her bag. He obviously hadn't sold it, if he wanted to sell it back to her. Or maybe he had, and this was just another scam to get money out of her. It was a profitable business for a man like him, who would stop at nothing to commit a crime, and had no respect for other humans. She wondered how far he would go, and so did Bart.

"Okay, call your friend." She gave Bart the contact information for Major Leopold, and the case number of the complaint she'd filed.

Bart called her back an hour later. "My friend is going to call the Paris office, and see what they can do to help. The French are touchy about interference from other law enforcement agencies, but you're an important person, you're famous, and it won't look good for them if they can't catch him, or if he does something worse. Let's go out to dinner tonight, you need to get out of the house and have some distraction." He felt terrible for her. "Ryan has to work late tonight, and Véro just wants to sleep right now. She feels awful in the evening. Let's go to a nice restaurant and forget the bag for the night." She wasn't in the mood, but he was being so kind to her, and so helpful, she didn't have the heart to refuse. And she was enjoying getting to know him.

"Okay, but nothing too fancy. I have nothing to wear except the dress I wore on New Year's Eve. And I'm afraid to go shopping, if he's following me."

"You would look gorgeous in a potato sack. And I loved that dress on you. I'll call you back when I get a reservation, and let you know what time."

"Thank you, Bart, for everything," she said warmly.

"Thank me when I accomplish something. I haven't yet." It was a good excuse to see her, and he felt genuinely sorry for her, and worried about her. He didn't like the turn it was taking.

After they hung up, she called Major Leopold, and said that a friend had contacted the FBI.

"We don't need outside help," he said stiffly, "we're doing all we can within our department." He sounded defensive.

"I'm sure you are, but maybe they can make some suggestions, or offer their help. And actually, if you don't mind, I'd like you to check out the guardian here. He is so overtly surly and disagreeable, maybe he's in cahoots with the thief now." She gave him Henri Laurent's name, the name of his employer and their address, and guessed him to be in his late forties or early fifties.

"I'll see what I can find out," the major said. She hated to hurt his feelings with the FBI contact, and they hadn't had long to solve the case, but she was grateful for any help they could get. If they took too long, the thief might sell the bag in a panic for any amount before they caught him. If there was any hope of getting her bag back, she wanted to at least try.

Bart sent her a text that said he'd pick her up at eight, but he didn't say where they were going. She didn't care as long as it was with him. His presence was very comforting and kept her going, from one day to the next. She felt strangely disoriented being in a foreign country with a thief threatening her life.

She tried to continue editing her manuscript that afternoon and couldn't concentrate. Both her daughters called her. They were sad to leave the boat and had loved their trip. They conferred after they talked to her, and even Olivia thought she sounded fine.

Halley started getting ready at six, and at seven-thirty, she was sitting in the study, waiting for Bart to arrive. She was wearing the same black dress she had worn on New Year's Eve, with a different necklace and big gold flower earrings with diamond centers. The doorbell rang at the dot of eight and she let Bart in with a broad smile.

"Thank you for all the time you're spending with me. I know you have things you want to do with your son."

"I do, but they're both working, and they won't miss me. And they want to spend quiet time with each other."

He had a car and driver outside, and they left the house quickly. The reservation for dinner was at Alain Ducasse, where Bart knew they'd get an extraordinary meal. He wanted to distract her and impress her. She was quiet and poised on the way to the restaurant, and she relaxed visibly as the evening wore on. He could see how stressed she was before that. She put a good face on it, but he could tell she was nervous. But with a little glass of Château d'Yquem at the end of the meal, after an excellent Bordeaux before that, she was in a warm haze as Bart paid the check, and a few minutes later, they walked out of the restaurant and through the Plaza Athénée hotel to his car waiting outside. He had Halley get in quickly in case they'd been followed, and gave the driver the instruction to take them to Halley's house. It had been a delicious meal and a lovely evening, and they headed toward the Alexandre

III Bridge to cross over to the Left Bank. For Halley, being with Bart put the stalker into perspective. As unpleasant as it was, it was a nasty episode and having her bag stolen and everything in it had upset her, but it wasn't fatal or a tragedy, and she felt safe again being with Bart. The bag and the thief shrank in importance, balanced by a civilized evening. She felt as though she was getting her bearings again. The calls from the thief had made her feel helpless and vulnerable.

They passed in the vicinity of the Faubourg St.-Honoré as they chatted in the car, and were suddenly faced by a wall of police, and additional squads in riot gear. They were all carrying machine guns, and the riot police had bulletproof shields. It looked like a war zone, and Bart frowned as he glanced out the car window. There was a tank, and police buses and vans lined the streets. A wall of riot police stopped their progress, and a police officer holding a machine gun approached the car, with a fierce expression, with his partner right behind him as backup. Bart and Halley were being driven in a Mercedes, and were obviously a respectable couple with a driver, as both police officers signaled to lower the windows and glanced into the car. Nothing they saw was alarming, but they were expressionless as they demanded everyone's ID papers. Terrorists hid in many guises, and no one was exempt.

The driver handed over his license, and Bart handed the police officer his passport. Halley didn't react for a moment, and whispered to Bart.

"I don't have a passport yet." He nodded, and spoke calmly to the officer, who was flipping through Bart's passport and handed it back. His partner had given the driver back his license. They looked expectantly at Halley, and she showed empty hands. She spoke to them in her limited French.

"I'm American. My passport was stolen a week ago. My bag was stolen, it was in it." The policeman answered her in heavily accented but adequate English.

"You must have an identity card or passport," he said firmly.

She showed him the copy on her phone, getting nervous as Bart stepped in. The driver had checked his phone by then and knew what the problem was. There had been an attempt on the president's life by armed gunmen at the Élysées Palace. Two of the terrorists had been killed at the Palace, but four had escaped and were at large. A massive manhunt was on in the area to find them. Traffic had been stopped all over Paris, all emergency vehicles and riot squads were deployed, and the exits from the city had been blocked.

"Please exit from the car," the first police officer said to her, and conferred with his partner, who went to get his superior.

Bart spoke to the officer. "My friend was the victim of a theft a week ago. All of her identification papers were stolen with her bag," he explained again, and Bart spoke to Halley over his shoulder. "Do you have a copy of the complaint with you?" he asked her. Her eyes were wide as she shook her head. She had left it at the house, not thinking she'd need it.

"Exit the car now," the officer said in English. Bart opened the door, she stepped out, and he got out with her. "Stand aside," the officer said to Bart, and it was clear that this was not the time to argue, with half a dozen machine guns pointed at them, since there appeared to be a problem. Halley stood alone with the police a few feet from her, in her black dress and coat and high heels. She looked like what she was, a very attractive, chic woman, who appeared to be totally harmless, but the police were taking no chances.

A senior officer approached then, assessed the situation, and spoke to his men in French, as Bart spoke up again from where he stood and didn't attempt to approach. He didn't want to exacerbate the situation, and remained visibly calm and cooperative.

"This woman is a famous American writer," Bart said clearly in English. "If you have access to the internet here, you can look her up. Her name is Halley Holbrook, and I can vouch for her." He took a card out of his wallet, making slow, smooth, measured gestures so as not to startle them. He handed them the business card that said he was a CEO, and he looked important.

"She must have a passport or an identity card, not a copy on her phone," the superior spoke firmly. "You have one, she does not." He signaled to his men then. "We must keep her in custody, in *garde a vue,* in supervision until she can prove her identity. Paris is under a state of emergency, monsieur." And before Bart said anything, there was an officer in riot gear on either side of Halley, and they were leading her away, with a determined grip on her arms. She glanced over her shoulder at Bart, trying not to panic, while he wanted to stop them, but doing so would have risked both their lives in the circumstances. They could have been shot if the slightest movement was misunderstood. She had to go with them, and be taken into custody.

"I'll take care of it right away," he called out to Halley, and she nodded, and followed her police guard looking docile and scared.

Her life felt totally out of control suddenly. Bart had his phone immediately in his hand when he got back in the car, and called his friend in Washington. It was still early there. He didn't answer and Bart left a message. Before they put Halley in a police car, they searched her and took her phone.

"Could I keep that?" she asked in French. It was her lifeline and it frightened her even more to give it up.

"No." They pointed her to get in and she did, and Bart saw the police car leave the scene almost immediately, and they told his chauffeur to drive on a few minutes later. By then the driver had informed Bart of the attempt on the president's life. They had pulled out all the stops to find the four fugitive attackers. Bart's heart was pounding as they left the scene. He felt terrible for Halley. They'd had such a nice evening until then.

"Do you know where they'd take her?" Bart asked the driver, and he shook his head.

"To a police station, but they won't tell us which one. They won't let her go until she gives them proof of her identity." Bart called his friend again and got no answer, and then remembered that he had Major Leopold's contact information in his phone, to share with the FBI, when Halley had given it to him. He quickly called him, got no answer, and left an urgent message, explaining what had happened, and asking for his assistance.

Five minutes later, as they reached the bridge to the Left Bank, after driving between walls of riot police, Bart's cell phone rang. He hoped it was his FBI friend, but it was Major Leopold.

"I have located Madame 'Olbrook, and vouched for her," he said calmly. "I am very sorry. Paris is in an uproar, with a manhunt for the men who tried to kill the president. And she had no physical papers. I need to give her a temporary identity paper. I should have thought of it," he said, feeling sorry for her.

"Thank you very much, Major. Where is she?"

"At a police station, being held until someone picks her up. I can assure you, she is well. I told them that she is a very important American. They took her out of the cell, and put her in an office at the police station. Can you pick her up? Or I can send an officer from our detail," he explained.

"Tell me where it is, and I'll go straight there." She was at a station near the City Hall, the Hôtel de Ville.

"I'm very sorry. This is an unusual circumstance," the major explained. "She is a foreigner with no identity she could prove, and they had to follow regulations in a state of emergency, particularly an attempt on the president's life. This is very serious. They are mobilizing all our forces." Bart had never seen so many police in his life, in all manner of uniforms, although mostly the heavy-duty CRS riot police.

"I understand," Bart said. "The poor thing has had a rough time between the theft of her bag, the thief's threats and stalking her, and now being taken into custody."

"Please extend my profound apologies to Madame. It was a formality," Leopold said regretfully, and Bart told his driver to go as fast as he could to the address the major had given him. Bart was eager to get there and rescue her from the traumatic end to their evening.

He expected to find her in a state of hysterics, or fury, when he got there, but neither was the case. Bart gave his passport to the officer at the desk of the police station at City Hall. The officer in charge had already been notified that an American VIP had been rounded up at the Faubourg, and she had been cleared by a senior officer of the Sûreté Territoriale. Someone would be arriving to get her.

They had Bart wait while a female officer went to retrieve Halley from the office, and handed her her cell phone as they walked her back to where Bart was waiting.

Halley thanked the officer politely with a small smile. It had been quite an evening. The officer was surprised that Halley wasn't complaining or hysterical, and was calm and polite. She told a colleague that a Frenchwoman would have been raising hell, but the American was astonishingly gracious and well mannered. They walked her back to where Bart was waiting and tears filled her eyes the minute she saw him. She tried to look composed but it had been upsetting and frightening for a few minutes. They had refused to tell her what was happening, until they came to inform her that Major Leopold had cleared her, and she would be free to go when someone came to get her. And without her phone, she couldn't call Bart.

She walked straight up to Bart and he put his arms around her and held her tight. He could feel her shaking even with her coat on. "It's all right, Halley," he said softly, smoothing a hand over her hair, and then holding her tight again to calm her. She had been very brave until then. "Let's go home now," he said gently, and she nodded and regained her composure as they left the station. She looked dignified when they left.

She took a deep breath of the night air when they left the building with all its shouts and ominous noises and uniformed officers running everywhere. Bart looked her over carefully. There was no visible damage and she still looked impeccable.

"Are you okay?" She nodded with a cautious smile.

"Yes," she said as she exhaled. "It was pretty scary for a minute. I didn't know what they would do to me, or where they would take me. I'm sorry to have caused you all this trouble, Bart. I didn't even think of needing ID papers."

"You couldn't know, and even if you did know why it was happening, you couldn't have stopped the police without the proper ID. Just put it behind you. I'm sorry it happened at all, to spoil our evening," he said sympathetically.

"I had a wonderful time at dinner." She smiled at him, and was relieved when they got back to her house. She wanted to take a shower and get rid of all the dust and grime and terror of the police station.

Bart walked her into the house and was sad to see how exhausted she looked. It had been an upsetting experience. She'd had too many lately and they had taken a toll. There were shadows under her eyes.

"I thought they were going to keep me there, or arrest me for not having ID."

"Thank God you had given me the major's number. He called me back very fast and got right on it." She nodded, almost too tired to speak, and he kissed her and left a minute later. She walked upstairs, took her phone out of her pocket, and glanced at it as she dropped her coat on the bed. She saw that she had four messages that had come in while the police had her phone. Two from her daughters, who must have wondered where she was. And two from a blocked number, and tears filled her eyes when she saw them. She knew they had to be from the stalker, and she suddenly had the same feeling she used to have as a child with her mother, that no matter what she did, or where she hid, she could not escape the beating that was coming. It had taken her years of therapy to get over that feeling of dread and a punishment she could not avoid, no matter how fast she ran, or where she hid, or how good she was. She crawled into the bed then without getting undressed, and curled into a ball, as the tears rolled down her face. Like her mother, Tomás Maduro, the bag thief who was stalking her, was an evil she couldn't flee, and no one could save her. She was powerless and alone again. It was déjà vu, and a feeling that brought the past rushing back to her with a vengeance, and in her heart, she became a helpless child again, no matter how old or big or successful she was now. There was no escape, and she thought he would find her and kill her in the end.

Chapter 13

The morning after she'd been detained by the police, Halley
woke up feeling as though she had been beaten up. Every inch of
her body ached, though they hadn't laid a hand on her or been
rough with her. She looked like what she was. A respectable, ex-
pensively dressed woman, middle-aged by technical standards, no
matter how young she looked. And even the police had guessed
that the matter would be cleared up quickly. If the president hadn't
been attacked and almost killed, no one would have cared about
the absence of Halley's passport. But in light of a terrorist attack,
they couldn't overlook a single detail of protocol. They had been
careful about how they handled her, suspecting that she could be
the wife of someone important, and that all hell would break loose
when her husband found out she had gotten locked up by the
French police. Those things could easily get out of hand and had
before, so they handled her with kid gloves, but she didn't feel like

it the next day. They had still detained her and briefly put her in a cell.

Her little black dinner dress was badly wrinkled when she woke up still wearing it. She took it off and took a bath, and felt slightly better. She was starting to recognize the danger signs that had plagued her over the years at times of great stress. It had only happened a few times when the twins were young, and it had all come back in a rush when Robert died. She had spent six months with a therapist, every day when she needed to. His assessment was that she was suffering from post-traumatic stress disorder, and when they went over the major traumas in her childhood, it didn't surprise Halley or the therapist. Halley always knew what it was and where it came from. She knew she was one of the lucky survivors, but the scars of her trauma were deep.

After Robert died, she had had nightmares for months, dreaming that her mother was coming after her, to kill her. Halley was drowning in the dreams, and Robert couldn't save her. And then she would find Robert dead on the beach or in a forest, and her mother would appear and come after her, and would kill her too. The dreams were easy to decipher, and harder to get rid of.

"You've lost your savior and protector, and you're afraid your mother will come back and you'll be helpless again, and this time she'll kill you. Robert dying is the loss of your happiness, you think forever, and in your dream, you're a helpless child again," Dr. Thacker had explained. Halley had had several acute anxiety attacks before she asked her doctor for the name of a therapist. She didn't want to spend the rest of her life having panic attacks and nightmares. She'd been happy for a long time, and even without Robert, she wanted to get back there. It had taken longer than she wanted, but a year after Robert died, she felt like herself again. She missed him, but she wasn't plagued by the ghosts of the past. The therapist had helped her finally put them to rest and bury them. Now they were back, having risen from the grave again. She wanted to deal with them quickly this time before they made themselves at home.

She hadn't particularly liked Dr. Thacker but he specialized in trauma, and was good at what he did. He had carefully led Halley through a minefield of pain, to all the most agonizing memories in her life that she had buried for decades. She'd had therapy before, but the recent time was the most effective. She wanted the ghosts out of her life forever now, even though she hadn't forgiven them and knew that she probably never would. The therapist didn't ask her to. He said that Halley didn't need to forgive them, but she had to be willing to leave them, forever this time, and give up the dream of winning their approval or their love. Therein lay the key.

They had gone through all her most painful experiences, and the worst forms of abuse, the beatings, the injuries, the stitches, the broken bones, and worse, the broken heart of a child that her mother didn't love, and the realization of it. Halley had had to almost physically wrench herself away from the idea that her mother would emerge from the grave and finally love her.

"Sabine was incapable of it," Dr. Thacker had said matter-of-factly. He wasn't gentle with Halley, but he wasn't cruel either. He reminded her again that she was no longer five years old, or three, or six, and that her mother, the most dangerous person in her life, hadn't killed her, probably because she didn't dare, not wanting to face the consequences, but would have liked to. That had always been a hard idea for Halley to stomach, but she knew it was the truth. Being hated by her mother was one of the hardest hurdles she had to clear. Her mother had been so excessively narcissistic that there was no way for her to love a child. Halley represented the ultimate narcissistic injury to her mother, even more so because she was beautiful as a little girl, and her mother saw her only as competition, not as her own flesh and blood. Her mother had been the evil queen in *Sleeping Beauty,* the villain of every story Halley had ever read, and of many of her own books. Sabine had a textbook pathology, and there was no way Halley could conquer or escape it. It was just bad luck that she was her mother. That was an accident of nature, or of Fate, but the deck had been stacked against Halley from the beginning and she knew it. And her father was weak, immoral, and almost as narcissistic as her mother. He simply ignored Halley most of the time and hoped she'd disappear, which she had obligingly done in closets and under stairs. Until he perceived her as sexual, and then would have loaned her to his friends for their amusement, if she had let him, which amazingly she hadn't. And he had decided to try her out for himself one drunken afternoon, with no thought of what it would have done to her, except that she hadn't allowed him to do that either. He was her enemy from then on, just as her mother had been. They were people she could never trust for an instant.

The only remarkable part of the story, in the therapist's eyes, was that Halley had the courage and the wisdom at a tender age to protect herself from the ultimate blow, from her father, which might have been the final one that pushed her over the edge. She might not have recovered if he had raped her or seduced her. Her own powerful survival instincts had saved her by not letting him do it. Instead, she had fought with all the wiles available to a child her age to escape both her father and his friends, who had touched her and tried to abuse her, but she had fled and never let them rape her. They had never touched her soul. Dr. Thacker pointed out that some grown women wouldn't have been as brave or as resourceful. But somehow, Halley had instinctively known that if she let them, she would never have been whole again or able to lead a normal life.

"Your preventing them is probably why you were able to love Robert so fully, and have a healthy sex life with him." It had been one of the most fulfilling parts of their relationship, which might not have been the case otherwise. It was the only part of her psyche and her body that her parents hadn't succeeded in battering. It was hard to understand people like them, and what motivated them. Many sociopaths actually did succeed in killing their children, and Halley had no idea why they hadn't. They had come close at times, especially her mother, while her father's crimes against her were more subtle. She blamed her mother more, because the injuries she inflicted were so obvious, and involved tissue damage. Those inflicted by her father were frightening in a different way. But she had been old enough to outsmart him and his friends and protect herself, like a child in a war zone fleeing the enemy. From her mother's abuse at the age Halley was, there had been no hope of escape, and there had been no one to protect her or save her. Only Robert, many years too late. She simply had to endure the abuse. Then Robert left too, and could no longer protect her from the ghosts that returned after his death, once she was helpless and alone again.

Halley could feel the ghosts hovering now, ready to reenter her life and try to crush her again, or kill her this time. Tomás Maduro had opened the door to them when he threatened her and brought the memories back again. The man who had stolen her bag had let them in. The trauma of the sense of violation she had, and the helplessness, had awakened her childhood abuse and trauma again. Not wanting to let the ghosts settle in, she looked for her therapist's number in the New York directory, and found him. She hadn't spoken to him in two years. Her life had been peaceful since then.

Halley had been reading the morning paper, and saw that two more of the French president's would-be assassins had been found, and killed in a deadly gun battle with the police. The remaining two suspects were on the run, still at large. Halley found herself crying as she read the story and didn't know why. She was crying for the president, the dead men, their mothers, and all the children in the world who had suffered as she had and she didn't know. And in the end, she was crying for herself, and the child she had been who had been so mercilessly beaten and abused, so frightened every moment of her life for six years, and then neglected and abused in other ways for another eight years until her father died, and after that, she was alone.

She was crying for all the loveless years, until her twins were old enough to love her, and later Robert. Locke had been in her life too briefly and inconsistently to give her comfort. She had lived for twenty-four years without a gentle touch or a kind word. It killed some people and might have killed her. But by some miracle, it hadn't. She didn't know why it hadn't killed her body or her soul. She didn't think she was stronger than anyone else, or braver, or more clever. Some part of her simply refused to be broken, like some people in concentration camps. Some died and others didn't. There had been studies comparing the survivors of severe child abuse to the survivors of concentration camps, and there were notable similarities, and comparable aftereffects, some of which Halley had experienced in her youth, and recognized the signs of now. It was familiar to her.

She had never let her children know the horror of it. It was too ugly for them to know.

Dr. Julian Thacker was a small wizened older man, in his sixties when Halley met him. At first she thought him cold, but Halley realized he wasn't one day when she saw that he had tears running down his face as she told of a particularly horrific episode with her mother that had required fourteen stitches in her arm. For Halley it was the shedding of memories that had lain dormant for years, the way it was for the concentration camp survivors coming back from the camps and chronicling what the Germans had done. It was digging the bullets and shrapnel out of her soul, after a war, and not letting it fester. The brutally painful sessions had freed her in the end, more than ever, but she also knew that she was the survivor of a special kind of war, and some days, due to weather, or something someone did or said, the scars would ache for a moment, and then settle down again.

When she finished the year of therapy, they were scars, no longer wounds. The wounds had healed. And an important part of healing was not seeing herself as ugly because of them, but as a beautiful person who had been injured, as if a mine explosion, or an erupting volcano, or an avalanche had buried her through no fault of her own. Fate had caused her to be born in an enemy camp. It wasn't something that she had caused or deserved. All her life until then she had tried to figure out what she'd done to provoke it. She hadn't. She had done nothing to provoke it, nor to deserve it, and once she fully understood that, for the most part she was healed of the aftereffects. And no one who truly loved her would ever find her ugly because of it, no matter how many stitches she had had or how many wounds had been inflicted on her. She had never tested out that theory, and had never told her daughters what she had experienced. She didn't want them to know. She thought they were too young and it was too gruesome to tell. She had told Robert all of it, and he had only loved her more. And she had mentioned it casually to Bart. She didn't know yet if she would tell him or not. She didn't know if he would stay in her life long enough to really love her. It was too soon to say.

Julian Thacker was a traditional psychiatrist who had a few unorthodox theories of his own, but his style of confrontational therapy had worked for Halley. She had faced all the painful events in her life squarely to rid her of the post-traumatic stress symptoms.

She waited until it was eight A.M. in New York, which was his call hour. He didn't seem surprised to hear from Halley, as though they'd spoken the day before, when it had been two years. Halley knew she could say anything to him. Nothing shocked him. He had helped her to be proud of being a survivor, not ashamed.

"Where are you?" Dr. Thacker asked.

"I'm in Paris," Halley said, and there was obviously more to say, or she wouldn't be calling.

"Are you alone?"

"Yes, sort of. I came alone, but I met someone here."

"Is there another man in your life at the moment?"

"No. I haven't dated anyone since Robert. I'm just starting now. The nightmares are back," Halley said with a sigh.

"Do you think it's because of the new man? Are they the same nightmares as before?" Dr. Thacker went straight to the heart of the matter. He always did. And she was scrupulously honest with him, and in her life. The honesty was an important part of the healing.

"It's not him," Halley said quickly. "And the nightmares are similar. My mother tries to kill me, and succeeds in the end."

"And your father?"

"I think he's gone."

"Did something happen to revive the trauma?"

"Something stupid," Halley said. "My purse was stolen the day after I got here. It's an expensive bag I loved, but so what? It's just a bag. It got stolen with everything in it, money, passport, keys, credit cards, personal stuff. The thief has been calling me wanting to sell me the bag for an extortionate amount, trying to blackmail me, and he says he's going to kill me. He keeps saying he controls me, and he will kill me if I don't do what he says. I feel helpless again."

"Ah, so your mother's back," the therapist said, and Halley was startled. She hadn't made the association. "Do you believe him, that he'll kill you?"

Halley thought for a minute. "Yes. I guess I do. I know I don't deserve it, but I think he might try."

"You're not five anymore, Halley. Have you told the police?"

"Yes, they've been terrific. They know who he is. They're trying to find him, and the bag. And the man I met here has been wonderful too."

"So you're not fighting the forces of evil alone this time. You couldn't stop Robert's death. But the police can stop the thief."

"He keeps calling me and threatening me," Halley said in a frightened voice. The fear made her feel weak and defenseless, as much as the threats.

"My guess is that they'll protect you, and ultimately they'll catch him. Your mother can't come back. She's been dead for forty-two years. Dead people don't come back. She's not a ghost. She was a very sick, disturbed woman who died, who didn't love you, and it was never your fault." It felt good to be reminded of it. "The thief is powerless. You don't have to give him any power. He's not your mother."

"He makes me feel the way she used to. Helpless."

"There is nothing helpless about you. You're a strong woman. That's your old PTSD talking. It's a flare-up, like a broken arm or a knee that aches before it rains. It's raining in your world right now. I doubt that the police will let him hurt you. And you can protect yourself. Are you being careful?"

"I am."

"Remember, he's not a ghost and he's not Sabine. The threat he poses is real, but there are people in your world to protect you now." Suddenly Halley wondered if she had made the association because her mother was French. She mentioned it to the doctor who thought it was an interesting detail.

"It's possible. I think it's a flare-up. I'm not dismissing it. Abuse will always remind you of her, like a familiar song, and stealing your bag is a major violation, or it feels that way, even to people who've never been abused. What he did is very personal and shocking for anyone, not just you."

"I feel stupid being so upset about it," Halley admitted.

"A), it would upset anyone, b), the bag is incredibly valuable, which is also upsetting, it's a real loss, and c), the thief has been stalking you and threatening to kill you. I don't think 'stupid' applies here, not even remotely." Halley smiled at what Dr. Thacker said and felt better. "Feel free to call me whenever you need to, Halley," he said, more warmly than usual. It had been a good session. "And we can get together if you like when you get back. I hope you'll feel better by then. Try to enjoy your stay in the meantime. Try not to obsess about the threats. And realize that he's real and not a ghost from your past."

They signed off then, and Halley sat thinking about what the doctor had said. It always helped to talk to him, to clear things in her head. She was still mulling it over when Major Leopold called her, to apologize again for her being detained the night before, and tell her that he and the agent from the FBI were meeting later

that afternoon and he'd like her to join them. She agreed immediately and called Bart to tell him about it.

"Do you want to come?" she asked him.

"I'd like to very much," he said. "Do you mind?"

"Not at all, I'd like you to."

"How do you feel today?"

"Kind of beaten up," she said. "I just called my old shrink in New
York. I feel better now. He's good at helping me clear out the cob-
webs and the fog in my head sometimes. I get confused about
what's real, and what's the echo of the past. He gave me permis-
sion to be officially upset about this." She smiled. "I thought maybe
I was overreacting." She didn't tell Bart about the nightmares, or
the associations they had for her. She had always kept that to herself, except with Robert. Bart was too new in her life to share such
heavy stuff with. The bag theft was heavy enough, and the stalker.
And he'd been great about that. She didn't want to overload him
with her past. He already knew enough.

The meeting was set for that afternoon.

"I'm meeting Ryan at his gym. My club in New York has a recip-
rocal arrangement with a club here. I'll meet you at the police office," Bart said, and after they hung up, she got up from the kitchen
table and went upstairs to dress, thinking about him. She felt lucky
to have met him. He was a real person and a kind man, and she
already respected him.

Bart was already at Major Leopold's office when she arrived. The
major was looking very official, and there was a tall, thin, serious-

looking, youngish man in a dark gray suit. He looked American, with short dark hair, and he introduced himself as Special Agent Bernard Dexter, of the FBI. They chatted for a few minutes and then the major got down to business, with everyone present.

"First, I want to mention your guardian. He's a bit of an unpleasant character, but I don't think you have anything to fear from him. He served time in prison for six months ten years ago, for bank fraud, bad checks, but he's had no problems with the law since. It's not a high recommendation for him, and I don't know if his employers are aware of it or if they care. Only slightly more interesting is that he is a member of the Communist Party, and apparently takes it very seriously. He goes to party meetings regularly, and he's been to Russia, but I don't think he's a spy or anything dangerous. He apparently has a passionate hatred for the rich, but his employers are extremely wealthy, so he probably dislikes them as much as he does you. He has no girlfriend, and he sounds like a bitter, unhappy person, from what people say about him. One of my operatives checked him out. He sounds disagreeable but harmless. I don't think he's a real concern, just an annoyance." It was a relief to hear it.

"The same is not true of Tomás Maduro, the man who stole your bag. He's a professional thief who caught our attention several years ago. But now we've been told that he belongs to a very active militant anarchist cell. We're waiting for more information on him from Interpol. He had trouble with the law in Colombia, but most of the time he has stayed below the radar, and he has several aliases. His main source of income is from the high-end goods he steals and resells. I think he got too lucky this time, and is finding that your very expensive one-of-a-kind bag is not so easy to sell. If he sells it in a reputable place, he needs a bill of purchase. If he sells it through the underground, he won't get anywhere near what it's worth. They can't pay him that kind of money, because they can't sell it for what it's worth. Possibly in Asia to some avid collector. At the moment, you are his best potential customer, and we think he's going to try to sell it back to you, just as he said to you, if you are attached enough to the bag to want it back for a high price. As you know, from what Hermès told us, it could be worth as much as a hundred thousand euros today. At a high-end auction, it might bring double that, if two collectors battle for it. I think he'll try to sell it to you for somewhere between fifty and a hundred thousand. That's big money for him.

"He has a wife and three teenage kids in Colombia, and a mistress here with two young children of his. We know he lives in the suburbs outside Paris in the 'ninety-three' district. We haven't narrowed it down yet, but we're very close. We think you'll hear from him again soon. He doesn't want you leaving when you get your new passport and slipping through his fingers. He's never been violent before that we know of. He's been very typical of that kind of thief. Steal, sell through his usual resources, steal again. He's said to live well, and he's well dressed. He has a visa for France, which we could revoke and send him back to Colombia when we catch him, or we could keep him here. He may cooperate with us, which would be simpler. His brother is a drug dealer who goes between here and Colombia, and a very dangerous man. He served time in prison in Venezuela and Argentina. Our man has been involved in anarchist demonstrations and riots, we've learned. Mostly for what he can steal when they break into and loot the high-end luxury stores. He's a real pro, and he only steals important brands.

"I think we need to wait for him now, until he contacts you again, and see what he says. I think he'll suggest a meeting and a price."

"And then what?" Halley asked.

"It depends what he says, and how badly you want your bag back. Of course, we would go to any rendezvous and intercept him. And if we get information on him before that, we'll arrest him, and hopefully he'll still have the bag, unless someone offers him a lot of money first. But I think he'll assume you're his best client, thinking it has sentimental or personal value for you. For now, we wait and see what he does."

"I'll see what we can dig up on him too," Bern Dexter said. He looked like he approved of everything the major and his department were doing, and what they had found out. They had a wealth of information about Maduro.

The meeting broke up after that, and Bart took Halley home. He was having dinner with his son and daughter-in-law that night, at a restaurant with their friends. He enjoyed joining them, and Halley was going to work on her book some more and have a quiet night at home.

He dropped her off with a quick kiss, promising to call her later and went back to Ryan's apartment.

* * *

Peter was bringing Savannah and Sophia to visit Olivia at her studio that afternoon. They were spending a week with their father after he got back from St. Bart's. He'd been busy with them, and hadn't seen Olivia since they got back. She couldn't wait for him to be free again. He had only suggested the meeting with the girls the night before. Sophia had had a cold for two days and was out of sorts. Savannah had had sleepovers with friends, and he hadn't wanted to overwhelm Olivia with additional kids. The stars had lined up perfectly for their meeting that day. She was nervous about it, and had bought pastries and cookies for them, and she was going to serve them pink lemonade.

Peter had briefed Olivia about the girls' preferences and warned her that Sophia was allergic to nuts, so Olivia was careful about what she bought. Sophia was four and Savannah was six. She was missing her front teeth and had red hair, and Sophia had dark hair and eyes like her father. Olivia watched them get out of his SUV in front of her house. They were both in booster seats in the back, and were laughing and talking when they got out. Peter held their hands as they walked through the garden to the kitchen. Olivia was standing in the doorway, smiling when they walked in. She devoured Peter with her eyes, she had missed him, and he kissed her chastely, but with a hand on her bottom, which his daughters didn't see. She was wearing paint-splattered jeans with a pink sweater and pink ballet flats, with her blond hair in a braid down her back. He introduced the girls, and they eyed the cupcakes and cookies and miniature eclairs on a big plate on the kitchen table, and the two pink balloons she had tied to each chair to make it look more festive.

"Is it your birthday?" Savannah asked her.

"No, is it yours?" Olivia asked her, and Savannah shook her head solemnly. "Is it Sophia's?" Sophia laughed and squealed "Noooo!" "Then we'll just have to have a regular old every day party. How about that?" Both girls giggled.

"Why do you have paint on your pants?" Savannah asked her, looking her over carefully.

"Because I paint paintings. Do you want to see them?" She had nothing else of interest to show them. She didn't have dolls or toys or children of her own for them to play with, or even a dog, which put her in the category of boring. She led them into the studio, and they stared at the paintings, puzzled.

"There are no people, just shapes," Sophia said. "That one is a red circle, and that one's a blue square," she identified them.

"And over here there are four orange triangles with a big purple splatter," Olivia said, showing where some of the purple paint had landed on her pants. "I got some on my shoe that day too." The girls laughed.

"Our mom gets mad if we get paint on our clothes."

"Mine used to too. Now all my clothes have paint on them, so it doesn't matter." She smiled at Peter, and he melted. She was being so sweet to his girls, and he knew she'd been nervous about it. She called him a dozen times to ask for advice before they came.

"Can we try?" Sophia asked, eyeing some red paint and a brush with a big smile. Olivia glanced at Peter and he shrugged.

"Sure, why not?"

"Mom will get mad if we come home all covered with paint," Savannah warned.

"Okay, then we'll be careful," Olivia said, pulling two garbage bags out of a box. She cut a hole at the top and two holes for their arms, and slipped them over their heads to cover their pink jeans and sweaters so only their pink sneakers showed. She told them to take their shoes off, and a minute later they were standing barefoot in front of an easel, looking like elves in garbage bags. She set two small canvases down on the easel, side by side, gave them each three colors of paint and some brushes, and told them to paint whatever they wanted. They squealed with delight, and started painting right away. Sophia swished the brushes across the canvas, and Savannah was carefully trying to paint a tree and a dog, and Olivia helped her, standing right behind her. She glanced over at Peter, who was enjoying the scene and took a video of them.

They painted for almost an hour and then they went back to the kitchen table and had the cupcakes and cookies and pink lemonade. They made a bigger mess with the cupcakes than the paint and had cake all over their faces. When they finished, she washed their hands at the sink and took the garbage bags off, and they looked as pristine as when they arrived.

Olivia had them sign their paintings, and she had used acrylic paints so they were dry by the time the girls left. They took their paintings with them and the cupcakes and cookies and the balloons.

Olivia helped them into the car and Savannah looked at her with a toothless smile.

"Can we come back and paint with you again?"

"Of course!" Peter had told them that Olivia was their new aunt Valerie's identical twin sister, which they found fascinating. They waved as they drove away, and Peter gave her a longing look and thanked her profusely before he left. They had a date the following night and were starving for each other. They had talked every night and texted all day. He took his paternal duties seriously, and had spent a good week with his girls, but he had missed Olivia fiercely.

He called her when they got home to thank her again.

"That was amazing. You said you weren't good with kids."

"As long as they like to paint, that I can do. They're so sweet, and so polite."

"They liked you too. They think it's funny that you and Val are identical, and they said you're more fun, and I agree, and I'm definitely more fun than Seth," he teased. "I can't wait till tomorrow," he whispered. "I love having them here, but I missed you all week." He was very circumspect with his girls around. She was the first of his dates they had ever met. And it had gone perfectly. Olivia couldn't remember the last time she was as nervous, but it had definitely been a hit, with the painting and the garbage bags and the cupcakes.

She smiled as she put things away and loaded the plates in the dishwasher. She couldn't see herself with children yet, and not for many years, but doing things with Peter and his might be fun. It had all gone better than she'd expected.

Valerie called her later to check. "How did it go with Peter's kids?" she asked her casually. She'd been wondering all afternoon, but didn't want to call until after they left.

"Really well. They painted and we had a cupcake party with balloons and lemonade," Olivia said proudly.

"Wow, that's new for you." Valerie was impressed. "Maybe you don't hate kids as much as you think."

"Yes, I do," Olivia said with a grin, "but Peter's are really cute. They invited me for a sleepover at their mom's house. I'll bet she'd be thrilled." They both laughed.

"So do you have a boyfriend?" Valerie asked her, desperate to know.

"Wait a minute, I haven't even seen him since the boat. We each have a life, you know."

"His is all smoke and mirrors with a lot of girls he doesn't care about, and you don't even see who's in the room unless it's on an easel. He's a good guy, Ollie."

"Yes, he is." Olivia sat down at the kitchen table with a sigh, and picked up a little pink sock someone had forgotten. It looked like Sophia's. It was tiny, and Olivia held it, wondering where her life was going. She didn't want to be a soccer mom when she grew up, or live in the suburbs, and she wasn't sure if she wanted kids of her own. But a guy with two very sweet little girls might actually work. She was willing to check it out, keep an open mind, see how it felt. And if it didn't work out, she was going to run like hell, just as she always did.

Savannah and Sophia asked for her when Peter tucked them in that night. They shared a room at his house, and their paintings were propped up on the dresser.

"Can we go back and visit Olivia again?" Savannah asked him.

"I think that can be arranged," he said noncommittally.

"I want to do a BIG painting next time," Sophia said, stretching her arms wide.

"Me too," Savannah added. "I love her," she announced to the room at large.

"So do I," Sophia said with a grin.

Peter was dying to say he loved her too, but he couldn't. It was too soon to share it with the kids, and even too soon to know, as Olivia said too. But that ship had already set sail, and it was picking up speed.

Chapter 14

Halley had been editing her manuscript and starting to make headway with it after she met with Bart, Major Leopold, and Bern Dexter, and it unnerved her that they were all waiting for the other shoe to drop now.

They were waiting for Tomás Maduro to make contact about Halley buying back her bag. At least he hadn't disposed of it or sold it, or sent it to a foreign country, unless he was lying and no longer had it. Anything was possible. And getting her bag back in one piece was the least likely scenario. He might have already sent it away or sold it, and was just blackmailing her for extra money. She couldn't count on seeing her bag again, let alone its contents. She tried to keep her mind on the editing, despite the distraction of worrying about Maduro's threats and blackmail. He hadn't called her again.

Bart called her after dinner with his son to ask if she'd heard anything, and he was relieved she hadn't. They didn't have a final plan yet, and he was afraid that whatever the police decided to do would involve risk to Halley. Major Leopold wanted his man.

Bart and Halley talked for about half an hour, and then he said he was going to bed, and she decided to keep editing for a while. She was wide-awake.

The phone rang right on time at five minutes to midnight. The thief had established a pattern and didn't deviate from it. She saw the blocked number on her caller ID and answered in a calm voice.

"You want to speak to me, don't you?" he said, taunting her when she answered. His voice was silky and sensual and he was toying with her. "You want your bag back. How much is it worth to you? I know what it's worth now, so don't try to cheat me. A girl at Hermès told me it could sell for as much as a hundred thousand euros at a fancy Christie's auction, or even twice that. You can bid on it there, or you can pay me."

"You can't put it up at auction," she said firmly. "The police would catch you, and you can't put it in an auction without the receipt. The house would take twenty-five percent of the sale price as their fee. And you don't have a receipt," she reminded him. He was silent, trying to figure out how far she would go. She cut into his thoughts quickly. "I'll give you fifty thousand euros, that's all I can do for now," she said. She felt foolish even offering him that, but whatever she gave him, the police would get it back when they arrested him.

"I don't believe you. You have plenty of money, you're a rich woman, you make a fortune from your books. I read about it," he said angrily. "You're trying to cheat me."

"You stole the bag," she reminded him, and he was silent again, calculating, trying to feel her out. She was feeling stronger after talking to Dr. Thacker. She was not a child, not helpless, not an abuse victim anymore. The doctor had said just the right things and reminded Halley that she wasn't alone and that the police would protect her. They had so far. But meeting Tomás Maduro, if she agreed to, was risky. And he might destroy the bag if she didn't pay him, if he hadn't already. "How would we meet anyway?" She sounded skeptical. She didn't want him coming to the house.

"I'll meet you at the flea market in St. Ouen," he said, sounding excited at the prospect. It was a popular vintage furniture market on the outskirts of Paris. It was crowded, and in a dicey neighborhood, and easy to get to. "At the stall with the vintage slot machines," he added. There were always lots of people in the stalls. There was a maze of alleys, which made it easy to escape and get lost. There were young people who wanted to play with the old arcade games, and the owner let them, and the general chaos of the vendors, customers, spectators, and tourists made it an ideal place to go unobserved and disappear quickly.

"When? Tomorrow?" She tried to sound nonchalant, but her heart was pounding. Meeting him at the flea market sounded dangerous to her. What if the thief had a gun and shot her? But she'd be no use to him dead, and guns were rare and hard to get in France.

"No, the flea market is only open on the weekend. I'll meet you on Saturday." It was open on Friday too, but the crowds were biggest on the weekend, and he knew he could get lost in the mass of people cluttering up the alleys crowded with stalls after they made the exchange. "Fifty thousand euros, in small bills. Be there if you want to see your bag again, and all the crap in it. I already threw some of it away. A lot of useless junk, and your credit cards are dead anyway. But I'm sure you know that. I'll meet you at one o'clock on Saturday, at the old arcade game stall." It was crowded and noisy and the owner was a friend. "Put the money in a big envelope. And remember, if you call the police, I will kill you. If you want to keep your life and the bag, be careful who you speak to. I'll know if you set me up."

"Why would I do that? I want my bag back," she said quietly, trying to sound calmer than she felt. They had a date now.

"You're a fool to have paid that kind of money for a bag," he said with contempt, "but it's lucky for me you did. Remember, if you tell the police, I slit your throat. And I will find you to do it." The way he said it made her shudder. "I have a hunting knife and I know how to use it. Your bag isn't worth dying for. If you don't interfere, they won't catch me." Something about the way he said it made her think of her mother. She used to threaten to kill Halley, and she sounded like she meant it, just as Tomás Maduro did. They were both people to whom human life meant nothing. Her life hadn't mattered to her mother, it never had. And this stranger didn't care about her either. The children she loved needed her, and maybe now Bart, and the bag thief was willing to throw her life away. The concept of it enraged her. She was so insignificant to him. She was just a way to get money, even if he had to kill her to do it. She meant nothing more to him than an ant on the ground, to be crushed underfoot.

Halley slept on her bed in her clothes again that night, shaken by the call. It was too late to contact Bart or Major Leopold. She could notify them in the morning, But sleep eluded her for most of the night, except for a few minutes when she nodded off, and then woke up again abruptly with a start minutes later.

By morning, she was exhausted. She had a cup of coffee and called the major. He was pleased by the call. This was what they had been waiting for, an opportunity to catch the thief, and get the man and the bag, if possible. He reminded Halley that they were close now. And they would catch Maduro at the flea market. He would be surrounded by their undercover agents.

"May I come to your home to meet with you and Special Agent Dexter? We can set everything up beforehand. When you get to St. Ouen, you will know exactly what to do and where to walk. We will leave nothing to chance. You will see workmen and carpenters, moving men, painters, telephone repairmen, delivery people, but nearly everyone you see will be our agents, protecting you and ready to catch him. It won't take long. You will hand him the money, step away, and from that moment he'll be ours. The risk to you is minimal," he assured her, and she hoped he was right. She agreed to the meeting at the house where she was staying, and he said he would call Special Agent Dexter. They would arrive separately, both in street clothes, in case Maduro was watching, but they doubted he was. The meeting for the bag had been set.

With a shaking hand, she called Bart as soon as she hung up with Major Leopold. She needed to hear his voice. Two weeks before, he had been a stranger, and now he was a friend, someone she trusted. And this was no longer about her bag. It was about catching a criminal, a man who was threatening to kill her, had stolen from her, and was blackmailing her.

"Is something wrong? You sound upset," Bart said, as soon as he heard her. He was beginning to be able to read her voice and know when something was wrong.

"No, I'm all right. He called last night. And the major and the FBI are putting a fail-safe plan in place to catch him on Saturday at the flea market. Maduro wants to meet me there, and wants fifty thousand for my bag. All of a sudden, I wonder if my stupid bag is worth it. What if something goes wrong? It's just a bag. I'm supposed to give him fifty thousand euros in small bills, and they arrest him on the spot. He said again last night that he'll kill me if I call the police. But there's no way for him to know. Do you want to come to the meeting this afternoon?" she asked him. She hoped he would but didn't want to press him. In the end, this wasn't his problem, it was hers.

"Of course I do. Is it all right with you if I come?"

"Yes, it is," she said, feeling overwhelmed for a moment. She had been trapped in this dance with a thief ever since he had stolen the bag from her. He had stripped her of her identity and all the personal things in the bag, stolen an object of great value, and was making her risk her life. She had been there before. She had to keep reminding herself of what Dr. Thacker had said, that she wasn't helpless, the thief wasn't in control, the police would protect her, and she wasn't a child anymore. When Maduro threatened her on the phone he took her right back to those helpless days when there was no one to protect her from her mother. She could feel all her old scars again, and the shock that another human being wanted to kill her. And in her mother's case, the person who was meant to protect her. At least Tomás Maduro was a stranger. He owed her nothing.

Her mother had broken the sacred trust between mother and child. Not in a million years would Halley have done anything to risk or hurt her own children. It had been incomprehensible then, as it was now, that her own mother hated her enough to want her dead. It was something she knew she would never understand. It was the curse she had tried to break all her life. It was the mystery she could not solve or explain. And her father had let her mother do it, and then violated his own obligation to protect her as well. They had left her alone in a cold world of terror, and then battered her themselves, each in their own way. The conclusion she had inevitably come to then was if her own parents didn't love her, who would? There had been no answer to that for years, in all the groups she had gone to and the therapists she had seen, she hadn't found the answers. She had found them with Robert, who had loved her so purely and so simply, no matter what, unconditionally, with all her flaws and scars, just as her mother should have, and was unable to. Halley had been innocent, without guilt.

And now she had to prove to herself that she was whole, and healed. No one else could do it for her. She had to trust the police and the FBI to protect her from a man who didn't even know her but wished her harm. In a way, it was easier to survive that kind of hatred from a stranger than a parent. But now was her chance to prove that they hadn't damaged her forever. They had disappeared into the past and were dead. Halley was alive. The grown-up Halley. The woman she had become. The mother of her twins. The woman Robert had loved so generously, and whom Bart might love one day. She had to prove to herself and to them that this man who meant nothing to her and was a stranger had no power to hurt and control her by making her afraid.

She thought about it all through the meeting. Bart was the first to arrive, and the special agent and the major came together. They explained their plan to Halley and Bart, who listened intently. The entire area would be teeming with undercover agents, in the alley where they would meet and in the other alleys by which he planned to escape. There would be no way out for him. The flea market was a maze, full of pickpockets and petty thieves, and no matter how well he knew it, they knew it better. It would be a minefield of FBI special agents and Major Leopold's undercover agents. Halley would be well protected the entire time.

"We will have you covered at all times," Major Leopold told her.

"And we'll be backing his people up," Special Agent Dexter said confidently. He was a dedicated ally now.

"You want your bag back, and we want our man. We want to put him out of business." And they only had two more days to wait. Her bag was just a detail now, even to her. She wanted to prove he had no power over her. She wanted freedom and justice. The bag was just a symbol.

Halley tried to maintain an aura of normalcy for the next few days. She spoke to her daughters, but didn't tell them what was happening. It was as much an internal battle as an external one. She had something to prove to herself, that she was not a child anymore, and she couldn't be controlled by threats and abuse.

Bart was free in the daytime, while Ryan and Véronique were at work. He spent all the spare time he had with Halley, then left her in the evening, to spend time with his son. He hated to leave her, even then. And she edited her manuscript at night, since she couldn't sleep anyway. She was almost finished, and the book was smooth as silk. She had worked on all the rough parts. Her editor had done a good job, editing her and asking her the right questions, to make the novel tighter and the flow more natural and true to life.

The police, the FBI, Bart, and Halley were all waiting for something to happen, but they had to wait until Saturday. There was no going any faster. Only a few of the stalls were open on Thursdays. Business picked up slightly on Friday, and on Saturday, whatever the weather, the flea market was teeming with activity. It was one of two days that people went there to shop or browse, buy or sell, and the day that would provide the most cover for the thief to make good his escape, and he didn't doubt for a minute that he would get the money and get away.

Bart kept Halley company leading up to Saturday. They went for walks, and sat in her house talking quietly about the plan and other things. Sometimes they read, or sat in comfortable silence. Memories kept flashing into Halley's mind, good ones, of when Valerie and Olivia were small, and her happy days with them.

They went for walks in less populated areas. Her stride almost matched his but not quite. He was very tall with long legs. He had a sense that she was fighting some kind of personal battle. The thief had somehow invaded her space, mentally and physically, and he had taken away more than her passport. He had taken her freedom and self-confidence, her sense of balance. Half the time now, she felt like a compass gone awry. She knew that the only way out of the darkness was through it. She was inching her way along.

Bart was impressed by how solid she seemed. He knew that she was struggling, worried about the confrontation with the thief, but he couldn't see the inner turmoil, the things she felt she had to conquer herself, that last vestige of her broken childhood. Humpty Dumpty had been put back together, but she wanted to be sure the glue would stick.

It was the day before she was to go to the flea market. Bart could sense how tense she was and nothing seemed to relieve it.

"Are you okay?" he asked her, as they sat down to the lunch of pasta and salad she had made.

"I'm fine," she assured him. But he wasn't convinced. She was wrestling with her demons, trying to still their voices.

"Is there anything I can do to help?" He wanted to know, but there wasn't. This was her war now, but she was grateful for his presence and support.

"You're already doing it, by being here." It didn't seem like enough to him. It seemed so little. He spent so much time with her, and he was going back to Ryan and Véro that night. Being with Halley was something he wanted to do for her, to help give her strength to face the confrontation with the thief. She was dreading it, and almost sorry she had agreed to it, instead of just letting it go. But walking away from an object of such great value, and that she loved, seemed like a shocking waste to her. The bag was the symbol of her battles with herself, to recover from the past and move forward to freedom and lead a good life. She couldn't let another abuser win and taint her future, and mark her forever as a victim. It was a war between the two of them, a fight between good and evil.

Halley and Bart were sitting on the couch on Friday afternoon, lost in their own thoughts, when Bart moved closer to her and put an arm around her. He could sense that she was thinking about Saturday. It was heavy on her mind.

"By this time tomorrow, it'll all be over. You'll have your bag, and he'll be in jail," Bart reassured her.

"Do you suppose I'm just doing this for revenge because he took it?" That troubled her.

"You're doing it because it's right, and if you don't stop him, he'll do it to someone else." She nodded agreement. Bart had been reading old copies of *The Wall Street Journal*, to keep abreast of what he was missing while he was away. He felt peaceful sitting beside her, and was trying to share his sense of peace with her. And this time when he kissed her, he seemed more passionate than before. He wanted to hold her in his arms and hide her, so nothing could harm her.

They were breathless when they stopped kissing, and Bart didn't want to stop. He wanted more. They'd been spending so much time together that his desire for her was becoming overwhelming, and he knew she had other things on her mind. All she had to do was get tomorrow over with, and start living her life again.

Bart felt young when he was with her, and stronger than he had in years. He wanted to use his strength to protect her and keep her safe. He wished he could go in her place, but the police wouldn't let him. He didn't like their plan. In effect, they were using her as bait, which upset Bart. It seemed way too dangerous, but Halley had agreed, and Bart knew he couldn't stop her. At least they'd have a nice weekend afterward, with all of it behind her. And hopefully, Tomás Maduro would be in jail.

They kept kissing as they lay on the couch together, and the kisses only fueled their desire for each other, it didn't quench their thirst. They were alone in the house. The housekeeper had left. They gently took off each other's clothes, and their bodies found each other. They couldn't stop and didn't want to. There was no reason to. They abandoned themselves to the passion they had felt almost since they met. Everything he had learned about her told him that his feelings for her were right.

They tiptoed upstairs naked in the empty house, laughing like children, and made love in her bed. They were lying on her bed afterward, as he admired the long, graceful lines of her body, and he was overcome with desire for her again, and didn't try to stop himself. He hadn't done that in years, and he was smiling when they stopped.

"You make me young again," he said to her.

"You *are* young," she said, laughing, and so was she. They still had so much life to live, so many things to do that they wanted to do together.

He texted Ryan that he wouldn't be home for dinner, and called him later and explained that he wouldn't be home that night, and Ryan laughed.

"The tables are turning, now you're calling me, Dad, to say you're staying out for the night. What am I supposed to say to that?" They both thought it was funny, and Bart was laughing too.

"You're supposed to say that I'm a lucky guy. I just didn't want you to worry."

"Thanks, Dad. Enjoy it, you deserve it."

"Was he shocked?" Halley asked him after the call, looking slightly worried.

"No, he was happy for me. So am I."

"Yeah, me too," she giggled.

He wanted to spend the night with her before she had to face her ordeal on Saturday. Their timing had been perfect. The phone didn't ring that night.

It was a perfect first night. They had dinner in the kitchen together, and then went upstairs and made love again. He could feel her tense whenever she thought about the next day, but everything was different now. She wasn't alone. She felt strong and brave, and they had each other. The past week had proven that. It had put both of them to the test, and they were still there, closer than ever. She knew that Bart wouldn't let her down, and he knew she was a good woman, the best woman he had ever known, and he wanted to explore the future with her. The only thing standing between them now was the meeting at the flea market, and the risk to Halley. Major Leopold said he would keep her safe from harm. And Bart prayed that he could live up to that promise.

Chapter 15

Bart left the house with Halley when she went out the next day to go to St. Ouen. Something had subtly changed between them. A barrier was down. Halley felt closer to Bart than she had felt to anyone in years, and she felt better able to face what she knew she had to do, because he loved her. Everything had happened so fast between them. But what they had experienced since they'd met was intense. And the danger she was facing made his feelings for her even stronger. He wished that he could go with her. He had said it several times, but Major Leopold had been adamant, and Bern Dexter agreed. Bart's being there with her might somehow alert the thief that there were people at the flea market observing him. Bart didn't want Halley to feel alone in St. Ouen, but he didn't look like someone who would be cruising the stalls at the flea market looking for buried treasure. He didn't look like an antique dealer, or a merchant. He looked like an American businessman, and Halley loved his strong masculine looks. They had made love again that morning before they left the house. New doors had opened to them, and they had a whole world to discover together. It was a fresh start for both of them, and now all Halley had to do was get the bag incident behind her, and prove to herself that she could do it, and that Tomás Maduro couldn't intimidate or control her. She didn't want to be ruled by fear and threats anymore.

Bart left her on foot when she left the house, after kissing her one last time, and headed back to his son's apartment. He knew that Ryan and Véro were home, and Bart was sure he was in for some teasing when he got there, for sleeping out. It had been well worth it. Halley was an amazing woman.

While Bart walked the short distance to Ryan's apartment, Halley was driven to Saint Ouen in an unmarked car, by an undercover FBI agent. Major Leopold's officers were already in place all over that one section of the flea market, where the vintage game machines were. The agents were carrying furniture, or working in a rug stall, while two were in the antique silver stall next to the vintage game machines. Others, in overalls, posed as telephone line repairmen. Halley couldn't tell who any of them were, as she waited in the car for half an hour, and then strolled into the alleys chock-full of stalls selling vintage clothing, furniture, lace, antique military uniforms, every imaginable kind of object. She would have enjoyed it if she hadn't been on a frightening mission. She knew she was surrounded by police on all sides and had nothing to fear from the bag thief. He was outnumbered. Between the Sûreté Territoriale and the FBI, they had twenty operatives in place, more than enough to subdue one man when they needed to. But they had to let Halley play her part first. She could feel her knees shake as she walked deeper into the maze of stalls, and saw the vintage game machines, and a flock of young people pressed around them. She didn't see anyone who looked like the photos she had seen of Maduro.

She didn't recognize him at first when she saw him in a beanie, a leather jacket and pants, dark glasses, and motorcycle boots, standing in the arcade game stall. He had obviously come on a motorcycle for a fast getaway. And then she saw that he was carrying something in a brown paper bag. It was concealed by brown wrapping paper, and she knew instantly what it was. She looked at his face and recognized his eyes, when he removed his dark glasses. His eyes were deep and dark and they bore right through her like lasers. She walked toward one of the game machines, ignoring him, and he followed her. Her whole body was trembling as she stood there and paid no attention to him. She took the large envelope of cash out of her bag, the police had given her marked bills. She stood close to him, and handed it to him without looking at him. He slipped it into his leather jacket. She thought he would leave her then, but he stood watching the scene around them, to make sure the way was clear. His motorcycle was parked near the flea market.

Maduro glanced at a moving man carrying a chair, spotted a clumsy object strapped to his leg under the overalls, and knew immediately that he was heavily armed and surely an undercover agent.

Maduro turned and looked Halley dead in the eye, and spoke under his breath in the voice she recognized, which sounded distinctly more Spanish than French now. "You told the police, you bitch," he said, and with a single gesture he grabbed her hair, in a long ponytail, and he dragged her into the next stall, selling antique silver. He had no way of knowing that the owners had been replaced by expert marksmen, all watching him. He dragged Halley into the stall backward, pulling her hard by her hair, and holding it tight in a death grip as she stumbled backward with him. She saw a flash of something come out of his pocket. It was the hunting knife he had talked about and when she looked across the alley to the stalls on the opposite side, she saw Bart, in jeans, a heavy fisherman's sweater, and cowboy boots. She had had no idea he would be there, but he couldn't keep away. He was watching them intently and saw the knife come out of Maduro's pocket.

"I'll kill you now," Maduro said to Halley, sensing danger all around him.

"I didn't tell anyone anything," she said in a low voice. She didn't even have time to think or react. The crowd of people watching them backed away when they saw him put the knife to Halley's throat, and the only people left in the area were undercover agents in a variety of uniforms and rough work clothes. Maduro tightened his grip on Halley, as she saw Bart stare at them. The undercover agents stood still. No one moved for a moment. They froze, as he pressed the knife against her skin. He shouted to them, knowing full well they weren't innocent bystanders. No one wanted to put Halley at risk, and the man in the motorcycle gear with a knife to Halley's throat didn't flinch for a moment. His freedom was on the line now, and his life, and so was hers. She was his prisoner now. Halley thought he would make a run for it, to escape, but he didn't. He just pressed the knife closer to her throat until she hardly dared to breathe. The knife had a long, sharp edge, which he kept pressed against her throat. He looked as though he was going to decapitate her any minute, and a few random people were watching them in horror, from the distance.

Halley was watching Bart to see what he was doing, while the undercover agents kept their eyes on her. No one dared move, fearing for her life.

"If any of you come any closer, I'll slit her throat!" Maduro shouted at the assembled group. He correctly assumed that only the police were left. Everyone else had run away from the stall and were watching from a short distance down the alley, afraid to get caught in any crossfire if weapons were drawn. Some of the merchants were crouching behind large pieces of furniture, as the thief yanked Halley's head back further, and held the knife even closer. She didn't make a sound as she waited for someone to stop him, but none of them dared make a move for an instant, and then eight men in the crowd with their eyes on him drew their guns and aimed at him. If he had a gun, he couldn't reach it and keep the knife at Halley's throat, so he was at a disadvantage momentarily.

"You're a dead man," the chief agent said, as he moved forward at the edge of the crowd. Halley could see Bart clearly then. Their eyes met, and another man in painter's coveralls appeared holding a machine gun on her attacker. Within seconds another dozen men were holding weapons aimed at Maduro, just as Bart knocked over an enormous Chinese urn, which shattered into a million pieces as it hit the ground. It was like the sound of an explosion, just long enough for the thief to be startled and loosen his grip on Halley. Suddenly all the images and memories of her childhood rushed through Halley's mind, the endless beatings by her mother that she didn't deserve, the betrayals by her father. The blows and the injuries, the terror she had lived with and no one stopped. And this time, only she could stop it and save herself. With every ounce of strength she had, and her full weight, she kicked her attacker in the shin, and smashed her fist backward into his groin, as the knife clattered to the ground, and the agents rushed forward and had him face down on the cement within seconds. Two of them pressed him down while another agent handcuffed his hands behind his back, and another agent put a heavy boot on his back to immobilize him, as Bart rushed toward Halley.

"Are you okay?" He looked at her intensely. He was out of breath from the sheer terror of what he'd seen, as one more agent picked the knife up as evidence, wearing latex gloves.

"I'm all right," she said, her voice shaking. She was deathly pale and her heart was racing as plainclothes agents cleared the area, guns in hand, while others searched the crowd for any accomplices lurking near the scene. They found none.

Major Leopold came forward from where he had been concealed and made sure Halley was all right. He took one look at her and called for an ambulance on his radio, grabbing a chair and telling her to sit down, as Bart saw what the major had seen. There was a red stain spreading up the collar of her white sweater. Maduro had sliced through it as he dropped the knife. She was bleeding as Bart opened her coat. There was a cut through her sweater into her flesh, the shoulder of her sweater was bright red, and the knife had gone through her coat as well.

"You're okay," Bart said calmly, as two of the agents exchanged a glance—there was no telling how deep the cut was. In the excitement she hadn't felt anything. She touched her shoulder and her hand came away red.

Agents removed Maduro from the scene, as he attempted to spit on the agents, just as the paramedics arrived and put Halley on a gurney. She looked dazed and like she was going into shock.

"Don't forget my bag," she said to Bart. It was lying on the ground in the game stall, still in the brown paper bag. And Maduro had the money in his jacket. One of the detectives picked up the bag and gave it to Major Leopold, while Bart went to ride in the ambulance with Halley. The paramedics cut through her coat and sweater in the ambulance. Her bra was already bright red, but the paramedics said the wound was only superficial. They used pressure on it on the way to the hospital, as Halley looked at Bart. She said she felt dizzy as she held his hand.

"That was smart of you to create a distraction." She smiled at him, still very pale.

"I forgot to tell you I was a Navy SEAL. That was a pretty smooth move on your part too. You landed a hell of a blow in the right place." He was trying to keep her talking to distract her.

"He brought back some old memories for me," she said, looking vague for a minute. She had been able to fight back and stop the attacks on her. She wasn't a helpless child anymore, just as Dr. Thacker had said. It was finally over.

The sirens and flashing lights were on and they got to the hospital darting through the traffic, with a police escort ahead of them. Bart went into the hospital with her, and she was brave when they sewed her up. Being there reminded her of the countless emergency rooms she had been in as a child, and the many times she'd had stitches. She couldn't let it happen again, even if he had killed her, and luckily, he hadn't. She had reacted by reflex, with no thought for her life.

Bart looked as shaken as she did when they took her home. She had painkillers they'd given her to take with her, but she said she didn't need them. They had numbed her shoulder at the hospital, and given her a tetanus shot so she wouldn't catch anything from the blade that had injured her.

The police said they would come to her home later, with a statement for her to sign, and they had taken photographs of her shoulder before it was sewn up.

Henri Laurent saw them arrive with a police escort, scurried into his lodgings, and locked the door, closing the drapes a minute later.

Bart assisted Halley up the stairs to her bedroom and helped her lie down. She looked exhausted, but she was smiling at him. A door had closed on the past that she knew would never open again. The years of abuse and pain had ended years ago, but the weight of them had finally been lifted off her heart. No one would ever hurt her again. She wouldn't let them. She could defend herself now.

"You shouldn't have gone there, they told you not to. But I'm glad you did," she said to Bart in a tired voice. The distraction he had created had saved her by giving her the chance to save herself.

"I'm glad I could be of some use. You're a brave woman, Halley," Bart said, admiring her courage again, still shaken at the thought of what could have happened.

"I had to be brave. I had a dangerous childhood, with no one to protect me," she said simply. He realized that he had only just begun to know her.

"I'm sorry," he said gently. "I've had a crazy feeling since I first saw you on the plane that we were destined to meet. I didn't know why, and I don't usually believe in those things."

"Neither do I," she admitted. "You make your own destiny, and you play the hand you're dealt." In this case it was a good one. And she lived by what she said. She had had the guts to strike out at her attacker, and had saved her own life in the end, in spite of the knife wound in her neck and shoulder when it was over.

"Whatever happened before, I won't let it happen to you again," Bart said. "I won't let anyone hurt you." She believed him and she knew he meant it. He was an honest man.

Robert had been the right man for her at the time, and now Bart appeared to be. He was the best person she had met in years, and they were so well suited to each other. It was an incredible stroke of luck. She had known him for two weeks, they had already gone through a lot together, and he hadn't let her down.

The past was what it was. It had been hard, but she had survived. She lay in bed a little while later, thinking about it, and what had happened at the flea market. It could have ended so differently. Bart had closed the shades in her bedroom, and came upstairs with a cup of tea a few minutes later.

He sat on the edge of her bed while she sipped it. He was afraid to get into bed with her, he didn't want to hurt her injured shoulder. The memory of seeing her with the knife at her throat was terrifying.

"Why don't you come to bed?" she said, setting the cup down on her night table. The bandages made it awkward to move.

"I don't want to hurt you," he said gently.

"I'm okay, really. He scared the hell out of me when he took out the knife," she admitted. "I thought he'd kill me."

"Me too," he said, the vision still vivid in his mind.

"We have a few more days of our vacation here. We should make the best of it," she said, lying back against her pillows and smiling at him, and he laughed. "We've been pretty busy since we got here. And you just helped capture a dangerous criminal." She could say anything to him, she felt totally comfortable with him, and trusted him completely. He had held up to some pretty scary events and had been there for her, without fail. He wasn't afraid of the past or the present. They were fine qualities in a man. And she wasn't afraid of the past anymore either. There was nothing left to be afraid of. She was free of the past. All the ghosts were gone. Only she and Bart were left. Good had prevailed.

The police came with the statement for her to sign a few hours later, and brought her bag. She lay in bed afterward looking at it and touching it gently. Only a few of her belongings were still in it. He had thrown out the rest. It didn't matter. She had everything she needed.

"What were you thinking?" Bart asked her gently, as he took the bag from her and set it down when the police left.

"I was thinking that I should call the twins." She smiled at him.

"Later," he said, getting into bed with her carefully, so as not to hurt her. And then he kissed her, and she dozed next to him, while he watched her. He fell asleep lying next to her, grateful that she was alive. They had found each other at just the right time.

Halley was grateful for what she had, her life, her twins, a man who loved her and had already proven he was there for her, and wanted to be. What more could one ask? The ghosts of the past had been relegated to the distant history where they belonged, never to return, this time for good. She had understood at last that the shame they carried with them was never hers. She was free at last, to lead the good life she had always deserved. The future was theirs.

About the Author

DANIELLE STEEL has been hailed as one of the world's best-selling authors, with a billion copies of her novels sold. Her many international bestsellers include *A Mind of Her Own, Far From Home, Never Say Never, Trial by Fire, Triangle, Joy, Resurrection,* and other highly acclaimed novels. She is also the author of *His Bright Light,* the story of her son Nick Traina's life and death; *A Gift of Hope,* a memoir of her work with the homeless; *Expect a Miracle,* a book of her favorite quotations for inspiration and comfort; *Pure Joy,* about the dogs she and her family have loved; and the children's books *Pretty Minnie in Paris* and *Pretty Minnie in Hollywood.*

daniellesteel.com
Facebook.com/DanielleSteelOfficial
Instagram: @officialdaniellesteel

About the Type

This book was set in Charter, a typeface designed in 1987 by Matthew Carter (b. 1937) for Bitstream, Inc., a digital type-foundry that he cofounded in 1981. One of the most influential typographers of our time, Carter designed this versatile font to feature a compact width, squared serifs, and open letterforms. These features give the typeface a fresh, highly legible, and unencumbered appearance.